Beach Secrets

Rehoboth Beach Reads

Short Stories by Local Writers

Edited by Nancy Sakaduski

Cat & Mouse Press
Lewes, DE 19958
www.catandmousepress.com

PERMISSION AND ACKNOWLEDGMENTS

Cover illustration/book design by Emory Au. © 2021 Emory Au.

REPRINTED WITH PERMISSION:

"At the Water's Edge," Carly Tagen-Dye. © 2021 Carly Tagen-Dye

"Beach Misses," Lonn Braender. © 2021 Lonn Braender

"Billy's Night Out," Elizabeth Ellers. © 2021 Elizabeth Ellers

"Bug Spray and a Ponytail," Tony Houck. © 2021 Anthony E. Houck

"Chance Encounters," Sarah Barnett. © 2021 Sarah Barnett

"The Companion," Nancy North Walker. © 2021 Nancy Walker

"The Cruciverbalist," Katherine Melvin. © 2021 Katherine Melvin

"Driftwood Days," Steve Saulsbury. © 2021 Steve Saulsbury

"Grease Monkey Baby," Nina Phillips. © 2021 Nina Phillips

"Independence Day," Renée Rockland. © 2021 Renée Rocheleau

"Loose Lips," Peter Keeble. © 2021 Peter Keeble

"Lucky the Chicken," David Cooper. © 2021 David Warren Cooper, Jr.

"The Merrifield Affair," Linda Budzinski. © 2021 Linda Budzinski

"Out of the Blue," Justin Stoeckel. © 2021 Lyle Justin Stoeckel

"Posturing," Frances Grote. © 2021 Frances Grote

"Rock Star," Jeanie P. Blair. © 2021 Jean Pitrizzi Blair

"Say Yes," Renée Rockland. © 2021 Renée Rocheleau

"Secret Message," Carl Frey. © 2021 Carl Frey

"Secrets in the Attic," MaryAlice Meli. © 2021 MaryAlice Meli

"Snapshots in Time," Ellen Krawczak. © 2021 Ellen G. Krawczak

"The Summer Jar," Donald Challenger. © 2021 Donald Challenger

"Undercover Daughter," Doug Harrell. © 2021 Douglas Gaines Harrell

"A Well-Watered Mind," Kim DeCicco. © 2021 Kim DeCicco

"Where Do I Begin?" Phil Giunta. © 2021 Philip Giunta

Table of Contents

PREFACE

These are the winning stories from the 2021 Rehoboth Beach Reads Short Story Contest, sponsored by Browseabout Books. Writers were asked to create a story—fiction or nonfiction—that fit the theme "Beach Secrets" and had a connection to Rehoboth Beach. A panel of judges chose the stories they thought were best and those selections have been printed here for your enjoyment. Like *The Beach House, The Boardwalk, Beach Days, Beach Nights, Beach Life, Beach Fun, Beach Dreams,* and *Beach Mysteries* (other books in this series), this book contains more than just "they went down to the beach and had a picnic" stories. The quality and diversity of the stories is simply amazing.

For contact information or other Cat & Mouse Press publications, go to: www.catandmousepress.com.

ACKNOWLEDGEMENTS

Thanks to Browseabout Books for their continued outstanding support. We are so lucky to have this great store in the heart of our community. They have supported the Rehoboth Beach Reads Short Story Contest from day one and continue to be the go-to place for books, gifts, and other fun stuff.

I thank both the Rehoboth Beach Writers' Guild and the Eastern Shore Writers Association for their support and service to the writing community. These two organizations provide an amazing array of educational programming, and many of the writers whose stories appear in this book benefitted from their classes, meetings, and events.

I thank this year's judges, Tyler Antoine, Lois Hoffman, Pat Marinelli, Mary Pauer, Ron Sauder, and Candace Vessella who gave generously of their valuable time.

Special thanks to Emory Au, who captured the theme so well in the cover illustration and who designed and laid out the interior of this book as well.

I also thank Cindy Myers, queen of the mermaids, for her continued loyalty and support.

An extra-special thank-you to my husband, Joe, who helps on many levels and puts up with a great deal.

I would also like to thank the writers—those whose work is in this book and those whose work was not chosen. Putting a piece of writing up for judging takes courage. Thank you for being brave. Keep writing and submitting your work!

—*Nancy Sakaduski*

And now here is my secret, a very simple secret: It is only with the heart that one can see rightly, what is essential is invisible to the eye.
Antoine de Saint-Exupéry

Say Yes

By Renée Rockland

Page cranked up the volume on her radio as P!nk belted out, "Raise Your Glass." WZBH 93.5, The Beach—Delmarva's Rock Station—was keeping her company as she waited for the light to change at Five Points. And given the number of cars ahead of her, it was going to be a bit of a wait. But even the traffic couldn't squash Page's good mood. Her meeting this morning at Nassau Valley Vineyards had gone even better than expected, and they were completely on board with the surprise proposal Page was planning for her client. She could imagine it now. The ring slipped into a glass of Cape Rosé during a private tasting (with the owner herself, no less). *Raise your glass* indeed! Another guaranteed *yes* from Proposal Planning by Page.

Actually, the "guaranteed yes" wasn't her doing. That was the *Cape Gazette* reporter who'd written a very flattering feature article and asked her about the percentage of positive outcomes. Thus far, every proposal she'd orchestrated had ended with yes, but Page wasn't about to make that guarantee. She advertised: "Helping you write the next chapter in your relationship." And with over one hundred proposals under her belt in the past eight years, she'd helped plenty of couples write their next chapter.

It had started as a lark the summer after she graduated with a marketing degree from the University of Delaware. She'd returned to Rehoboth Beach to help her parents with their catering business when she ran into one of her friends from Cape Henlopen High School at the movie theater, and he told her he was planning to propose to his girlfriend.

"How are you going to do it?" Page had asked.

"Um … I'm going to ask her?"

"Sure, but where? When?"

He shrugged his shoulders. "This weekend?"

"That's all you've got—*this weekend?* That's not very romantic."

"Well, of course I'm going to get down on one knee. I'm not a complete heathen."

Page shook her head. He was hopeless.

"OK, how's this: I'll get donuts from the Fractured Prune and hide the ring in the box."

"Seriously, Ty?"

"You don't know how much she loves their donuts."

"What's Melissa supposed to say when your kids ask how Dad proposed? 'He just dropped to his knee after breakfast, but I had to wash the frosting off the ring'?"

"This is way too much pressure. Why does it have to be such a big deal?"

"Because it *is* a big deal. You're getting engaged! But it doesn't have to be a big deal in the way you mean. It just needs to be thoughtful. Let me help you."

So, Page asked the owners of the Fractured Prune for a special arrangement, and they were thrilled to help pull off the surprise. They made miniature O.C. Sand donuts, which they arranged in a circle and then put a powdered-sugar-covered strawberry shortcake donut at the top for the "diamond."

When Melissa opened the box Sunday morning, she said, "What's this? They made a ring?"

And Ty said, "That's not the only ring you're getting today."

It was totally cheesy—totally Ty—and Melissa loved every part of it. They had even served miniature O.C. Sand donuts at their wedding reception.

Page's phone rang as the light changed for the third time. Finally, she made it through the intersection and continued crawling south with the hordes of tourists descending on her little seaside town. It was almost noon on a beautiful Saturday in early June, and she had the top down on her bright-red Jeep, soaking up some vitamin D, which made dealing with the summer traffic almost tolerable.

She turned down the radio and pressed a button on her earpiece. "This is Page."

"Page, it's Derrick. There's … well … we've got a bit of a problem."

"Define *problem*." Page braked as the minivan in front of her with six bicycles strapped to the back came to a complete stop simply due to the sheer volume of cars on the road.

"So last night … we went dancing at northbeach," he said, "and, maybe I had a little too much to drink? I guess I danced with some girls, and now Mo's mad. She won't come out of our room."

"Let me see if I understand this," Page said with practiced patience that she hoped masked her irritation. Her good mood was rapidly evaporating. "On the eve of your engagement proposal, you left your girlfriend standing alone in a bar while you danced with some other women?"

"It sounds kind of bad when you put it like that."

"It *is* bad, Derrick! What were you thinking?"

"I don't know, but you gotta fix this. She's refusing to come down to the beach. We've got, like, forty-five minutes 'til the plane."

"You're on the beach?"

"Yeah. Just like we planned. I keep texting her but she's not answering."

Page switched into crisis mode. "OK, here's what I want you to do.

Call Bayberry Flowers. Tell them it's an emergency and use my name. Pick out something that says, "I'm sorry for being a first-class jerk," and with any luck, I'll pick them up in fifteen—maybe twenty—minutes. I'll take the flowers to Mo, and … I don't know, I'll figure it out from there."

"I'm on it! And Page, thanks. I mean it. You're getting a killer review on Yelp."

Page hung up and immediately called the company she used to fly proposal banners. Over the years, she'd cultivated several professional relationships, and the owners of Ocean Aerial were at the top of her list. For nearly four decades they'd been flying banner planes advertising everything from restaurant specials to insurance to marriage proposals. One time, they even flew a "please forgive me" banner all day for a guy who wanted to make amends with his wife, but when she found out what he'd paid for it, he was anything but forgiven.

Page had visited their farm in Berlin, Maryland, and knew what it took for the planes to pick up a new banner; it wasn't easy. It involved a quick drop in altitude, grappling hooks, PVC pipe, and an experienced pilot who knew just when to jerk back on the yoke to quickly gain altitude once they'd snagged the banner from the field where they were laid out in rows at the start of each day.

The pilot was probably already en route with Derrick's banner. Any other time, they would only need to make one pass, but Page wasn't sure that would suffice today. Over the past eight years, she had orchestrated countless banner proposals. They were a bit prosaic but nevertheless remained a popular choice. By now, she could practically coordinate them in her sleep. The personalized proposal scavenger hunts, which she was known for, were far more intricate and took a great deal more planning.

Page rubbed her temples as she sat, unmoving, near Home Goods, listening to "Hot Fun in the Summertime," broadcasting from the convertible next to her. It was definitely hot, but Page was not having fun.

She did some mental calculations; the plane would have to make two, if not three, passes. This was turning out to be a lot more complicated than she'd anticipated. But if she were being completely honest, she'd dealt with worse. After two beach proposals ended with rings lost in the sand, she'd bought Goldie, her trusty metal detector, which she always carried in the back of her Jeep. A lost ring was a far greater crisis.

She was passing Outlet Liquors when she finally hung up with Ocean Aerial and then made the turn onto Rehoboth Avenue. The florist was just ahead on her left.

"You're a lifesaver, Nate!" Page scooped the flowers off the counter. The arrangement was stunning—white daisies with lilies and roses and a few pops of purple statice. "Gorgeous, as always. I owe you," she called over her shoulder on her way out the door.

"No thanks necessary. Just keep sending the happy couples my way."

"Count on it!" Page waved farewell and rushed to secure the flowers on her passenger seat.

The Beach View Hotel, one of the premiere boutique hotels in Rehoboth, was only a mile away, but it still took Page ten minutes to navigate the endless stream of downtown traffic and pedestrians. There were absolutely no parking spots on Wilmington Avenue—no surprise—so Page pulled into the hotel parking lot, taking a spot reserved for their guests. Hopefully, this wouldn't take long.

"Hi, Elaine," Page greeted the older woman at the front desk. "How have you been?"

"Page! What a lovely surprise." Elaine was a natural at reception. She could make wrinkles and cellulite feel welcome.

"I was hoping you could help me. You've got a couple staying here, Derrick Davis and Monique? I'm wondering if you could call up to their room and tell Monique she's got a delivery? I'd like to give her these myself."

"I can do you one better. She's sitting right over there." Elaine pointed toward a cozy cluster of chairs just off the lobby.

"Oh!" The way Derrick had made it sound, Mo was still in their room. Well, at least this was progress. "Thanks, Elaine."

Page plastered a huge smile on her face. "Monique? Hi! I've got a special delivery for you. Aren't these just gorgeous?" Page needed to drop her pitch about three octaves. She was giving herself a headache.

Monique frowned. Frowned! Page tried again. "Someone named Derrick called the store and said he owes you an apology." Monique reached for the flowers, turning the vase around in her hands.

"I don't see a card." Page wanted to bang her head against the wall.

"That's my fault. Sorry. I left in such a hurry. You know, traffic and all. He paid extra for quick delivery. Said he feels like a jerk." She took a breath and tucked a stray strand of hair behind her ear. "I don't mean to pry, but, well, I hope everything's OK."

Evidently, a little sympathy was all Monique needed. Her eyes welled up and tears spilled over even as she tried to wipe them away. "I'm so sorry."

"Don't be," Page said, fishing a packet of tissues from her canvas shoulder bag as she sat down. "For what it's worth, and I mean, I'm no expert, but unless he hit you or something—"

"Oh, no! It was nothing like that." Monique looked horrified. "We just went out last night, and he was dancing with some other women." She took the tissue and dabbed her eyes, wiping away mascara that had migrated onto her cheek. "I told him it was OK. We've been together a long time, but I guess I just got jealous." She shrugged her shoulders. "Who knew?"

"That you're human?" They both smiled. "I'm Page, by the way."

"My friends call me Mo," she said, blowing her nose. "Do you have a boyfriend?"

Page nodded. "Jeremy and I have been together five years."

"Us too! Still, every time I start to talk about the future, Derrick gets all weird. But I can't imagine my life without him." She admired the flowers in her lap. "Even now, I can't really stay mad. He's down on the beach waiting for me."

"You should go," Page said, hoping she sounded encouraging, not desperate.

"Why don't you come with me? You can meet him and then maybe we can all hang out later?"

Oh dear, Page thought. She definitely didn't want to be part of Derrick's proposal. "I'd love to hang out, but I've got … a few more deliveries to make."

"This will only take a minute." Mo stood and grabbed Page's hand. "C'mon. I don't want you to leave thinking he's a complete arse. Only a partial one." She winked, and against her better judgment, Page followed her outside, both of them staring down at their phones as they walked the short distance to the boardwalk.

Page texted Ocean Aerial. She wasn't sure where the plane was, but she knew the pilot had made at least one pass.

"Derrick's near Zelkey's," Mo said.

They both removed their sandals before stepping onto the beach, and in a sea of rainbow-colored umbrellas somehow managed to find Derrick. He was relaxing under the shade of a canopy, wearing pineapple-print boardie shorts and jumped up as they approached.

"I'm so sorry, baby." He gave Mo an uncomfortably long kiss, and Page looked away. She'd done her part; Derrick could certainly take it from here.

"Derrick, this is my new friend, Page," said Mo, all smiles and smudged lipstick. "She delivered your flowers."

Page started to excuse herself when she heard the distant hum of an approaching propeller plane. Automatically, she looked skyward, along with everyone else. It was human nature. As the bright yellow plane passed overhead, Page had a clear view of the banner and nearly fainted. It said, "Page, Marry Me?" with a big red heart on either side of the words.

"Oh my God, Derrick! I'm so sorry." Page's sandals slipped from her fingers. Her stomach turned cold. How could she have let such a terrible mistake happen?

This entire proposal had been a disaster from start to finish today. She'd orchestrated proposals aboard the Jolly Trolley and the ferry, in the top of the observation tower in Cape Henlopen State Park, and even in Funland's haunted house. There'd been a flash mob at the bandstand using Clear Space summer stock actors and a kayaking adventure with Dogfish Brewery. She'd coordinated drones to fly in engagement rings and commissioned artists to build sandcastles and ice sculptures. She knew every rooftop in the area with a view of the sunset and was on a first name basis with countless chefs who would happily help pull off a surprise. She had even bought Goldie, her trusty metal detector, for God's sake! And in the end, it was a simple banner proposal that had unraveled her.

She could barely breathe. "I'm so sorry. I don't know what to say."

"Say yes." The familiar voice came from behind her, and when she turned around, Jeremy was down on one knee, an engagement ring extended toward her.

Page's heart was beating a rapid staccato so loudly she was certain everyone could hear it over the distant hum of the receding propeller plane. Still, it was beating. That was good, right? She covered her mouth with her hand, not trusting herself to speak.

"You always said I wouldn't be able to surprise you." Jeremy grinned. "But you should know by now how much I love a challenge."

"So D-D-Derrick?" She stammered.

Derrick shook his head. "You can catch Mo and me at Clear Space tonight. We've got the leads in *Grease*. Gave Jeremy tickets. Front row."

"You're actors?" she asked, wide-eyed.

Mo put her arm around Page and playfully bumped her hip. "Pretty good ones, huh?"

Page shook her head in disbelief. Then, as everything started to crystalize, and her heart rate slowed appreciably, she stared down into Jeremy's blue eyes and said, "Wait a minute! Are they even staying at the hotel?"

"Nope," he said, clearly enjoying himself. "Elaine was in on it too. And Ocean Aerial was awesome. They were dying when you called in a panic about the plane."

"Well," Page said, finally recovering herself, "if you're trying to make this a family business, I think you've got a good shot."

"Does this mean we're going to be a family?"

Page furrowed her brow.

Jeremy held the ring aloft. "I'm still waiting for an answer."

"Yes!" Page threw herself into his arms, effectively knocking him backwards and sending the ring flying through the air. Immediately, everyone dropped to their knees and began frantically sifting through the sand. Everyone except Page, who took off running toward her Jeep. Goldie to the rescue! At least she was prepared for one emergency today.

RENÉE ROCKLAND IS AN EDUCATION PROFESSIONAL WHO WORKS IN ELLICOTT CITY, MARYLAND, DURING THE SCHOOL YEAR AND PLAYS IN REHOBOTH BEACH, DELAWARE, DURING THE SUMMER. A LIFELONG WRITER, RENÉE USED HER TIME IN QUARANTINE DURING THE COVID-19 PANDEMIC TO RECONNECT WITH HER FIRST LOVE AND EMERGED WITH SEVERAL SHORT STORIES, TWO OF WHICH ARE PUBLISHED IN *BEACH SECRETS*. ADDITIONALLY, HER AWARD-WINNING STORY, "NO DOGS ALLOWED" IS PUBLISHED IN *THE BEST DOG STORIES OF 2021*. RENÉE IS A MEMBER OF THE REHOBOTH BEACH WRITERS' GUILD AND EASTERN SHORE WRITERS ASSOCIATION. SHE IS CURRENTLY AT WORK ON HER FIRST BOOK, A COLLECTION OF HEARTWARMING SHORT STORIES SET IN HER BELOVED REHOBOTH. YOU CAN CONNECT WITH HER ON FACEBOOK.

A Well-Watered Mind

By Kim DeCicco

I was on Lewes Beach, reading under my umbrella, when I overheard the family's spat:

"Leave that T-shirt on over your bikini," the father said.

"Why? None of the other women are."

"You're a kid, not a woman."

"I'm thirteen!"

"Exactly."

"Mom!"

"I agree with your father."

"Arrrrrr!" the girl exclaimed as she stormed toward the bay, T-shirt in place.

I understood the girl's frustration. I could even smile about it. But my smile didn't spring from relief because I was now a middle-aged adult. No. My smile arose from the memory of the woman who helped me through my thirteenth year.

* * * * *

It was July 1989. I was three months past my thirteenth birthday, and my mother and I seemed constantly at war. I was more interested in spending time with friends than with family. I wanted to wear makeup and fashionable clothes—meaning tighter and shorter. I preferred dance class to homework, and I definitely preferred talking with my friends about boys over doing chores. According to my mother, I burst into argumentative fits if she dared question my choices.

That wasn't true. *If* I responded poorly, it was because she *always* told me no.

My parents, my grandmother, and I lived in a two-family house outside Philadelphia. Dad worked for the navy; Mom was a curator at the Philadelphia Museum of Art; and Gran, a recent retiree, volunteered three days a week at the library.

On a bright Friday morning, Gran, who lived in the apartment upstairs, stopped by our kitchen on her way to the library. She was in time to witness another of the many heated arguments between my mother and me—this one about the miniskirt, on loan from a friend, I wanted to wear to the mall.

"What happened to the nice girl you used to be?" Gran asked as I stomped, red faced, around the room.

Her words stung, and they fueled my anger. "I *am* nice! *She's* the problem!" I pointed an accusatory finger at my mother.

"Anna!" Gran whispered and shook her head in warning.

I had gone too far.

With nostrils flared and lips pinched tight, my mother picked up the phone and dialed. She made three calls: the first was to her job, saying she wouldn't be in until after lunch; the second was to my father, advising him that she was driving to Delaware but would be back that afternoon; and the third was to Oma, my great-grandmother.

"Go pack for the weekend." My mother looked at her watch. "We're leaving in fifteen minutes."

I was being sent away.

Oma and Opa, my great-grandparents, came to America from Germany in 1926, and they spent the next forty-two years building a new life in Philadelphia. When they retired in 1968, they wanted nothing more than to spend their remaining years in a quiet town near a beach, so they purchased a cottage in Lewes, Delaware. Opa passed seven years ago, leaving Oma alone in the house. She was happy by herself and made a point of saying so whenever my mother or Gran tried to convince her to move in with us. *"Nein,"* she'd say. "I love the beach. I will go back to Philly when I need burying."

Late-morning sun highlighted short gray hair curled thick around a face lined for each of Oma's eighty-six years. Rheumy eyes took my measure as I stood in the doorway, a small suitcase clutched in one hand and a book hugged to my chest with the other. Her lips pouted with sympathy as she opened her arms wide. Dropping my belongings, I flung myself into her embrace.

"It's OK," she soothed. "Let it out." Her warm hand stroked my long brown hair. I knew her nails would be trimmed and unpolished, practical and square like her age-spotted hands. She pulled an ever-present handkerchief from her skirt pocket and dabbed my eyes, then handed it to me for my nose. "They have forgotten their own youth, how this age was for them."

I nodded but didn't understand. Mom and Gran at thirteen? It seemed impossible. They were *Mom* and *Gran,* not … people.

"Come." Oma chucked me under the chin. "You are thinking too hard. Put your things away and we will have tea."

Oma's home faced a short side street that ran directly to the beach, giving us a clear view of Delaware Bay from the porch and front windows. The house remained unchanged since its purchase, except for the attic, which had been converted into extra sleeping space, with two dormer windows added to catch the breeze. That's where I slept. The main floor consisted of two tiny bedrooms, a bath, a small living room, and a kitchen large enough to fit a table and four chairs—as long as you pushed the chair in when opening the refrigerator.

A yellow Formica table already held a china pot and two mugs by the time I entered the kitchen.

"Sometimes, Anna," Oma began as she scooped loose tea into the pot, "the mind can be like these leaves—dry and brittle, not flexible.

But when you add water, the leaves become supple and can bend." She covered the pot and we waited for the tea to steep.

"So, how do we add water to our minds?" I asked, my attention on wisps of steam escaping the spout. They carried the scent of peach, my favorite.

"We walk the beach."

Questions gathered on my tongue, but my queries were halted when she asked that I hold the strainer so she could pour. We took our mugs and settled on the porch to look at the bay.

"We will walk in the morning, at half past seven. You can ask questions then. The rest of today we relax."

Morning sun warmed our backs as we strolled along the shoreline. Gentle waves lapped against the sand and swirled water around my feet. I bent to collect the remains of a mussel shell. Its edges were deeply chipped, but the two halves were still attached at the center, forming a silhouette. "It looks like people kissing," I said, and held it out to Oma.

She leaned close to inspect the shell. "Are you thinking about kissing?" she asked, her question light and curious.

"No," I answered quickly, my face warming.

She started walking again. "Then why show your stomach?" She waved a hand at my crop top.

My cheeks flamed. Like my mother and Gran, Oma didn't seem to understand my desire to wear trendy things, to be like my friends. However, her words conveyed disappointment, not reprimand, which made me feel embarrassed instead of angry.

"Anna, a kiss is fine. This shirt, too, when appropriate, like here at the beach." She took my arm to steady herself in the sand. "But if you want your mother to respect your choices, to trust your judgement, then give her reason to do so. From clothes to kisses, you are responsible for your decisions. So, ask yourself: 'What does this say about me? Does this benefit or hinder who I want to be?'"

"You mean like how I want to be a dancer?"

"Not exactly." She chuckled. "I mean *how* you want to be, *ja*?"

I flipped the shell around in my hand as we continued along the shore. How *do* I want to be? No one had asked me this before. The question made sense when I thought about Gran's words: "What happened to the nice girl you used to be?" Did I want to be *nice*? Sure, but not always—not when I felt pushed. "Oma? Do I always have to be nice, even to my mom and Gran?"

She tilted her head from side to side as she considered my question. "Not always."

This was good news!

"But you should always be kind."

"How?" I asked. "They won't even listen to my side of things. It's frustrating."

She asked for the shell I carried. She looked it over, rubbed its rough surface with her thumb. Then, she kissed my temple. "You tell me," she said, and tossed the shell into the bay.

"I was going to keep that!" Annoyance shot through me.

"I know."

Shock slackened my jaw, but anger started to twist and grow in my chest. "Then why'd you throw it away?" I asked, stomping a foot in the sand.

"I wanted to."

"Oma! That wasn't nice, or kind."

"No, it wasn't. Yet, you are being kind—asking me why and pointing out that I wasn't nice instead of accusing me of being mean." She smiled.

I exhaled my remaining anger. "It was just a shell."

She patted my arm. "Good. Now you understand what it means to water your mind." She gently tapped my nose. "Maybe tomorrow I will throw away your little shirt."

"Omaaa!"

I had to hold her steady while she hooted with laughter.

Scents of flour and yeast greeted me the next morning. A towel-covered bowl sat on the table, and Oma was at the sink washing measuring cups.

"Today we make challah," she announced as I kissed her cheek and retrieved a mug. I poured tea from the pot resting on the stove. It was light and didn't need sugar.

After drying her hands, Oma moved to the table and sprinkled a circle of flour from the canister. "People are like bread," she said as I took the seat opposite her. "Many ingredients mixed together to make something new." She punched down the soft dough a few times, scooped it from the bowl, and kneaded it for several minutes on the floured surface. With a sharp knife, she divided the lump into four segments. Together, we rolled each portion into tapered strands. "You, your mother, your grandmother, and I are like these strands," she said. "Four pieces of a whole."

I nodded.

She laid the pieces side by side, then pinched them together at the top. "Now, always using the strand on the right"—she demonstrated as she spoke—"weave it over, then under, then over the three other pieces. You do the rest."

"Over, under, over," I whispered while plaiting, the fragrant strands silky under my fingertips.

"*Ja*, good." She bobbed her head, then patted mine, leaving flour prints in my hair. "This is the secret to good challah, and to life."

"What do you mean?" I asked while following her gestured instructions to pinch the ends and tuck them under.

"Braided dough produces a strong loaf," she told me as she reached for a baking pan already lined with parchment. "But a braided loaf also understands its need to separate with ease if it is to nourish." Carefully lifting the bread, she placed it on the pan. "I learned this with my daughter, your grandmother, who learned it with your mother." Oma wiped her hands on the towel, slid into a chair, and looked me in the eye. "Now, your mother is learning how to separate while nourishing you."

"If she went through this with Gran, then why is she so tough on me? How is that nourishing?"

Oma shrugged. "Because it's easy to forget the hard parts of being young." She guided stray hair behind my ear. "But also, when you are a mother, you think mostly about protecting your daughter . . . and, also, yourself."

Herself? "What does my mother need to be protected from?"

"The heartache of losing her little girl."

"It makes her sad that I'm growing up?" I couldn't wait to get older, go to high school and then college. How could that upset my mother?

"Not sad, but . . . melancholy, *ja*? She *is* proud of the woman you are becoming, but also, she misses the child you were—the child who depended on her."

"Oh." I wasn't sure I understood. Shouldn't my mother be happy that I was learning to take care of myself?

"OK, time for you to water your mind again. Go sweep the porch while I make egg wash for the bread and put it in the oven."

"I thought walking the beach was how I watered my mind."

"That's one way; there are hundreds. Cleaning is the best."

I was suspicious. "You're making that up."

"Ha! I'm old, Anna. I don't need to make things up because I *know* everything."

Shaking my head, I grabbed the broom and walked toward the door—Oma's gleeful laughter followed me the entire way.

A warm breeze fluttered the curtains and carried the water's salty aroma to me as I settled into bed that night. I thought about everything Oma had told me and wondered what would happen tomorrow when my mother arrived to take me home. I didn't feel any different, so I didn't think I'd be able to stop myself from arguing with her in the future. And I certainly didn't know who, or *how*, I wanted to be. Earlier, when I told Oma all of this, she said not to worry, such things take time. She told me I'd naturally evolve into my best self if I remained mindful, if I kept the thought *How do I want to be* in my head as I made choices. This would also help when my mother and I disagreed. She said to not concern myself with *feeling* different. I'd know when a change occurred.

I looked out the window at the rising moon and hoped Oma was right. Yawning, I closed my eyes and let the bay's gentle rolling soothe my fears.

Oma was scrambling eggs when I entered the kitchen. A grapefruit half awaited me, and I happily dug a serrated spoon into its flesh. The tart juices puckered my mouth and made me feel as if I were swallowing sunshine.

"Your mother called last night. They should be here soon, maybe ten minutes."

The spoon froze midway to my lips. "What? So soon?" It wasn't even eight o'clock.

"*Ja.* They left early."

Wait a minute. *They*? "Is my dad coming?"

She scraped eggs into a bowl and covered it with a plate. "No, your grandmother."

"Oh, no!"

"What? Suddenly you don't like your grandmother?" She lifted an eyebrow.

"No, it's just … things were so bad that morning." Dropping the spoon, I slapped my hands over my face. "They're going to gang up on me the whole ride home."

Oma tapped me on the head with her spatula. "Stop being so silly."

"Hellooo," a voice called from the front door.

They were here. I had no time to hide.

Oma met Gran and my mother in the living room, where many hugs and kisses were exchanged. I sat on my hands and waited. Minutes ticked by like hours until, finally, my mother entered the kitchen. She greeted me with a smile. That was good sign. Maybe everything would be fine.

Her forehead creased. "Anna, why is there egg in your hair?"

Or maybe not. I kept my mouth closed and shrugged.

"That's my fault," Oma said as she and Gran joined us. "Mina, get the plates." Oma pointed Gran to a small stack on the counter. "And the bread, Janie. We need that too."

My mother picked up the loaf Oma and I had made yesterday and set it on the table. Sitting, she cut several pieces and passed them around while the rest of us served ourselves eggs.

Silence settled over the table as the others ate. I pushed my food around, appetite gone, and peeked at my mother. She had stopped eating and was staring at the loaf. Then, she looked at me.

"Anna, I brought you here because we needed a break from each other."

An ache knotted in my chest. Her words hurt, even though I had thought the same thing at the time.

Oma knocked her fork against the hand my mother had resting on the table.

Pink color seeped into my mother's cheeks as she brushed egg from her hand. "And, because I knew Oma would teach you how to make challah. I remembered how much her lessons helped me when I was your age." Her blush deepened. "I fought with my mother too."

Curiosity pushed through my hurt. "About what?"

She lifted a shoulder. "The same things: clothes, makeup, chores."

"Smoking," Gran added.

Whoa! I looked, wide-eyed and slack-jawed, at my mother.

She scowled at Gran, who shrugged. Oma smiled and continued eating.

My mother sighed and popped a bit of bread into her mouth. Her expression turned thoughtful as she chewed. Then, she touched the hand Oma had bumped earlier and color crept into her face again. "Oh, Anna." Her eyes filled with remorse. "I'm so sorry. I never should have said we needed a break. That must have upset you."

I nodded as a lump settled in my throat.

"I'm also sorry for bringing you here without any explanation. I was mad, but that's no excuse."

I took a shaky breath. "I'm sorry too—for being mean."

She came over and hugged me and kissed my head, then stayed to pick the eggs left by Oma's spatula from my hair. It felt good to have her close.

She looked at Oma. "Thank you for nudging me. I'd forgotten the most important part—to be mindful. It was such a long time ago."

"*Pssht*. You don't know 'long time ago' yet." Oma squeezed the hand my mother offered. "But now the memory is fresh again, *ja*?"

I felt my mother nod.

"Did Oma tell you that cleaning is the best way to water your mind?" my mother asked as she combed her fingers through my hair.

I chuckled. "Yeah, but I think she's fibbing."

"Me too." Gran said, shooting her mother a sideways glance.

"Bah." Oma waved her fork in the air, sending bits of egg everyplace. "None of you know anything. It's a good thing I'm still here."

Our laughter rang through the cottage loud and long, and something shifted inside me. The atmosphere was different. I was different—and knew it, just like Oma had said. I felt connected to my mother and Gran. It was no longer *me* and *them*, it was … us.

* * * * *

The girl's terse "No!" pulled me from my reminiscing. Her father had joined her in the water and offered to tug her around on an inflated raft. Her mother watched from the shoreline with rigid shoulders—I expect she foresaw a quarrelsome afternoon.

I rummaged through my beach bag for a pen, then turned to the blank page at the end of my book. I fervently wrote down the recipe for challah and directions for braiding a three-strand loaf—including that each strand represents a person. I also included sage words from the wisest woman I've known: "Keep your mind supple by 'watering' it with simple pleasures or tasks—like walking the beach or baking bread. A supple mind helps shape *how* you want to be."

I tore out the page, creased it in half, and slipped it into the mother's tote while they were still in the bay.

A smile spread across my face as I closed my umbrella and folded my beach chair. Oma would be delighted to know I had secretly passed on her wisdom. I imagine it's something she would have done herself.

I left my beach things on the porch and went into the cottage to start water for tea. As I scooped leaves into the china pot, I swore I could hear Oma's voice:

"Anna, you forgot to tell them cleaning is the best!"

Kim DeCicco is the 2020 Delaware Division of the Arts Fellow in Emerging Fiction. Her short stories appear in several anthologies, including *Beach Dreams* and *Halloween Party 2021*. Born in New York, she now lives in southern Delaware and divides her time between writing and peddling antiques.

Inspiration for "A Well-Watered Mind" came from Kim's recollections of the relationship she had with her mother and grandmother during her thirteenth year.

Judges' Comments

A coming-of-age story with daughter, mother, grandmother, and great-grandmother takes you back to those rebellious years everyone goes through. And sometimes a walk on the beach is not just a walk on the beach. This well-written story has visual and sensory details to entice the reader forward. Secrets are subtle—not only what parents did before they were parents, but also a recipe—and we cherish both. Appreciate how the story develops without cliché or twists to reveal—solid, and poignant as well. Kudos to the author; no soft spots here.

Loose Lips

By Peter Keeble

Frank's been gone eleven months now, and I have no idea where he is. Well, I do in a way, in that he's on a navy destroyer. Somewhere.

He's good at writing to me, but he's not allowed to say anything much, other than he misses me and what sort of wedding we're going to have when the war is over. That, of course, is all I really want to read about anyway. He had a good job up at the menhaden fisheries in Lewes and was out in any weather, so of course he was a natural for the navy, and they snapped him up the minute he set foot in the recruiting office down on Rehoboth Avenue. Now, he's escorting convoys across the Atlantic.

It's just Mom and me at home now. Dad passed five years back; his heart had never been good, and when my sister, Nancy, married, that just left the two of us in the house. It's a good-size place with four bedrooms, two blocks from the ocean and an easy walk to most places, which is just as well. Try getting gas for a car these days! I quit my peacetime job, as I thought I should do my bit in this war along with Frank. So, I went to work on a local farm as part of the Women's Land Army program. I'm out there come rain or shine, along with the other girls, hauling bales of hay, digging up potatoes, and even driving the tractor.

I badgered Mom about her getting a job to help the war effort, but going out to work is not really her thing, as she's always been at home looking after all of us. "Well," I said, "carry on doing just that but earn some money out of it." So right then and there we wrote up an ad for the *Rehoboth Beach News* (two bedrooms for rent, evening meal, etc.)

and along comes Mrs. Turner and her daughter, Elsa. Mom was thrilled, as she'd been a bit worried about having men in the place, what with me being single and passably pretty, if I do say so myself.

Mrs. Turner was stout with flat feet, and she smiled a lot. She and Mom hit it off right away. Elsa was just a couple of years older than me, so it was an easy fit all round. They had been living in Washington DC, but Mrs. Turner said if anyone was going to drop bombs on Uncle Sam, Washington was the place they'd do it, and she didn't want to stick around to find out. Can you blame her?

I've mentioned how I am passably pretty, but Elsa was a stunner. Movie star looks with natural blond hair, dazzling blue eyes, and a figure that, in our shorter wartime skirts, was really showed to advantage. Well, I was suited with my Frank, so there was never any competition between us.

Elsa loved going to the dances, which happened every Saturday night down by the boardwalk. We usually teamed up to go, as no decent girl would show up by herself, and we had a good laugh into the bargain. Elsa loved a man in uniform. All the lads from Fort Miles would turn up, and she always made sure she ended up with one of these "Boys from the Battery," as we called them. Of course, I'd mentioned all this in my letters to Frank, and he said, "Go off and have a good time, love, but remember—straight home afterward." He's one in a million, my Frank.

We'd have bands visiting from Wilmington or Baltimore, and they were really good. Toward the end of the evening, they always played Glenn Miller's "Moonlight Serenade," which got the couples dancing close, and from there they drifted out onto the boardwalk for their own "Moonlight Serenade." Some wandered down onto the beach where apparently you could "see the moon better."

At home over the evening meal, Elsa would often relate the latest news she'd picked up from her Saturday night strolls on the beach. It seems the guys up at Fort Miles were tracking enemy ships by triangulating their positions from the watch towers along the coast. This was important, as enemy vessels might enter the Delaware Bay and could do a lot of damage to the shipyards in Wilmington and Philadelphia.

I asked Elsa how she got them to tell her all this. She drew me close and in a conspiratorial way said, "When I get those boys down on the beach, there's nothing they won't tell me. I call them my beach secrets, and like all good secrets of course I promise not to tell a soul." She laughed. "It makes them feel big to tell me what they're doing; regular Errol Flynns, some of them."

Mom frowned and said, "Well that's all very well, but I don't know those boys should be talking about their jobs like that. After all, as the posters say, "Loose Lips Sink Ships."

Elsa smiled broadly and said, "Don't worry, the only ships those boys up at Fort Miles will be sinking are German ones." We all had a good laugh over that.

I would often wander down to the beach—what I liked to think of as my "quiet time" with Frank. Living here on the coast, with Europe just across the water, the nights are when you really felt you were at war. Looking up, I'd sometimes see our fighter aircraft from Dover Army Air Base going goodness knows where, but wherever it was, it wasn't going to be good. Straight ahead, there were shipping convoys out at sea, maybe the very one Frank was escorting, silhouettes on the dark water with smoke billowing out of the funnels and disappearing into the night sky. Meanwhile, German U-boats, unseen, could be circling under the waves, waiting for them. It made me feel scared, but more than that it made me scared for Frank and somehow helped me understand what he must be going through.

Elsa and I drifted apart. We still went to the dances, but as soon as we arrived, she was off on her quest for Fort Miles's boys. Most times as the evening got later, I didn't bother to wait for her but just made my own way home.

I missed Frank awfully, and my walks down to the beach after dinner became more frequent. Despite the cold and the chill of fall, I felt closer to Frank down there in the dark, listening to the same ocean he must be listening to.

One October night, I just couldn't sleep. Despite the lateness of the hour, I wrapped myself up and went down to the beach to "be with Frank" for just a few minutes. I thought it might send me off to bed with lovely dreams.

The beach was dark, cold, and damp—the sort of marine chill that gets into your bones. I was sitting with my coat wrapped around me, thinking this wasn't such a good idea, when through the mist I saw something out at sea. A shape, not a ship but more of an oblong shape, with a bump on the top. I stared and then my blood went cold. *A U-boat.*

I didn't know what to do, so I just sat there. I noticed a second, much smaller, shape making its way toward the shore. I could just make out a rubber dinghy with two men paddling it. Luckily, my coat was a dark one, and I must have blended in with the night. I spotted another figure running down the sand toward the water. The three of them pulled the dinghy up on the beach. They talked for a while, exchanged something, and then the dinghy and the two men headed back toward the submarine. The figure on the shore called out something in German then turned and walked up the beach and onto the boardwalk. The person passed fairly close to me but didn't see me, thank goodness. It was Elsa.

I stayed rooted to the spot. The submarine had disappeared, presumably diving once the two men had reboarded. My mind was spinning, but one thing was making sense—Elsa's obsession with only going out with guys from Fort Miles and taking them down on the beach to learn their secrets.

I wanted to tell Mom, but what was the point of scaring her half to death? The next day dragged, and that night Elsa went up to bed cool as you please, but I lay down fully clothed, drifting in and out of sleep. It was well after midnight when I heard a bedroom door open. I was fully awake in a flash, all senses on overdrive. I heard footsteps going down the stairs, not those of a middle-aged woman, but those of a younger one. I slipped out of my room just in time to see the front door close. I went out to the street and saw nothing at first, but then I could see a figure in the shadows, heading toward the beach. It had to be Elsa. I followed, and with our blackout requirements it was easy to blend into the dark. I made sure to keep Elsa in sight.

When we reached the boardwalk, Elsa went down onto the beach. I felt helpless, but then I thought, *I'm not helpless*. Frank wouldn't love a girl with a yellow streak, and I owed this to him. I had to protect him. Who knows the secrets Elsa was passing on, or what orders she was receiving about things to find out from the loose-lipped, besotted, Fort Miles soldiers? I had to stop it.

I stepped onto the beach and called out, "Elsa!"

She stopped, turned, and saw me. She hesitated, then walked back up to the beach as I moved down to meet her.

"Hi there. So you couldn't sleep either," she said.

I could have gone along with it, but it would have sounded pretty weak, and I knew she wouldn't believe me. I answered, in a voice I could hardly credit as my own, it sounded so assured, calm and icy. "No. I came to watch you meet your submariner friends."

Elsa's eyes widened, and her mouth drew tight; those perfect movie star lips turned into a snarl. She walked up to me, twisted my arm, and in one swift movement was behind me. "Then, my dear, you'd better come and meet them too."

I felt something hard in my back. I have never seen or felt a pistol, but somehow you know it when one is stuck in your back.

We walked down to the water. It was pitch black, and a stiff breeze was bringing the sea mist in. All I could make out was white surf crashing onto the sand.

"What are you doing, Elsa?"

"I'm doing my bit to win the war, as you put it. Except I'm winning it for the German Reich."

"But Elsa, this is our country. You and your mother are as American as Mom and me.

"No, we are not. And she's not my mother. She was just provided to give me a credible cover."

"I don't understand any of it."

"We have a few more minutes to wait, so you may as well hear the whole story before we get aboard the submarine. There is no going back for me now my cover is blown. And, my dear, there's no going back for you either."

She went on. "My name is Elsa Schafer. I got a degree in modern languages from Heidelberg University and worked as a translator for the German government, but then transferred to, shall we say, the espionage division. My faultless English and my looks made me a perfect choice for this mission. You can't believe what secrets some of those soldiers will tell you down on the beach. Their brain is in their pants, and they will tell you anything you want to know in exchange for a few kisses and a little grubby fondling."

Somehow, I didn't feel afraid, now that all doubt was removed. We walked down to the edge of the surf. I knew once I was on that sub it was over for me. I had to do something. Frank was doing all he could to win this war, and damn it, so would I.

Elsa was still close to me, with the gun in my back. It was now or never. I spun my body around and grabbed her. Fortunately, she was taken by surprise and by the time she thought of pulling the trigger, my hand was locked on hers. I kicked her legs out from under her and threw us both down into the waves. I still had surprise on my side, and I started to drag us into deeper water. Elsa grabbed me fiercely, letting go of the gun. She was biting and kicking, but I was able to pin her arms tightly.

The rip currents in Rehoboth during winter can be deadly. We were now out of our depth, so Elsa's legs were no longer a threat. She needed them to keep herself afloat as we got pulled further out. Our clothes were heavy with the water, and we were both getting tired.

Having lived in Rehoboth all my life, I was used to swimming in the sea, and those months on the farm had made me incredibly fit. I now summoned all of that strength.

Rather than fighting to stay afloat, I pulled us both down. I had taken a deep breath, but Elsa, not knowing what was coming, hadn't. I held tight and could feel her writhing to gain the surface, but I held us down as she tried to kick up. My lungs started to ache. I was able to surface briefly and took a gulp of air before pulling us under again. Her struggles became less frantic, then suddenly just stopped. I knew it was over.

I surfaced and pulled Elsa up. My instinct was to try to resuscitate her, but why, only to have the whole fight start over? She was an enemy agent, and in war you behave differently and do things you would never think yourself capable of during peacetime.

Then I saw it. The submarine had surfaced about five hundred yards away. We were pinpricks on the dark ocean, so hopefully they couldn't see us. A dinghy set off for the shore as before, but after waiting for no more than a few minutes, they rowed back, and the submarine submerged.

I let Elsa go. She drifted out with the current until I lost sight of her. I dragged myself up on the shore, exhausted. Shivering uncontrollably, I made my way back home. In my bedroom, I wrapped myself in blankets and just cried.

The next morning, Mrs. Turner dismissed Elsa's absence by muttering something about her romantic trysts. Then she put on her coat, grabbed her shopping basket, and wandered off to the shops to get us something for lunch. Or so she said. We never saw her again.

I wasn't sure if I should tell the police or some government ministry. I decided to just go up to Fort Miles, and I told everything to an older man in unform with a lot of stripes on his sleeve. Well, almost everything. I left out the very last bit. I told him Elsa left me on the beach, aiming a gun at me as she got into the dinghy, then boarded the submarine and disappeared. He told me to go home and said I might be called upon later.

Indeed, a few days afterward a man in a dark overcoat with a briefcase turned up on the door and asked to speak to me. He was from the War Department in Washington, but I told Mom he was from the insurance company about our roof.

Mom couldn't work out what happened to the Turners. I told her Elsa had mentioned she and her mother were thinking of moving back to DC after all. This seemed to satisfy Mom, but she still thought it odd that they never said goodbye or left a forwarding address. Still, she had their one month's deposit, and I assured her it was quite all right to keep it in lieu of notice.

Some weeks later, there was a paragraph in the *Rehoboth Beach News* about a woman's body being washed up along the coast in Maryland, with a request from the police for someone to come forward and identify her. Of course, no one identified Elsa, and I assume the case just passed into one of those unsolved files at the police station.

About a month later, I got some marvelous news. Frank's ship was due to dock in Norfolk, Virginia, and he would have a week's leave before they were off again. I didn't want him wasting any precious time getting up here, so I arranged to travel down to Norfolk to be waiting for him as he comes ashore.

I don't know if I'll tell Frank absolutely everything; he may be the one person I do tell, but I'll see. I don't want anything to get in the way of our perfectly blissful week. After all, it was only Elsa and me on the beach that night. And the beach can keep a secret.

PETER GREW UP IN LONDON, ENGLAND, AND THEN HIS JOB TRANSFERRED HIM TO SILICON VALLEY IN CALIFORNIA, WHERE HE BECAME A US CITIZEN. SOME YEARS LATER, HE SETTLED IN LEWES, DELAWARE.

TAKING ONE OF THE EXCELLENT GUIDED TOURS THROUGH FORT MILES PROVIDED HIM WITH A LOT OF THE BACKGROUND FOR THIS STORY, AND AFTER A CAREER OF WRITING CORPORATE EMAILS, IT WAS NICE TO WRITE SOMETHING A LITTLE MORE INTERESTING.

Where Do I Begin?

By Phil Giunta

For the first time in nearly a decade, Dustin was on his way to a date.

He was meeting Shannon for supper at Zogg's Raw Bar & Grill in thirty minutes. Of all the women who had responded to his profile on midlifesingles.com, she was the most compatible and genuine—or so it had seemed from the messages they exchanged.

He checked his watch as he stepped onto the boardwalk from St. Lawrence Street, where he now lived after inheriting his parents' house last year. Zogg's was nine short blocks away. *Plenty of time to get there via the beach. Maybe it'll calm my nerves.* He slipped off his sandals and made his way down the ramp, nodding to a young lady as she passed.

She returned a wink. "Love that spring smile."

He did a double take at the auburn curls beneath a wide-brimmed sun hat. *Jessica …* In the blink of an eye, the woman's hair was blond and straight. "Uh, thank you."

"Enjoy your evening."

"I'm gonna try. You too."

It's a whole different life here, or it could be if I put the past behind me. Despite his anxiety about dating again at fifty-two, Dustin took solace in the briny scent of the early May sea breeze, the churning waves that crashed onto the sand and receded in soothing repetition, and the thin bands of gossamer clouds that striped an otherwise clear sky.

In all of his travels, Dustin could count on one hand how many places had brought him peace. The Delaware Coast was one of them. Yet that peace was tarnished by the hell he'd gone through to get here. He knew it would take time to heal, to jettison the baggage of his past, but he wanted to move forward sooner rather than later. After all, he wasn't getting any younger.

Stop worrying. Shannon's probably nervous too. Not many people reach our age without scars. Just be yourself.

"By all means, be yourself and show her what a loser you are."

Dustin closed his eyes and rocked his head back. Even a year after their divorce, his ex-wife still occupied space in his head, beating him down with incessant recriminations, just as she had during their marriage. *Don't start, Brandi. Not tonight. Get out of my head.*

"I wonder how Shannon will react when she finds out you're an alcoholic."

Recovering *alcoholic. I've been sober since we split.*

"Once a drunk, always a drunk. You tried to keep it from me until you spiraled out of control. You were still grieving over Tyler and, yes, Jessica. I couldn't live up to her. Neither could Kirsten before me. You denied it, but I know all of your secrets, Dusty. I only wish I'd known them before I married you."

I was battling severe depression, Brandi. I should have been upfront about it and not tried to hide it from you. I made mistakes, but I never meant to hurt you.

"You can change location, but you can't change the fact that you're damaged goods, Dusty, and when Shannon figures that out, she'll run from you like I did. You'll be alone for the rest of your life."

"Yeah," he muttered. "Maybe you're right, Brandi."

As Dustin trudged across the sand, laughter from a family standing at the water's edge shook him from his reverie and silenced Brandi's verbal onslaught. He stopped to watch as a mother and father clutched their toddler's hands, lifting him into the air each time the next wave advanced toward their feet.

"We were like that once. Those were good days ... before it all went to hell."

I don't need the reminder, Kirsten. I think about it every day.

"Then it should be easy to tell Shannon how you were an absent father to a son who wanted your love and approval, to spend more time with you, to know that you were proud of him. Instead, you ignored him, pushed him away."

I didn't push him away. I took that new job and had to travel. It was good money. I was trying to build a better life for us.

"I would have preferred a better marriage. You were working to avoid me, to avoid being a father. By the time you realized the consequences, it was too late."

Don't go there again, Kirsten. Please. Dustin's stomach clenched. She always knew where to hit him. *I was young. Immature. In hindsight, I was still a mess after Jessica. I wasn't ready for parenthood.*

"I had to find that out the hard way, but I don't care that you neglected me. I'm sure Shannon would love to hear about your suicide attempt after Tyler overdosed on heroin, or will you keep that from her? Your skeletons follow you everywhere you go, Dusty. Turn around now before they ruin another woman's life."

Dustin snatched off his sunglasses and wiped the tears from his face. "Yeah." His voice cracked. "Maybe you're right, Kirsten."

"*She* is *right*, boy."

I don't need a lecture from you, Dad.

Kirsten was gone. Now, Dustin imagined his father limping along beside him from the leg wound he had suffered during the Vietnam War.

"*You gonna tell your new girlfriend what a lousy, no-good son you were? How you left me to rot in a nursin' home, just waitin' for me to die so you could get the house here? You think you deserve to be happy, boy? You failed as a son, a husband, and a father. You're no good to anyone.*"

I had the best teacher, or did you forget that the only time you were around was when you were drunk? Who was it who spat in my face and told me I was an accident who should never have been born? *The things you did to me and Mom when you were trashed I could never tell anyone. Thanks to you, I suffered a lifetime of depression and—*

"Oh, shut up. You still cryin' about that after all these years? Jesus Christ! You're a grown man. Get over it! I did what I did to prepare you for the world, to make you tough and strong. Take responsibility for yourself and stop blamin' me for your failures. Ain't no woman ever gonna want you."

"Yeah." Dustin's gaze fell on the spiraled coil of an ivory whelk shell protruding from the sand. He dropped to his knees and scooped it up. It was hardly a perfect specimen. One side had been punctured, leaving a gaping hole, and the tip of the spire had snapped off, along with a few of the knobs that studded the shell's wide top. Dustin ran a thumb over the cracked jagged edge of the opening. What had once been a beautiful shell was now hollow and broken. The world had taken its toll. *You can't change the fact that you're damaged goods.*

"Maybe you're right, Dad." He tightened his trembling grip on the shell. "Maybe all of you were right about me."

"No. They're wrong. Dusty, you were the most responsible and loyal man I ever knew. You were by my side every minute of my battle with cancer. You took care of me and loved me like no one else in my life—right up to the end, babe."

Right up to the end, Jessica. Dustin's tears were drops on the sand. I never got over losing you.

"I know."

Of course, I tried to keep that from Kirsten and Brandi.

"They knew it, too, and it destroyed your life with them. Whatever happens tonight, Dusty, don't let it ruin that too. I told you before I … before I died … go out and find love again. Be happy."

Dustin snickered. *Clearly, I don't know how.*

In his mind's eye, Jessica knelt before him, the evening sunlight casting a vermilion halo around her auburn curls. *"Why did you move to Rehoboth?"*

To start fresh. Find inner peace. To be near the ocean, the boardwalk, the festive atmosphere. Remember those summer nights when we strolled down Rehoboth Mews to the Coffee Mill? You would get Caramel Kiss …

"And you got Toffee Crunch."

And we would sit outside, listening to live guitar music under the soft white lights that crisscrossed the alley. We were young and didn't have a worry on Earth. I want to feel that way again.

"You can, Dusty. The ocean, the boardwalk, the coffee shop, they're all still here. You have another chance to be the Dusty I knew, the Dusty I loved. He's still in there. The past can only stop you if you let it. Take it slow with Shannon. Don't dump it all on her at once but be honest with her. No more secrets. If she's the one for you, it'll work out."

You were always the wise one, Jess.

"Just flash that spring smile."

Alone on the beach, Dustin stood and squared his shoulders, drawing himself to his full height. He had a fleeting urge to hurl the shell into the ocean but thought better of it. Instead, he brushed it off and slipped it into his jacket pocket. *For luck.*

* * * * *

"Look for a pale green baseball cap and long-sleeve yellow T-shirt," Shannon had said when they scheduled their date. As Dustin passed Zogg's outdoor bar and strode into the restaurant, he spotted that exact combination at a booth against the windows. He fiddled with the seashell in his jacket pocket in a feeble attempt to ignore the quivering in his chest. *Just be yourself.*

She was scrolling through her phone as he approached. "Hi, Shannon. I hope you weren't waiting long."

She gazed up at him and returned his smile. "Hey, Dustin! Not at all." She tucked her phone into her purse. "I got here early. I haven't been to Rehoboth in a few years, so I decided to make a day of it. Did some shopping, took a walk on the beach."

"You, too, eh?" As Dustin slipped off his jacket and slid into the booth, something clattered to the floor.

"What was that?" Shannon ducked beneath the table and emerged a moment later, whelk shell in hand.

Dustin chuckled. "Just something I found during *my* walk on the beach today."

She examined it for a moment before handing it to him. "Do you collect them?"

"Not really, but for some reason, this one appealed to me."

"It's seen better days."

He shrugged. "Maybe that's why."

"Our waitress is bringing water. I was going to order a Corona, but according to your profile, you don't drink, so I didn't want to do anything inappropriate in case …"

Dustin raised an eyebrow.

"What I mean is … my ex-husband was an alcoholic who tried to quit drinking more than once. As much as he tried to control me, he couldn't control himself."

"I see." *Not many people reach our age without scars.*

After the waitress took their orders, Shannon folded her arms atop the table and leaned forward. "So, tell me more about yourself—beyond the rosy façade we all write in our profiles. I want to know about the *real* Dustin."

"The real Dustin." He returned a wry smile and ran a thumb along the seashell's coarse, pitted surface. "Where do I begin?"

Phil Giunta's novels include the paranormal mysteries *Testing the Prisoner*, *By Your Side*, and *Like Mother, Like Daughters*. His short stories appear in such anthologies as *Love on the Edge*, *Scary Stuff*, *A Plague of Shadows*, *Beach Nights*, *Beach Pulp*, the *Middle of Eternity* series, and many more. He is a member of the Horror Writers Association, the National Federation of Press Women, and the Greater Lehigh Valley Writers Group.

Phil is currently working on the final draft of a science fiction novel while plotting his triumphant escape from the pressures of corporate America, where he has been imprisoned for over twenty-five years. Visit Phil's website at www.philgiunta.com.

Phil's story for *Beach Secrets* is dedicated to his friend Jessica Headlee, who lost her yearlong battle with cancer in June 2021 at the age of twenty-five.

Chance Encounters

By Sarah Barnett

If a photo existed of us during that year, I wouldn't recognize myself. What were we doing? Besides making a huge mistake.

A stranger looking at that imaginary photo would see a short, slightly overweight woman next to a taller, slimmer, younger man. A second grader would see the mismatch and wonder why we stood so close to each other.

My marriage to Ryan was coming apart, so I was hiding out in Rehoboth Beach. For fifteen years I'd rated our relationship as "almost happy." As silly as it might seem, our major problem was the beach. Ryan considered the ocean his enemy. The sea threw sand everywhere—sand that lingered in his shoes, migrated to feet and toes, and from there to … well, everywhere. He sneered at boardwalk food and souvenir shops filled with tacky trinkets. I considered the beach my true home and tried to appreciate each of its seasonal personalities. I spent as much weekend and vacation time as I could in the condo I'd inherited from my parents, while Ryan stayed at our house in Virginia and went on mountain hikes with his buddies or binge-watched whatever sport was in season. When I daydreamed about retiring from teaching, I saw myself breakfasting on the condo's patio that overlooked a small pond. I did not share this vision with Ryan.

October 2018

We met at trivia night at Fins. Larry and Marian stopped by our table to talk to Lana, my best Rehoboth friend. Lana knew many locals from her work at the library, and we'd bonded over our appreciation of the same novels. When she introduced them, she united their names in one breath: "LarryandMarian." It almost rhymed. They held hands as we chatted. Larry's mustache matched his tortoiseshell eyeglasses. I admired Marian's streaky blond hair, which she wore in a sculptured layered style that said "salon-do."

Next day, I was in Safeway looking for sea salt when I spotted Larry crouched in the aisle. He was talking to the spices.

"Get outta there. You belong over here."

I couldn't resist. "Do they listen to you? Or are they like my sixth graders?"

He looked up and laughed. His brown eyes laughed too. "Stephanie, right?"

I nodded.

He gestured at a basket at his feet filled with canned soup, cake mix, and cereal boxes. "Makes the job easier. People put stuff anywhere." The tag on his shirt read "Manager."

Ten minutes later we sat drinking coffee at one of the Starbucks tables in front of the store. Small talk. He liked his job. It left time for biking and fishing. Marian had a front-desk job at a local hotel. He liked living on the edge of the country, where the land was flat, and you could bike or walk for miles. So many places to see the sun rise and set. He worried that Marian was more driven by her career. She hoped to find work at a bigger hotel that hosted meetings and conventions—in Philly or DC. As we talked, he twisted his napkin into a spiral. "My family's here. I can't imagine living that far from the ocean."

Then he turned the conversation around. "You like coming to Rehoboth by yourself?"

I didn't want to make a speech about Ryan, the beach, my confusion. I shrugged. "It's complicated."

"I was just …"

"No, it's OK. Let's just say I'm at a point in my life, my marriage, where I need a break. It can be lonely, but in a good way. Being alone helps me think."

"I get that," he said. And I thought he did.

February 2019

I told myself it wasn't cheating. But it wasn't not cheating either.

It began innocently enough on a sunny November day.

I was walking south on the boardwalk holding an ice cream cone, while I watched the waves as they crested and broke toward the shore.

I didn't recognize Larry in street clothes walking toward me, but Bogo, his super friendly golden retriever, veered over to say hello. They stopped and I bent down to scratch Bogo's ears and tell him how beautiful he was. And then the three of us continued walking together as if we had planned it.

After that, we did plan it. Larry would consult his phone. "How about Saturday at nine?" He'd suggest a meeting place. Marian worked most weekends, so before or after Larry's Safeway shift, we'd walk on the Junction and Breakwater Trail, in Cape Henlopen State Park, in Prime Hook.

We walked side by side, talking easily, with periods of comfortable silence. Once, we stopped to watch a woodpecker digging into a dead oak tree. The temperature hovered around freezing and when I pulled my scarf a little tighter, Larry put his arm around my shoulders. It felt so natural I wanted to turn in for a full hug. I didn't.

"How are things in Virginia?" he asked as we climbed the steps to the Hawk Watch.

I wasn't sure how much to share, but I'd just figured out something about my marriage. "You know how sometimes you argue over some small thing? And you keep going back and forth? In other words, nowhere?"

He nodded. We went over to a bench and sat.

"Did you ever think the thing you were arguing about was not the *real* problem?"

He drew his eyebrows together in a frown, so I went on.

"Lately, I can't do anything right. I told you he hates the beach, right?"

"And ..."

"And now I don't load the dishwasher right, and I drive too slow, but I don't make a full stop at a stop sign, and he picked up one of my library books to read and didn't like it. And I finally realize this is not about the beach or appliances or driving or reading. It's *me* he doesn't like."

I think he wanted to hug me then. Instead, he took me by the elbow, and we got up to continue our walk. After a while he said, "Marian's going to DC for an interview with Marriott."

"How do you feel about living in DC?"

"The truth? I'd hate to leave here. But she's set on having what she calls *a real career*. He made air quotes with his hands. "I always thought we'd stay here, but she wants to try city living. It's her dream."

And then I found myself wanting to hug him.

June 2019

Ryan and I agreed to a trial separation. We both knew we wouldn't try terribly hard. He was seeing Allison, his ex-wife.

"You two are dating? I asked.

"Kind of," he said.

I planned to spend summer in the condo and look for a teaching job in Delaware. I'd always planned to live in Rehoboth someday, and someday was arriving earlier than expected.

My walks with Larry made me realize how much I'd missed talking to someone with no hidden agenda or points to make. He'd tell me how he'd made Italian-style "gravy," which is what non-Italians call "sauce." I told him about my grandmother's "secret" cheesecake recipe, which was really the recipe printed on the cream cheese package. We went back and forth about favorite beach foods. He liked the Ice Cream Store; I favored Kohr's. He was a fan of Grotto's; I preferred the pizza at Louie's. He put ketchup on his hot dogs; I went for mustard and sauerkraut.

We had an unspoken agreement to keep our friendship, if that's what it was, to ourselves. A forty-five-year-old woman and a thirty-three-year-old man taking long walks together while sometimes discussing their respective marriages—weird, right?

I was at the farmers market buying tomato plants when I looked up and saw Larry biking through the park. He stopped and pulled off his helmet. "Hey, Steph," he said, "Let's get cupcakes." Ryan had called me *Steph-an-ie*, sometimes dragging out the syllables and using a tone that suggested he was about to discipline a toddler. I liked that Larry had shortened it to Steph. I could be a different person when I was with him.

He got vanilla. I chose chocolate. Then he stopped to buy apple cider doughnuts for Marian. Apparently, she was feeling down because she didn't get that job she wanted but was still determined to advance her career. She'd driven to a shopping mall almost two hours away to find professional-looking clothes you couldn't find in Rehoboth.

That chance encounter with Larry reminded me that Rehoboth is the kind of town where you're always running into someone you know. At the library, you meet a friend from yoga class. At yoga, you meet the woman who served you lunch at Summer House or Dogfish. Sooner or later, one of us was going to run into someone who would wonder what we were doing together.

I was wondering the same thing. I was attracted to Larry, but whenever I considered romantic possibilities, I saw all the reasons it would be wrong. For both of us. His marriage, of course. And for me, a twelve-year age gap that felt like a chasm I hesitated to, and maybe couldn't, cross.

I couldn't shake my uneasiness, but I didn't want to give up what we had.

Summer was my least favorite Rehoboth season—sluggish traffic, crowded restaurants, parking that resembled a spectator sport, and a general feeling that "lower, slower, Delaware" had crawled to a stall.

The thunderstorm before the holiday weekend signaled trouble. I was supposed to meet Larry at Lake Gerar, but he texted me a foggy photo of the Henlopen Hotel with the message, "rained out." It was around four, the loneliest part of the afternoon. I settled down with a book and a cup of tea and was beginning to think about dinner when my doorbell rang.

Larry. In a sodden hoodie. At my door. We looked at each other for several awkward seconds. I couldn't read the expression on his face. "I'm … I'm lonely," he said.

Those two words triggered all that came next.

I tried to tell him with my eyes that I understood. *I know lonely*, I wanted to say. I know how it feels to be *with* someone and lonely at the same time.

Maybe nothing would have happened if I hadn't pulled him inside and lifted my arms to hug and be hugged. We made our way to the couch, where I put my arms around him, and he rested his head on my chest. The kisses that came later felt like promises.

Did I think about my list of reasons why sex with Larry was a bad idea? I'm sorry to say I didn't. Our lovemaking surprised me. It was slow and tender. Like a goodbye.

Later, he sat on the bed, buttoning his shirt, when I came out of the bathroom wearing my robe. "This is not why I came here," he said, waving at the tangled bedding.

"I know." I sat next to him.

"No, really." He turned to look at me. "I came to tell you that Marian and I are leaving Rehoboth. There's a job offer for her in DC. We're going to try living somewhere in Maryland—Silver Spring, maybe."

"I'm sorry." What could I say that would make him feel better? *Silver Spring is lovely!* I could babble about DC's museums, theater, professional sports, but that was all meaningless to him. "That's nice for Marian," I said. Strangely enough, I meant that. Part of me was glad that this woman would get what *she* wanted, instead of going along with her husband's desires.

"It'll be good for us," Larry said, as if repeating something he'd read in a magazine. "We'll come back to visit my folks. And we'll vacation here too."

We shared a long hug at the door. Then he was gone.

August – September 2019

In the weeks that followed, I had a lot to think about. How did I become the "other woman" in some melodrama? Or was it a soap opera? Sure, Ryan's rejection still hurt, but that was no excuse. "Illicit" is the word that popped into my head in the morning while I scooped coffee into the filter and waited to hear the machine groan in acknowledgment. *Illicit,* I thought, while I sat on my patio, the fountain burbling, the birds twittering.

I checked out piles of books from the library—literature, beach reads, mysteries, romances—anything that offered clues on how single women managed their lives. Self-help didn't help, but novels offered multiple views into the lives of women I could identify with. I admired the successfully single ones. Women who were happy dining alone and didn't need a romantic relationship to feel complete.

I missed seeing Lana and my other Rehoboth friends. Lana and I intersected at the library, but I always pretended to be on my way somewhere. The problem was I hadn't told anyone about Larry. I had a secret to keep, so I couldn't talk about missing him. On nice days, I'd rise early and drive downtown to the beach, walk the shoreline, watch the sun rise. When the water began sparkling with reflected sunlight,

I'd get some coffee and sit on a bench to watch the town come to life.

You can only wallow for so long. My divorce would be final soon, and I was about to begin teaching math at a nearby middle school. So one day, I headed to the outlets to shop for school clothes.

I stepped out of the dressing room to get a better look at myself in a full-length mirror about fifteen feet away. *Who was that woman?* The dress that was cute on the hanger had turned me into a little old lady. I almost laughed aloud at my idea that someone spotting Larry and me would get suspicious. More likely they'd take me for his mother.

That wake-up call sent me to the gym and spin class, where I met Kim, also a teacher, who invited me to join her and some of the other "spin-aholics" for coffee after class. Our coffee klatch consisted of six to eight women, ranging from thirty-something to seventy-something. We were single, divorced, widowed, married to men, married to women. We never ran out of things to talk about.

"Where have you been all summer?" Lana asked when I ran into her at Safeway's deli counter.

"Long story," I said. "I'll tell you some time. How are things at the library?"

Lana tossed her packages of provolone and turkey into her cart. "Our book club's starting soon. You in?"

I'd been hoping for an invitation. "Definitely. I've been doing a lot of reading lately."

November 2019 – February 2020

Each day, I felt more at home in Rehoboth. On my few weekend trips to visit friends in Virginia, I'd look forward to the watery landmarks on the return trip—Bay Bridge, Kent Narrows Bridge, Red Mill Pond— then finally signs that read "Beaches." I'd turn into my driveway, admire the evergreen shrubs I'd planted, think about accenting them with a rose bush or two, maybe some daisies and dahlias. This contentment came with a side of restlessness. I wasn't ready to think about dating, but I needed something besides plants to care for.

I fell in love with Ziggy at a Humane Society adoption event. He had a wiry gray coat and enormous, pointy ears that were out of proportion to the rest of his smallish body. Just looking at him made me laugh. When we arrived home, his ears perked up and his eyes studied the living room. He chose the sofa and made himself comfortable atop one of the throw pillows.

March – December 2020

Life changed dramatically when the COVID-19 pandemic arrived. The first semester of school went well, but by spring, classrooms were empty, and I was teaching math on Zoom to kids in their pajamas. My book club and coffee klatch friends became talking heads on my laptop screen. Some of us started meeting outdoors for socially distant walks on the boardwalk or around the neighborhoods near our homes.

One day, Lana joined Ziggy and me on a favorite jaunt. Starting at the library, we walked down Rehoboth Avenue to the boardwalk, then south to Prospect Street, where we turned west and walked up and down the blocks that ran perpendicular to the beach. We took turns pointing out houses we'd like to live in. I admired a cute bungalow; Lana liked a two-story home with a wraparound porch. We walked another block without speaking, each of us perhaps thinking that these dream homes close to the ocean would always be out of our reach. When I stopped to let Ziggy check out a mailbox post, Lana said, "Remember Larry and Marian from trivia night?"

What made her think about them? "Sure," I said. "I saw Larry a few times in Safeway."

"They've been living in Maryland. Marian got a hotel job in DC."

"I guess that's why I haven't seen him lately." My voice sounded funny. My face felt warm. *Was I blushing?*

"Well, you'll be seeing him again. The hotel business is kaput. Marian's been laid off. They've moved back to stay with Larry's folks until they can find an apartment."

I'd managed to wrap up my memories of Larry in a folder called "the past." If I was lucky (and careful), the story would stay hidden.

March 2021

I didn't recognize him right away, as we both wore the required face masks on the boardwalk. Ziggy swerved to check out an oncoming dog. *Was that Bogo?* It was. And the man walking toward me wearing sunglasses and a Washington Wizards sweatshirt was Larry. Our dogs did the usual meet-and-greet act, touching noses, circling, sniffing butts. If only people had a simple formula to smooth over awkward moments.

"You got a dog," Larry said.

"Yeah. And you're back." There's nothing like stating the obvious when you don't know what to say.

He explained about Marian losing her job. He was working at Fresh Market, hoping a management spot would open. Marian was looking into becoming a sales rep for a line of beauty products and nutritional supplements.

"Still talking to the spice jars?" I asked.

He smiled. "How 'bout you?"

I told him about teaching and book club and the gym, and ended with, "I'm sorry things didn't work out for Marian." What else could I say? I was searching for a graceful getaway or some way to convey, *it's over; let's not talk about it,* when Bogo pulled hard at the leash and barked a loud hello to a German shepherd he seemed to know. Larry gave me an apologetic look and trotted after his dog. I waved him away and we parted.

As I walked back to my car, I replayed the scene in my head and graded it C+. Probably the best we could do.

Life slowly returned to almost normal. Restaurants, stores, beaches, and boardwalk hummed with activity. I was checking out a silver jewelry display at a craft fair when I spotted them in the distance. It was like a scene from a movie: Marian placing hand-decorated hats on Larry's head one at a time, shaking her head while he pulled them off. Larry laughing, then grabbing a handful of hats to place on Marian's head. Marian laughing.

I should be happy for them, I thought. And I was, though the feeling was muddled with sadness and regret.

I moved off to an exhibit of small art works that I thought were paintings. When I got closer, I saw that the detailed scenes were composed entirely of colorful, intricate stitchery. I marveled at one small work—a tiny cottage with a thatched roof and a garden of roses, lilies, and daisies. I wondered at the artist's patience in stitching each tiny flower, a brick wall, a wrought iron gate. How many hours went into fashioning the cottage's minute stained-glass window? And I wondered, after weeks, months, maybe years, of painstaking work, how could the artist ever manage to let go of her creation?

Before retiring to Delaware and discovering the joys of creative writing, Sarah Barnett had careers as teacher, librarian, and lawyer. She is vice president of the Rehoboth Beach Writers' Guild and enjoys leading free writes, teaching writing classes, and dreaming up story and essay ideas while walking her dog on the beach. In 2020 she received a Delaware Division of the Arts Fellowship as an emerging writer.

Sarah loves living in Rehoboth and wrote "Chance Encounters" in part to celebrate year-round living at the beach. Her work has appeared in *Hippocampus*, *Delaware Beach Life*, *Delmarva Review*, and other publications, including several Cat & Mouse Press books.

Secret Message

By Carl Frey

"Mom!"

"Yes, dear. I just want the best for you. It was only a suggestion."

"I am not, repeat not, going to start nagging Roger."

"It's been five years, dear. That's all I was saying."

"OK, OK. Let's change the subject. Just do your crossword and let me handle Roger."

"I do have to get back to this puzzle. The deadline for the next edition of the *Beach Paper* is tomorrow."

"You've done them every week for, like, forever. It should be a cinch."

"Usually, I have them finished a week early, but I decided to design this puzzle with a theme and it's taking a bit longer than usual. You'll find out when you do it."

"Roger's the puzzler. When he finds out what it is, I'll know. I gotta run. Meeting Roger at Blue Moon for dinner."

Tina Rodney kissed her mom goodbye, pulled on a Cape Henlopen State Park ball cap, threaded her blond ponytail through the notch in the back, and left the Maryland Avenue house by the back door.

Evelyn returned to her puzzle construction, laboring over the upper right corner until it worked. When she finished, she emailed the completed puzzle to her editor with a note to not make any edits that would interfere with the puzzle theme.

$\star\,\star\,\star\,\star\,\star$

Roger Dewey had made it halfway through a Dogfish Head 60 Minute by the time Tina arrived at his Blue Moon corner table. She gave him a kiss on the lips, lingering a bit longer than usual. He had not seen her in days. Roger gave her waist a squeeze and sniffed her hair, enjoying the lingering fragrance of her shampoo. They sat and talked, sipping drinks and catching up, as they had not seen each other in over a week.

Tina peeked over her menu at Roger, watching him stroke his trim beard as he considered the menu, a habit of his that used to annoy her but no longer did. When Roger shaved his beard last year, she realized she liked it and encouraged him to grow it back. It returned and has stayed. He has too. She liked that.

At the end of the meal, they made plans for his return next week. He would stay a few days for beach time. Leaving the restaurant, Roger picked up a free *Beach Paper* so he could work the latest puzzle from Tina's mom when he had some free time in DC. He worked challenging puzzles every day from the *Post* or the *Times*. The easier puzzles in the *Beach Paper* often were part of his conversations with Evelyn, a classy lady who always made him feel at home in Rehoboth. Roger dropped Tina at her mom's and drove to DC and a pile of work.

* * * * *

Roger returned to spend an August week with Tina. Sitting under an umbrella at the beach, a refreshing breeze off the water rattled the newspaper in Roger's hands. With a pen he worked Evelyn's latest puzzle while Tina started a beach read she had picked up earlier in the day at Browseabout. Roger leaned over to Tina.

"OK, I need some help with this one. Your mother is getting crafty in her puzzle making. There's a clue: 'Actor Elwes in *The Princess Bride.*' I never saw that movie."

Tina lifted her sunglasses and stared at Roger. "You never saw *The Princess Bride*? Really? Inconceivable. I must have seen it half a dozen times. It's fun. I have to show it to you. We'll download it."

"I never saw it. Sure, let's watch it, but now—who is Actor Elwes in

The Princess Bride?"

"Cary. Like Cary Grant. That would have been too easy a clue for Mom."

"Thanks." Roger returned to his puzzle and Tina resumed reading.

When Roger finished, he clicked his pen closed and said, "Done." He gave Tina a nudge. "Your Mother created this puzzle with a secret message."

"Oh yeah, what's the message?"

Roger read the message and smiled. Tina beamed, nodded, and said, "Yes."

Message From an Admirer
Puzzle by Evelyn Rodney

ACROSS

1 I love ___
4 Ship pronoun
7 Mont Blanc for one
8 It can be a little piggy
9 Singer ___ Lang
10 Last instructions
11 Join or match
13 Actor Elwes of The Princess Bride
14 A partner for Pa
16 Point an arrow
17 Just wild about
18 Football 6 pointers
19 Last part

DOWN

1 Himalayan cattle
2 Queen of Spades
3 Heads ___ or 7 ___
4 Bond martini no-no
5 Divine fellow
6 Slithery sea creature
10 Dryly humorous
12 Some chairs have two
13 Meow maker
15 Combine or sum
17 Kiss ___ Kate

For message, read: 10, 1, and 11 across; 17 down

For help solving the puzzle, see the solutions page at the end of the book.

After Carl Frey retired from forty-one years working in flavor and fragrance chemistry, he hung up his lab coat, moved to Lewes, Delaware, and enrolled in writing courses at the Osher Lifelong Learning Institute. That leap led him to the Rehoboth Beach Writers' Guild and publishing a picaresque adventure/comedy novel: *Caldonia Cafe*. Cat & Mouse Press published his short story "Rehoboth Beach in Crisis" in their anthology *Beach Pulp*. He currently leads Guild-sponsored freewrite sessions on alternate Monday mornings at the Rehoboth Beach Public Library and constructs crossword puzzles for the Friends of Cape Henlopen State Park monthly newsletter.

Snapshots in Time

By Ellen Krawczak

Dorothy was in the middle of a blissful epicurean daydream, savoring a crusty French baguette with creamy, slightly smelly cheese running down the side, when the phone rang. She saw that it was Don, one of her twin brothers, and said to herself, "this cannot be good." Don rarely called her and never called with good news. "He better not throw a monkey wrench into my trip to the south of France next month," she said, even though there was no one there to hear her.

She and Aunt Betsy, her mother's sister, had planned this trip for three years. The first year, the travel agent canceled due to the coronavirus. The second year, she and Betsy canceled, concerned about flight quarantines. And now that this trip was so close, Dorothy did not want anything to upset her plans. She traveled with Aunt Betsy every summer, and the trips were always amazing. Aunt Betsy knew exactly where to travel, where to stay, and what to see. Money was never an issue.

"Hi," she said as she picked up the phone.

"Great news!" Don's voice boomed as Dorothy's stomach lurched.

"Tell me," Dorothy said, "did you win the lottery?"

Don laughed. "Not quite. A space has opened up in Brandywine Living at Seaside Pointe in Rehoboth for Mom, and she is thrilled to be moving into independent living. She will be in her new place by the end of the week, and we won't have to worry about her falling down the stairs in the river house."

"That is good news," Dorothy said, but she knew there was a catch. Don wouldn't be calling unless he wanted something.

"Listen," Don said. "I'm going to take care of sprucing up the house. Dan is going to handle the real estate end of it. Mom asked that you go through all the papers in the attic and keep what you think is important."

Dorothy groaned. She hated going to that house. Her memories of it were not one of a happy childhood. The house, which was on the Nanticoke River, had a long driveway with lots of pine trees and little sunlight, and the shadows always made the house feel sinister. The building was old and creaky, and the attic was dark and musty. She couldn't imagine sitting up there going through papers. "Why me?" she asked Don. "How am I supposed to know which papers are important and which are not?"

"I don't know. I offered to do it since I know your trip is coming up, but Mom said she wanted you to do it."

"Can I do it when I get back? I will only be gone a month, and the timing would be so much more convenient."

"Sorry, but Mom wants to get the house on the market as soon as possible. I've already started tackling repairs and Dan plans to list the house within the next few weeks. I promise that this won't interfere with your trip. Besides, Mom almost never asks you to do anything because she just can't deal with the attitude."

Don's words hurt, but they were accurate. Whereas Mom doted on the twins, she had never really warmed up to Dorothy, and Dorothy understood why. She was prickly, chafing at her mother's rules. She wanted her mother to be more like Aunt Betsy, spontaneous and fun. If Aunt Betsy had been Dorothy's mother, she would have let her skip school to travel and let her parachute jump when she had the chance. Her mother played it safe and boring.

Dorothy agreed reluctantly because she really did not have much choice—her summers were relatively free. She had become an English professor, not out of a love of literature, but because it afforded her time off to travel each summer. Dorothy talked to herself as she finished doing the dinner dishes. "I can do this. She is only asking me to clear out the attic and there is probably nothing worth saving anyway."

Dorothy decided to go to the river house the following Friday, although she grumbled about it for almost the entire week. "I am not happy about this," she muttered as she pulled out of the driveway, "but I guess complaining won't help. I sure hope she's not a hoarder." Dorothy brought a notebook to make a list of items to keep, along with boxes to put the items in. Her mother had several large recycling bins, which she hoped would hold the items she'd be pitching.

Dorothy arrived mid-morning, dressed in jeans, long socks, high-top shoes, a long-sleeved shirt, and work gloves. She prayed that her clothes would protect her from the spiders or other creepy crawlies skittering along the attic floors and walls. Carefully climbing the rickety stairs sideways, she placed one foot on each narrow riser.

The attic was as dank and musty as she expected. Even with the two small bulbs hanging from the ceiling, the room was dark and unwelcoming, but it was surprisingly uncluttered. She wondered why her mother didn't toss everything when she had the chance. There were a number of old cookbooks, and that made Dorothy laugh. Dorothy was a terrible cook, but her mother kept sharing recipes, hoping that one day Dorothy would come to enjoy cooking. "Not going to happen," she said out loud.

At the end of the first day, Dorothy had divided almost all the books between a pile for the twins and giveaways for the library, and she had tossed the moldy ones into the recycling bins. She stopped for the day, showered, and then drove into Rehoboth, treating herself to a Grotto pizza on the boardwalk. She had forgotten how much she loved being at the beach in the early evening, watching people walk by and listening to the roar of the ocean. She decided to return to the beach the next evening for dinner.

Dorothy had thought that going through her mother's attic would be tedious, but it was not. She set up a radio to provide background noise, although she found herself interrupting it with frequent utterances of, "you've got to be kidding," and "unbelievable." She found the old magazines dated, with their portrayals of the perfect wife who was gorgeous, cooked gourmet meals each evening for dinner, and had two unbelievably cute children. But she had to admit, she also found the magazines interesting. They were a snapshot of what was going on in the world at that time—the latest food trends and hair styles, changes in mores, and progress toward women's liberation and civil rights. When she came across her old Nancy Drew books, tears filled her eyes. She would take the books home with her. It might be fun for her students to read them, to compare them with mystery books written today. She smiled. "Thank you, Mom."

As Dorothy finished sorting the books and magazines, she came across a shoebox wrapped in a lovely blue lace ribbon. She opened it and found letters nestled within the blue satin. *From Dad?* she wondered. But when she picked up the letters, she realized they were from Caroline, her mother's college roommate. Dorothy had never met Caroline because she lived on the other side of the country, but she had been her mother's closest friend and they had corresponded throughout the years. *That's funny. She was never sentimental.*

Dorothy brought the letters downstairs to read in better light. The letters were newsy, although of course, she only had Caroline's to read. Mostly they were about Caroline and her family, with comments on what Dorothy's parents were doing (skiing, house hunting, preparing for twins). Then the tenor of the letters changed, and it was almost as if Caroline was giving her mother a pep talk.

Dear Laura,

I know how terribly disappointed you are that you won't be joining Ed and the twins for a year in Switzerland. How ironic since you did all the legwork in getting the boys internships and renting the chalet. I'm sure you thought your baby days were over with both boys finishing college and headed for a new life. But, a baby, what joy, what fun.

So, she was an "oops" baby. She had come along just before the entire family had planned to spend a year in Switzerland. Dorothy could only imagine how unhappy her mother must have been not to be able to ski the Alps or travel through Europe with the rest of her family. *No wonder she resented me. I would too.*

There were a number of other pep-talk letters to her mother. Apparently the "oops baby" was not an easy child—sullen and prone to temper tantrums. It seemed that Caroline was doing her best to keep her mother's spirit's up. "Well," Dorothy said indignantly, "what do you expect from an unwanted child?"

Dear Laura,

I am sad that you decided to put off law school until Dorothy is a bit older. I wish that Ed was around more often to help you. Having a husband in the diplomatic service and not being able to always travel with him must be so difficult. Please reconsider law school—I know how much you were counting on a career in law. Do you think that Betsy would be willing to sit for a few hours each day while you are in school?

Mom wanted to go to law school? She could only picture her mother in the kitchen with an apron, not in a courtroom with a legal brief. "I really don't know you at all, do I," she murmured. Dorothy had to admit to herself that she had never thought of her mother as a person with hopes and dreams. She decided to read the remainder of the letters the next day and returned to the beach to treat herself to an early dinner at Victoria's Restaurant in the Boardwalk Plaza Hotel.

The next afternoon Dorothy did a final sweep of the attic. She put the books for the twins and the Nancy Drew books in her car and consigned magazines, old check registers, and receipts to the recycling bins. After dropping off three boxes of books at the library, Dorothy stopped by the supermarket to buy a microwaveable dinner for that evening. She found herself looking forward to reading the rest of Caroline's letters. She began to feel that not only was she getting to know Caroline, but also she was getting to know her mother.

Dear Laura,

You must have been scared to death. I remember when Brian had croup and how frightening it was staying up all night, counting each breath. I wish Betsy was more of a help to you. Isn't she able to sit with Dorothy even a little bit so you can get some rest? Does she really need to be traveling for months on end? I wish I lived closer so I could help you.

I'm glad Dorothy is feeling stronger and hope she gets better soon. And I hope Betsy stops being so selfish.

The letters were interesting. Caroline was a good writer, and she came alive in the letters. She clearly loved Dorothy's mother and Dorothy began to see her mother as a younger woman, someone who had a life and dreams and a beloved friend who truly cared for her. *I wonder if I would have liked you—if we would have been friends. Would you have liked me?*

Dear Laura,

I'm sorry. I should hold my tongue, but honestly, how do you put up with her? What do you mean she didn't come to Dorothy's high school graduation? Was flying to India to go to an ashram that important? Sometimes I would like to shake some sense into that woman. Really. Did Dorothy feel bad, or did you gloss it over like you've done so many times before? When is Dorothy going to realize that the yearly trips and outrageous gifts are nothing? Sigh—I'm on my soapbox again. You, my dear Laura, are an amazing mother and I hope Dorothy realizes it someday.

Dorothy had to think for a minute. Aunt Betsy did take her on a trip every summer, which is why, Dorothy guessed, she liked traveling so much. And she did give her wonderful, completely useless presents. Dorothy remembered an airplane flying over with a huge "Congratulations!" banner when she turned twenty-one. But did Aunt Betsy come to her graduations or the family's Thanksgiving or holiday dinners? Dorothy couldn't remember seeing her on those occasions. Did Aunt Betsy have any relationship with the twins?

Dorothy was getting ready to box up the letters when a photograph, which had been stuck on the bottom, fell out of the box. It was a gorgeous picture of two women in their late thirties at the beach. They were standing at the water's edge, splashing each other. Dorothy recognized her mother. Her head was thrown back and her smile was one of pure elation. Dorothy turned the picture over and saw the writing, "Laura and Caroline in Rehoboth, June 30," and in parentheses, the year. She turned the picture over again. Her mother looked so carefree, so completely happy and joyous. Dorothy did not need to look in a mirror to see herself as she truly was—a resentful middle-aged woman, unable to let go of past grievances. Had she, she wondered, ever smiled with such abandon? Did she have any friends who loved her so completely?

She looked at the picture. Something was wrong, out of kilter. She turned the picture over again, and then again and again. It didn't make sense. The date on the picture was late July and Dorothy was born in early September. Her mother did not look the least bit pregnant.

"Oh, God," she cried out loud, rocking back and forth as she began to realize how wrong she had been all her life. Her resentment had been misplaced. The woman staring back at her in the photograph was not her biological mother, as she had always assumed, but her mother nevertheless. This was the woman who gave up going to law school, gave up a career, gave up traveling the world to be her mother. This was the woman who counted her breaths when she had croup, who baked cakes for her birthday parties, who taught her to ride a bike, who encouraged her to pursue her academic studies. Dorothy was not an "oops" baby; her mother had chosen her. And Dorothy had punished her by always comparing her mother to Aunt Betsy, carefree and without a responsibility in the world. She couldn't imagine Aunt Betsy giving up her jet-setting life to change a diaper or wipe a feverish brow with a wet cloth. But she could picture Aunt Betsy giving up her child, handing her to a sister to raise. It explained so many things.

She sat on the edge of her chair and sobbed until her shoulders were heaving. She then slid into a hot bath and wept some more. A wall of shame washed over her. The woman she thought had given her nothing had actually given her everything. And the woman who had given her everything had also given her up. *How could I have been so blind?* She knew she couldn't undo the past, but she could march forward into the future.

That evening, Dorothy sat in the kitchen, eating her microwaved dinner, accompanied by a full glass of red wine. It would be her last visit to the house. She took out her notebook and wrote down her plans. She would take pictures of the house in the morning and have them framed so her mother would always remember the home where she raised three children. She would try to establish an adult relationship with her mother. And she would screw up her courage to tell Aunt Betsy that she would not be accompanying her to France this summer.

* * * * *

It was a beautiful, sunny, summer day when Dorothy drove up to Brandwine Living. Her mother greeted her, but her smile looked wary. Her eyes popped a bit when she saw that Dorothy had made muffins for her.

"Did you actually bake them?"

"I did," said Dorothy, smiling, "and I promise that if you drop one on your foot it will not break a toe. I've been practicing."

While they were having tea and muffins, Dorothy said, "Mom, I read Caroline's wonderful letters."

"Ah, yes," her mother said. "I thought you might find them interesting."

"Oh, more than interesting, Mom. Ever so much more."

Her mother took a sip of tea and slowly put her cup down. "Would you like to keep them, Dorothy?"

"Yes, Mom, yes. I was hoping you would ask. A thousand times, *yes*."

"Then, that is my gift to you, but it is also a gift to me that you read the letters and that they meant something to you."

"And, I have a present for you," Dorothy said, handing her mother the two framed photographs of the house. Dorothy had spent part of her last morning at the house walking around, taking pictures. A friend who taught photography edited them and the local art studio framed them. Dorothy had caught the sunlight streaming through the trees, and somehow the house looked more friendly to Dorothy.

Dorothy's mother smiled, her eyes crinkling around the edges. "Why, they are lovely," she said. "Did you take them?"

Dorothy nodded. "Home is where the heart is. Your old home has traveled to join you in your new home."

Her mother walked around the room and picked out a spot for both pictures. "This will be the perfect place for them."

"I agree. And, speaking of travel, pick out a place you would like for us to go and let's start planning." Dorothy clasped her mother's hand as they sat down to look at the brochures that Dorothy had spread out on the table.

Ellen Krawczak is enjoying the quiet life on Maryland's Eastern Shore. She lives on the St. Martin River and loves watching the ducks and gulls and birds from her sunroom window. Before she retired, she was a paralegal in a New York City Law firm, a real estate settlement officer, and a substitute teacher.

Judge's Comment

Secrets about self, especially long-held ones that affect who we are and where we came from, are the most difficult to reconcile and forgive. This is especially true when the secret has been held by the family members closest to us. This story reminds us that forgiveness benefits all involved.

The Summer Jar

By Donald Challenger

June 2021: North Shores, Rehoboth Beach

In the end, Lyle Cathcart begins his memoir at the beginning. Laptop screen pallid in the glare, he calls up nine pages that read like the barroom swagger of nearly every guy he's worked with for thirty years: the effortless shrug of alpha-male preening. He jumps to the end— "did the math on my phone at the end of the day and saw that seven figures had become eight"— and in a spasm of disgust, punches the delete key, watching it all vanish: boarding school, Georgetown, Wharton; free-climbing through futures, options, hedge funds; the bulletproof rush of eight-balls vacuumed in the backseats of cabs at two a.m. with this week's girlfriend on one hip and a "personal assistant" on the other, materializing from somewhere, courtesy of someone, en route to some other club. *Delete.*

Begin. He pours another tumbler of single-malt and stares at the Atlantic from his third-story crow's nest. An actual crow dozes on the handrail. Tenacious heat. It's early for a second pour, maybe eleven a.m., but today it feels as though the screaming light, the spangled water, the bottomless sky are drinking *him* in.

The beginning could be childhood memories, day-tripping from DC with his mother, or, later, as a teenager bent on anarchy along this strip of sand then known as Whiskey Beach, home to underage parties into the '80s. He'd roamed the dunes here as a kid, ransacked on weed and Colt 45, and it felt like uncharted wilderness. Now it's conquered, tamed by new money like his own. Yet Lyle has triangulated it several times and is pretty sure that he once got serious with a cheerleader far out of his league right *here,* on what is now his own private beach. Which is kind of why he bought it.

Along the tide line, an old man with a metal detector straggles past.

In fact, Lyle knows where to begin, has known since he slid out of bed three hours ago and tiptoed from the room so that the smack of feet on hardwood would not wake her. Jennifer? Geraldine? An old-fashioned name he'll remember when he needs to. He still sees that real beginning with the quicksilver clarity of an old snapshot: his mother tucking him in, her face exhausted from another marathon shift at the dry cleaner. He was ten. He could smell the solvent she bore at night, summon her grinding cough. Her feet were leaden on the stairs, but her face would glow when he sang her name as she reached his door. "Lily?" She loved the sound of her name, banished "Mom" early, would always have a ghost story ready—pseudo-spooky tales that ended with a hand grabbing him under the covers.

But on this night the story had been different. Given the trauma that followed, he doesn't remember much—some creepy Indian thing about a spirit trapped in a clay pot every winter, maybe some eco-myth—but he recalls being transfixed.

Then she kissed him goodnight, shuffled down the stairs. Later, slipping into sleep, he heard the door close. When the car started in the driveway, he jolted awake and piled downstairs in panic. He was too late. He never saw her again. Nor, to his knowledge, has anyone else.

He pours again. "The secret beginning," he writes, "is the moment when the world you know burns down behind you."

✶ ✶ ✶ ✶ ✶

June 1956: Camp Arrowhead, Sussex County

In the end, Mildred Duffy's wheezy Plymouth expires on a thin gravel road skirting Rehoboth Bay. Fireflies stutter a semaphore in the trees. She finds the hood latch, which leads to the discovery of steam spitting from a kinked hose winding to a screw cap that says *Warning!* at the top and *Pressure!* at the bottom, which pretty much leaves her where she was before finding the hood latch. She'll have to walk the last stretch to Camp Arrowhead in the twilight. She spits some choice incantations, climbs back in, and squeezes into her storytelling costume. It's part blowsy, bejeweled gypsy, part Glinda the Good Witch—whatever she could piece together from Rehoboth's only thrift shop. She flattens a mosquito in the amber glow of the dash light, checks her wristwatch, smears on some stage makeup. Then she steps out and unlocks the trunk. To her left, a whip-poor-will is crestfallen; otherwise, the road lies silent.

She pries a flashlight from under the spare and peels open her notebook. The night before, she'd cribbed the kernel of a campfire yarn from an old Federal Writers' Project book of Delaware history and lore. She'd planned on a half hour or so to whip those arid paragraphs into a real ghost story before meeting the kids in the story circle. She loves getting the voice right, the gestures, a first sentence that opens like a creaky door. Stories matter. But tonight, that ship has sailed. She's late. It's dark.

She looks at the Sussex roadmap in the scanty light. She'd passed the last service station, the last pay phone, the last streetlamp at least forty minutes ago. She curses her poor choice of shoes. Then Mildred Duffy tests the gravel with one foot, breathes deeply, and summons Angelica in the warm, calm woods—good gypsy, plausible seer, paid fifteen dollars tonight to frighten children.

"A long, long time ago," she tests the silence, "before your grandparents' grandparents were born, an Indian holy man from the Nanticoke tribe tricked the summer into—" She gags theatrically, imagining nine-year-olds nodding off. Tries again. "Did you know that every season has a spirit?" No, too philosophical. A girl needs a story and, beyond everything, a *secret*. She waltzes the flashlight beam through the scrim of trees, kicking up gravel.

"This very summer—this very *week*—just down the beach from here, a sister and brother were digging in the sand and uncovered something frightening," she finally says. "An ancient secret. Let's call them Patsy and … Thomas. And let's call what they found 'the summer jar.'" Pause. "Because the *real* names for who they are and what they found are too *terrifying*, even for brave girls like you."

That'll work. She smiles and finds her footing.

* * * * *

In the End, Sleuths Shelve Search for Lost Writers' Project Author

By Orville Wickes, Jr.

REHOBOTH BEACH — One year after a young woman researching the history of Sussex County vanished in broad daylight, police admit their investigation is at an impasse.

Miss Denise "Dini" Rose, 23, was last seen departing from the Zwaanendael Museum in Lewes June 21, 1937, at 2:45 p.m., according to investigators. No sign of foul play or ill intent has been unearthed.

Ironically, Miss Rose had just made a discovery of quaint Indian lore recorded by the region's first Dutch explorers.

"We never close the book on a riddle like this," said Capt. Bryce Carmichael of the Delaware State Police, who took command of the case days after the disappearance. "However, with no witnesses, no evidence of foul play—no evidence, period—it is time to direct the resources of our men in blue to more pressing matters."

It is believed that Miss Rose, a strapping but boyishly attractive "physical culture" enthusiast who enjoyed the outdoors and strenuous pursuits, intended to walk northeast to Cape Henlopen Point and then south down the shore to Rehoboth Beach, a distance of about ten miles.

Though a forbidding trek for a young lady, "that was her way, to walk or run or ride her bicycle everywhere," said her dear friend and roommate, Miss Agnes Gould, who reported Miss Rose missing when she did not arrive at their apartment by nightfall. "Why, Dini did not even drive an automobile!"

Yet no witness has ever come forward to report seeing Miss Rose along that route, police said. That is puzzling, because it was a balmy Monday afternoon, with sun worshippers and fishermen out and about as the beach region's "high season" began.

Miss Rose, an avid swimmer, may have stopped along an isolated stretch of sand between Lewes and Rehoboth to take a dip, found herself in trouble, and succumbed to the waves, police say. However, coastal records for that day indicate neither rip currents nor high surf.

Miss Gould dismissed such speculation as "poppycock" in any case. "That's about as likely as Gertrude Ederle drowning in the bathtub," she said. "Dini could swim the whole way if she wanted."

A final curiosity is that Miss Rose departed the museum with a satchel of notes from her research. A student of history at the University of Delaware, she had been hired by Professor Harold Deakyne of that august institution to study the beach region for a forthcoming book-length history of Delaware. When published this year it will be one of forty-eight such volumes, one for each state, commissioned by the U.S. Works Progress Administration under the aegis of the Federal Writers' Project.

Neither satchel nor papers have been found.

(Continued on Page 8)

✶ ✶ ✶ ✶ ✶

1631: Zwaanendael Settlement

Charred fragment of letter, Jacobus Wolfert to unknown recipient, presumed 1631/32; recovered from earthenware jar at site of original Walvis colony, provenance unproven. Zwaanendael Museum, Lewes, Delaware. Archived 1937: Miscellaneous Correspondence, Pre-colonial. Box 3, Folder 23.

In the end, I come to know these savage folk as a curious and intelligent people. They are greatly our masters in the nurture of crops. They abide by a system of governance that is orderly, if mysterious, and they commune with a hierarchy of gods and spirits that, while heretical by any Christian measure, in sum honors virtuous action. With prayer and reflection, I humbly have come to believe the Nantaquak, our brethren in many means, excepting of course, with reluctance, the Grace conferred by the Sacrament of Baptism under the Beneficence of Our Holy Father.

Yet many in the colony are of far darker estimate. Our Dear Reverend Bastiaen, for his measure, observes them to be "joyous in their wickedness, contemptible in their comportment, beyond all reason," as I recall his words … [charred, indecipherable] and thus, around the long finger of shore we speak of as Zuijt Hoek, and into a wilderness of sand and pine, though God preserve us has in these few months provided scant bounty … [indecipherable]. As we faced the quieting sea, discouraged, we bore in our nets and spoke a penitential grace in Divine Service, considering upon the Holy Supper of the Lord.

On the path to Blommaert's Kill some whispered of the visitor, a native yet again encountered down the strait of sand below Zuijt Hoek … [indecipherable] claims not to be of the Nantaquak, nor the Tshapetank. He shares our tongue with a facility remarkable even to

Rehoboth Beach Reads

Bastiaen, who is learned in many languages and poorly inclined to credit any savage … [charred, indecipherable] greeted by the natives not with tumult, but with empty eyes, as if the visitor is not seen, or has passed in the night beyond the ears of sentinels.

He arrives in twilight or early morn, seen always by a lone brother at toil or at prayer. He is by accounts tall—benevolent—standing in a humble light that cannot be confused with a visitation of Our Savior. He speaks patiently and nobly, with one eye lost to some ancient battle … [indecipherable] nothing of his approach but his voice behind me: "I bear a secret: Knowledge lest your people fall in winter." This secret, he said, is imparted only to a holy man or woman—that only one among a people could hold this vision without wrath descending.

When I objected that I was none such, he said that he had some days earlier pledged this secret to Reverend Bastiaen but had been rebuked and cudgeled. The visitor did bleed. He therefore now believes another among us, some worthy, must bear this burden of knowledge, and that we of the Walvis must observe a profane ritual if we are to survive the winter. But this worthy must also maintain a vigilant, eternal silence.

He then spoke, in the manner of parable, of a spirit of the heat that must be held through the barren moons. This spirit must be captured in an earthen pot when the three sisters are harvested and kept buried with a strip of deerskin tightened around the pot so that it cannot go free until next planting, the first song of the whip-poor-will. Kept so, he said, we suffer in our turn but are protected from the worst of the storms and the cold.

Each time, he said, you will be tempted to free the spirit, to "fill the world again with heat during the short days. But those who do are taken, and many innocents are taken with them."

Finally, this: At great cost have we learned to wait, to serve the world through the seventh generation.

Thus, I am chosen. I have discovered that the three sisters of the

Nantaquak are their maize, squash, and beans. I so understand the visitor's secret as a legend that their fertility spirit must be held close through the region's frigid months, to be released at the time of planting.

I thanked the visitor for his concern but assured him that, on the contrary, our True Christian God would in his Providence nourish us.

Yet I wonder more strangely now if *we* must somehow hold the summer at bay, as if this fell to man and not to God? And I awake in disquiet at the thought that Our Lord does beseech and command us to protect the world in our toil. Numbers 35:33-34, "Defile not therefore the land which ye shall inhabit, wherein I dwell." Revelation 11:14, "Thy wrath is come … and shouldest destroy them which destroy the earth."

I share with you my own doubt: Are _we_ not the visitors here?

I write privately of this to you. I commend myself to your favor across these immeasurable fathoms,

Jacobus Wolfert

＊＊＊＊＊

June 1938: Delaware Coast News

(In the End, continued from page one)

Mr. Tobias Gleason, curator of the Zwaanendael Museum, recalled that Miss Rose had made a remarkable find on the very afternoon of her disappearance.

"I was at first hesitant to have such a … *unique* student rummaging about in our research materials," Mr. Gleason said. "But Miss Rose quickly demonstrated herself to be a capable scholar.

"On the tragic day, I permitted her access to some boxed papers not yet archived. Among them turned out to be what is apparently a letter written by one of the original Zwaanendael settlement's Dutch explorers, from the ship *Walvis*. The letter was of course never sent.

Rehoboth Beach Reads

The settlement was razed before the next Dutch West India Company ship passed. But these scant glimpses into the activities of the colony now survive in our archives because of Miss Rose's work."

That artifact now stands as the final legacy of a remarkable young lady who combined beauty, brawn and brains in equal measure before vanishing one June afternoon in one of the Delaware coast's most perplexing and disturbing mysteries.

* * * * *

June 2021: North Shores, Rehoboth Beach

Her hand on his shoulder scares the hell out of him, but in that moment, Lyle remembers her name: Gwendolyn. He looks up, instinctively spins his laptop away from her, vaguely irritated but forcing a grin. "Hey, sleeping beauty," he says. "Good morning. No, afternoon." He tops his glass and hands it to her. "Refreshment?"

Gwendolyn takes it, downs the single-malt in two swallows, and squints across the sloping roof and miles of whitecaps. She's wearing last night's hilarious boardwalk T-shirt that says, "Cool story, bro. Tell it again!" When he'd driven her home in his vintage Shelby and brought her up to the crow's nest to seal the deal, she'd looked young enough to be his daughter. Today, she is as old as he is, the lustrous raven hair now matte black in this unforgiving light, decades of relentless nightlife unfurled across a corroded face that is somehow regal in its failure to repent.

"You're drunk," she says, without inflection. "Known you for fifteen hours and haven't seen you sober yet." She extends the glass for a refill. "What you writing?"

Lyle sighs, pours, and wonders if he can just throw her some shorthand to get her out of here. He decides full-tilt boredom is the surer path. "My life story," he says. "I've had a *fascinating* life:

Georgetown, cum laude at Wharton, career in finance, early retirement, two wives?"

"Hmmm." Gwendolyn walks to the railing and peers over, distracted. The crow rouses itself, forages beneath a wing, veers off. Lyle sidles up. "I'm starting with a secret story my mom told me at bedtime. Amazing. She'd just, like, make them up on the fly, totally."

"Great stuff," she murmurs.

"Epic." He leans back against the railing.

Gwendolyn turns toward him, slow and close. "About that secret."

He gives her his best WTF look, all owlish eyebrows, but she keeps coming. "The particular story you're writing about? A trapped spirit?" Her eyes are hooded now, luminous. He starts to lean away. She smiles, but something is happening to her mouth. "Unfortunate. It isn't yours to tell. Or hers. It's … entrusted."

She kisses him, the connection electric but not quite erotic, and it feels vaguely accidental as they slip over the railing. Lyle has just enough time to wonder how this woman could possibly know his mother's stories as they fall slowly, with his forbidden knowledge, toward the patio, toward the tide, toward Whiskey Beach.

* * * * *

June 1956: Camp Arrowhead, Sussex County

After twenty-six pairs of eyes slide saucer-wide at the end of "The Summer Jar," after the shrieks of pleasured horror, after "Michael, Row the Boat Ashore" and "Kumbaya," Angelica's charges scatter into the woods toward their cabins. She's thrilled. They'll be awake for hours, retelling and re-imagining the story, dreaming and waking to it: the shattered jar, summer fled across the water, panic, mercy, horror, heat, ice. The wisdom of the Nanticoke; the desiccation of the world. They may tell their own children this story some night in a different life.

She's reminded them of the pleasure of burial alive in one's own bed, flashlight in hand, comfort in fear. A contagion of secrets.

She stands from her log perch. Her shins are scorched from the campfire, now in embers as a counselor shovels dirt. She inhales, shrugs her shoulders, and again becomes Mildred Duffy, due at her bookkeeping job at her father-in-law's Chrysler dealership at eight a.m. sharp. She's taken her first steps into the woods when a child emerges from the dark, straw hair tumbling around her face, arms circling herself, her body a rictus of dread.

"Honey!" Mildred drops to her knees and throws her arms out to the girl, maybe ten, eleven; the child retreats a step. "What is it, baby? Are you all right?"

The girl holds up her hands. "Why weren't they more careful?" she pleads. "They all broke the world!" She seems half-asleep. Mildred stares for a moment before realizing she is talking about the story. She laughs.

"Oh, sweetheart, no! Patsy and Thomas didn't really drop the summer jar. They aren't even *real*." The girl tilts forward and lets herself be held. "I made it up so we could all have fun being scared around the campfire," Mildred says. "We'll *always* have summer and winter. It's nature." Mildred sways until the girl begins to relax. "I'm not even real," she whispers. "I mean, *I'm* real, but I'm not a witch. I work in a place that sells cars. My name is Mildred Duffy, not Angelica." She hugs the girl. "What's yours?"

Mildred hears steps behind her and turns to see a young counselor, barely a teenager herself, hands on hips in mock dismay. "What am I going to do with you?" she says gently. She lifts the child's hand and tugs her back toward the cabins. "She's a little high-strung, this one," she confides to Mildred. "Sweet but so *serious*. Lily, say goodnight to the nice lady."

The girl clings to Mildred a last moment, then lets go. As she does, her mouth drags by Mildred's ear, and her voice seems calmer, older:

"*Now* you're telling a story." Then Lily Cathcart waves once, dismissive, hand like a pincer, and they are gone.

Mildred sighs and climbs up. She hasn't walked two minutes when she remembers that her own car is still far up the road, broken down. *Idiot.* She'll need to get a ride from someone at the camp. She roots through her bag for her flashlight. Did she leave it near the campfire? "Oh, Miss?" she calls out, turning. "Counselor?" She waits. "Lily?"

She inches back down the path, or what should be the path, for some time. Then she is crashing through the woods. Then comes an emerging calm, a dark clarity as she glimpses the ending, and she waits.

Donald Challenger is a retired journalist and teacher who most recently worked as an editor at Hamilton College in upstate New York before returning to his native Delaware. He is coauthor of *Contemporary Editing*, a journalism text now in its third edition with Routledge. He writes fiction and records original music in Lewes as half of the Beausage Brothers with longtime friend Charlie Everett, whom he met in their first high school band. "The Summer Jar" was inspired in part by the narrative possibilities of "nested" stories such as David Mitchell's *Cloud Atlas* but brought to life by childhood memories of the beach region. In the '60s, the author's father once got the family Plymouth stuck axle-deep in the sand on old Whiskey Beach, where the story's opening scene is set. And he was perennially envious of the friends who all sported T-shirts from Camp Arrowhead, where in reality he never set foot.

Beach Misses

By Lonn Braender

A reporter is much like a detective; sometimes you have to dig up someone's yard to find the story. I'm the literary reporter for the *New York Daily,* so not about to dig up a yard but digging was certain.

Daryl David, certainly a nom-de-plume, was whom I needed to dig up. Mr. David wrote a gentle book of short stories centered around Rehoboth, Delaware, called *Beach Misses.* It was first released by Cat & Mouse Press, a tiny publisher in Lewes. Each year, they hold the Rehoboth Beach Reads Short Story Contest and publish the winning stories, but they also publish other books of short beach reads. So, it wasn't a surprise the initial printing of *Beach Misses* was published by them.

I started by reaching out to Nancy, the owner of Cat & Mouse Press. Excited to be contacted by the *New York Daily,* she was happy to help. Nancy told me that Daryl David had contacted her out of the blue and pitched her *Beach Misses.* She was hesitant at first, but after reading the manuscript, agreed immediately. She detailed the entire process, but throughout the publishing interaction, she never once met the author. She edited the book via email, tried unsuccessfully to convince the author to change the title, and released the book in time for summer. In August, the book was reviewed by *LA Tribune.* The *Tribune's* literary critic—a friend of mine—was born in Rehoboth and goes back each summer for a visit.

The critic loved the book, raved about it. She said it was one of the best collections of short stories she'd seen in decades and put it on her must-read list. That fall, BOI Press, the country's second-largest publisher, bought the rights and printed ten thousand copies. Before the following summer season, the print run hit two hundred fifty thousand copies and kept climbing, making it a bestseller.

There are break-out books all the time, but we always know who the author is. I interviewed Nancy and everyone who had anything to do with *Beach Misses* at BOI Press. No one had met the author. He never came to the city, had no picture on his book (a must for bestsellers), did no touring or signing. He didn't have a website or a Facebook page. The only information the publisher had was an email address and a post office box. Even a hefty bribe got me nowhere.

So, I've come to Rehoboth to dig up Daryl David.

This was my first trip to Rehoboth. If New Yorkers want to go to the beach, it's Coney Island or the Jersey shore. So, I was surprised to find it was a cute bustling town with many restaurants, nightclubs, and a pristine beach. I wish I had had more time; a few days in the sun would be heaven. But I only had four days to find and interview the author. The Fiction Writers Gala was that Friday in Los Angeles, and I had an appointment to interview Stephen King about his newest novel.

My search started at Browseabout Books, an indie bookstore in the center of town. Naturally, *Beach Misses* had its own table, as did a book called *Beachcomber*. *Beachcomber* was a novel mentioned in one of the *Beach Misses* stories and was now selling out. I spoke to the owner at length. She didn't know Daryl David but made me promise to bring him in when I found him. I agreed, but she seemed to be playing it cool. So, I grabbed a copy of the book and headed to the counter.

The woman at the register was friendly and said she knew the book well. I leaned in and whispered, "So, how do I get my copy signed? My daughter loves it. I would be dad of the year if I got a signed copy." I held the book up like a prize.

"Oh, I'm sorry. He hasn't signed any books to my knowledge. That'll be seventeen fifty."

My next stop was the coffee shop. Writers are notorious for working in coffee shops, and there were a few nearby. Half a block from Browseabout, I stepped into the Coffee Mill, a bustling local cafe in an alley with a few small tables pushing against the picture window. It was *the* perfect setting. The barista knew all about the book and could only pray Daryl David would write his next best seller in their shop.

I got the same response from every coffee shop, in and out of town. The downtown librarian made me promise to call her as soon as I found him, the mayor offered the key to the city, and every shop in town swore to bend over backward to have an appearance by the author, especially the tiny pet store because of a short story called "Maddog."

Maybe Daryl David wasn't a coffee drinker; maybe he was a night owl—a pub kind of guy. That night I hit the bars, and there were many. I started with pubs, where someone might sit in the corner with a laptop. I asked each bartender, server, and manager; none had ever met the man, but most knew the book.

By midnight, I was exhausted and a little tipsy, so I Ubered to my hotel out on the highway. The next day, I went to other places an author, or anyone, might go. I stopped at grocery stores, liquor stores, and drug stores. I even stopped at a car repair shop. The man had to spend money someplace, but no dice; no one knew him. Could the entire town be sworn to secrecy?

The next morning, I dressed more businesslike and visited the banks. There were dozens of separate branches from Lewes to Dewey and not one of them knew Daryl David. A few secretly searched their system, now curious, but still nothing.

On my last day, I went to the only place positively linked to the man—the post office. The only information Nancy and BOI Press had was his email address and post office box. The post office was on the main drag in Rehoboth and thankfully had a bench out front. I didn't think the postmaster would appreciate me camping out in the lobby.

I was there when the building opened and I followed every person in, male and female. If someone went into the room with the post boxes, I stepped close and pretended to mess up a combination. But no one opened box #357, Daryl David's. And box #357 was stuffed. As a last-ditch effort, I asked the postmaster, knowing full well he'd tell me nothing. By the time the post office closed, I was spent.

So, that was it. I'd spent four days, spoken to hundreds of people, and hadn't uncovered a single fact about Daryl David. Nothing. It was like the man didn't exist. Why? It made no sense. I sent Mr. David one last email, the hundredth, inviting him, no *pleading* with him, to chat. No response—but also no bounce back, so I knew the email went to someone.

I drove out to my hotel, showered, and packed my bags. I had just enough time to grab dinner and then drive to Baltimore for the last flight to Los Angeles. I wondered, could Daryl David be planning to attend the Gala? That would explain the stuffed post office box, but he wasn't listed on the attendee's list—I had a copy.

I checked out and walked half a block to The Crab Hut. The restaurant was included in the *Beach Misses* story called "The Pink Ribbon." It wasn't a tourist trap. Located on the highway, the place was a bit shabby, but not shabby chic. There was bric-a-brac everywhere, all of it dust covered.

I approached the bar and knew my assumption was accurate. The bar was almost full, and the crowd was obviously mainly friends engaged in rousing conversations. Local is my favorite kind of restaurant—the food is generally good and affordable, and the people are usually friendly.

I took the one remaining seat at the bar, nodding to my neighbors. There was a lone man to my right on the last stool by the wall who nodded back noncommittally and a woman to my left who was totally enjoying the loud conversation. Still laughing, she glanced at me and I said hello.

"Don't believe a word those guys say. Liars, every one of them." She jabbed her finger at two men at the other end of the bar. "Tana," the woman called to the bartender, "you don't believe Benny, do you?"

"Honey, I don't believe any of you." Tana grinned as she stepped over, pushing a menu to me. "What can I get you?"

I ordered a draft. Tana quickly glanced at the gentleman to my right and stepped away. I picked up the menu but kept my eyes on the crowd. Surely if any of these people knew Daryl David, they'd divulge the secret. As soon as there was a break in the banter, I asked the woman next to me, "Tell me, have you ever heard of the writer named Daryl David?"

The woman scrunched up her face and shook her head.

"He has a best-selling book about Rehoboth."

"Oh, I heard about that. I'm a movie person." She turned back to her friends. "Hey! Any of you read that book, Beach something?"

"*Beach Misses*," the guy a few stools down said. "Yeah, pretty good."

I leaned over, "Do you happen to know who the author is?"

"Never heard of him."

The others agreed and before long, they were off on another rowdy debate.

Tana returned with a mug of beer for me; she also put a fresh beer in front of the man to my right. I hadn't seen him ask. I started to ask her about the menu, but she stopped me. "First time here?"

I nodded.

"The Steam Pot, honey. It's our best seller."

"Done. I'll take it." I slid the menu back. "But before you go, I have a plane to catch and must leave by"—I don't know why I looked at my watch—"eight-thirty."

She looked up at the dingy clock made of plastic driftwood, nodded, and moved to the order screen. Someone from the group on my left called for her, but she held up a hand and entered my dinner order.

When she finished entering my order, she turned and asked, "Benny, you ready for another?" She was already pouring it.

Glancing at the man on my right, I noticed he seemed oblivious to the rowdy crowd. I said, "I hope the Steam Pot is good. I'm starved."

"Can't go wrong with that." He sipped his beer.

"Mind if I ask a question?"

The man shrugged. "Doesn't mean I need to answer." He was the kind of person who had zero expression and less interest.

"Ever hear of Daryl David?"

"Wrote some book?"

"Right. I'm searching for him, but no one seems to know him."

"Check the phone book?"

"I think Daryl David is a nom-de-plume, a pen name," I added, in case he didn't know the term.

He shot me a disgusted look. I shrugged apologetically. "Sorry, habit. You know the man?"

"Try the bookstore."

"I've been to every shop, bar, bank, and even gas station from Lewes to Dewey. Not one lead."

"Maybe he's not from here. They write books nowadays without ever visiting the city." He sipped his beer.

The man wasn't engaged; he never really looked at me. He seemed to be looking someplace far, far away.

"True, but this book started here before it hit the best-seller list. And the stories are pretty much dead-on local. I checked each location mentioned in each story."

I sipped my beer in sync with him. He was watching Tana pour drinks, and so I guess our conversation was over.

One thing about traveling as much as I do, it gets a bit lonely, so I continued. "The thing is, how could a book sell half a million copies, and no one knows the author?"

The man looked back at me, surprised. "Where you from?"

"The *New York Daily,* I write the literary column." That response always made me smile, I was proud of my job, but he frowned.

"Should have told them you were from Lewes." He sipped. "Why do you care so much? Everyone writes a book these days."

"The thing is, there are oddities about this book. First, there's the title, *Beach Misses.* Nothing is missing that we can find, and "Misses" doesn't seem to pertain to women."

"We?"

"I've talked to the country's best-known critics; they all have the same questions."

He finished his beer just as Tana arrived with a fresh one.

"And the stories, there are twenty-two short stories, and each is exactly thirty-five hundred words long."

That turned the man's head and for the first time, he showed some emotion. "You counted?"

"We've all counted. Who writes twenty-two stories exactly the same length?" Just then a banged-up aluminum pot arrived. It was stuffed with clams, shrimp, and fish in an aromatic tomato broth. Steam rose from the pot like a nuclear tower, fogging my glasses. The aroma made me smile and salivate.

Tana came back and offered another beer. I declined, reminding her that I had to be in Baltimore soon.

I blew the steam off a clam and dug in. The Steam Pot was delicious. It confirmed my belief: eat where locals eat; you never go wrong.

After a few bites, I noticed the man next to me looking. He nodded. "Good?"

"Fantastic." I wiped my mouth. "So, tell me, have your read *Beach Misses?*"

He nodded. "You came all the way from New York to ask a guy why his stories are, what did you say, thirty-five hundred words?"

"Every newspaper in the country is trying to interview the author.

I was hoping for the scoop. But more than that, there's a reason this book is on the best-seller's list. The stories are wonderful. I laughed, I cried, I was holding my breath at the end of one. From the first page of the first story, I was hooked. The author took me on an emotional roller coaster ride and it's his first book. I've reviewed self-published and small-press books before, but never one this good."

The man raised an eyebrow at me.

"How is it that a first-time author writes a story about a beach volleyball tournament played in drag that made my sides hurt? I teared up when the girl got the guy in the end. Oh, and there's a story called 'Perfect Beach Day' about a differently abled guy who finds utter joy learning to bodysurf. I never cry from reading but did over that story."

I continued explaining the stories, probably listing them in order. I told the man, who now seemed interested, about each one: how they made me feel, which were funny or serious or mysterious. When I finished my dissertation, and the Steam Pot, he shook his head at me.

"Did you memorize the book?" He almost laughed.

"Just about. I've read it multiple times. Every critic I know has. But not one can figure out what's missing. That's why I need to find Mr. David. As a first-time author, he has a lot to say, but there are a lot of questions. Like why twenty-two stories, why not twenty-three or twenty-one? Why thirty-five hundred words, exactly? Who does that? And most important, what's missing?" I exhaled. I'd gotten pretty excited. "This guy is touching souls like few authors can. I need to know how he did that."

Taking the last scrap of bread, I sopped up broth and stuffed my mouth. I was ready to nap.

"Why not ask the publisher?" the man offered, just as Tana replaced his empty glass.

"They know less than me. I was the one who pointed out the word counts to them."

Just then Tana appeared, removing the empty pot. "It's after eight-thirty." She put the check on the bar and waited.

I pushed my credit card at her and checked my watch. To my surprise, the group on my left had gone. There were now a few new people quietly sipping drinks and talking. She came back quickly with the receipt. I over-tipped, thanked her, and hurried out. As I reached the door, Tana called my name. I stopped short and spun. She was holding up my credit card. *Ugh!* I raced back and just then, the man I'd been sitting next to for the last hour and a half grinned at me.

As if in a courtroom presenting facts, he said, without emotion, "Misses—twenty-two stories rejected by the Rehoboth Beach Reads Short Story Contest judges. Contest rules: fewer than thirty-five hundred words." He turned back and sipped his beer.

I blinked, then blinked again. *What?* My mouth dropped open.

"Daryl David?" I asked.

"Better luck next time." He shrugged and nodded at the bartender.

Tana wiped the bar where I'd sat. She glanced at the clock again, her eyebrows raised. The man sipped his beer, looking straight ahead as if I'd never sat beside him. The people to my left talked, oblivious of my dilemma.

Looking at my watch. I shook my head. No way could I miss an interview with Steven King, I'd lose my job. I wanted to scream. I didn't take my eyes off the man as I raced out the door.

I mentally kicked myself all the way to the airport. But as soon as I got there, I changed my returning flight from New York to the Salisbury Airport—the closest one to Rehoboth. It cost me a fortune, but I didn't care. And this time, I wouldn't be in a hurry to leave.

Lonn Braender is a Jersey-born artist, printer, businessman, entrepreneur, and writer. Lonn was a painter of landscapes and seascapes for more than twenty-five years, but due to life changes he found an alternative creative outlet—writing, which has become his passion. Lonn has written dozens of works of varying lengths. He had his first short story published in the 2016 Rehoboth Reads anthology, *Beach Nights*, where it won a Judge's award. He went on to be published in *Beach Life*, *Beach Love*, *Beach Fun* (in which his story won third place), and *Sandy Paws*, all published by Cat & Mouse Press. This particular story is based on a secret plot to make the story come true, within reason. Lonn lives and writes in Bucks County, PA, with his muse and husband, Bruce. To learn more about the writer and his work, visit www.lonnb.com.

At The Water's Edge

By Carly Tagen-Dye

Of the twins, Addy was the one in charge of sneaking out. She could tell which car was Pá's from the sound of its engine alone and had perfected shimmying her way back into her bedroom using the house's drainpipe years prior. Aside from getting caught, Joel was most concerned about getting abducted. As he and Addy slithered out their front door and away from the stillness of their house, Joel imagined all the ways they might get kidnapped over the course of the evening. This didn't stop him from following his sister, though.

Once they were outside, Addy and Joel walked out of their neighborhood and toward the closest bus stop. They took the route going out of their hometown and into Rehoboth, the beach town that was a haven for all manner of restless folks.

The 201 bus was deserted that night. Addy and Joel sat in the middle seats reserved for the elderly, Addy with the small JanSport backpack she used as a purse and Joel trying not to let his nerves get the best of him. The bus's inside lights were fluorescent, and Joel wondered if they made every hint of excitement or anxiety visible to a passing eye.

"You worry too much," Addy hissed at him. Joel hadn't said anything, but he knew she could tell. "I can see the gears in your head turning."

"Pá's going to come back early," Joel said, fidgeting with a hangnail. "I just know it."

"He's got a late class tonight." Addy crossed her arms. "And maybe he'll grab something to eat after."

"When was the last time he went to a restaurant?" The twins' father valued routine. He kept to his schedule, which included booking it home after work as soon as possible.

"You never know. Maybe he's feeling spontaneous tonight." Addy's voice dripped with sarcasm. Joel narrowed his eyes.

"He's going to come back, look in our rooms, and see us gone."

"That's only going to happen if you think it's going to happen." Addy smirked and pressed down on Joel's cowlick in the way that annoyed him most. "You're going to manifest it. It'll be your fault."

She wasn't being mean; but, as always, she had the last say. Addy, forty minutes older, was therefore forty minutes wiser. That unspoken rule had lasted sixteen years.

Joel swatted her hand away and turned to face the window. The bus rambled down Coastal Highway, past outlet shopping centers and hotels. The frenetic lights of passing cars illuminated his reflection. His eyes remained wide and unsure.

* * * * *

The night before Addy and Joel snuck out, the kitchen's only sounds were forks scraping against plates and the low hum of the air conditioning unit. The twins and their father sat around their small table. It was close to the refrigerator, where takeout menus hung limply, and gas station magnets were losing their grip. One of the overhead light bulbs had gone out, and the remaining one cast a dim yellow glow across the room.

"What do you two plan on doing with your summer?" their father asked in Spanish. He'd made *guisada*, and he pressed a stale tortilla into his meat as he talked, dark eyes masked behind thick, silver glasses. His spring teaching semesters, alternating between UD and Delaware State, always took a toll on him. The weeks leading up to finals were busy and long. Addy joked that this was why Pá always looked disgruntled; his eyes were giving out from staring at Scantrons for hours on end.

"Nothing." Addy looked up. "Absolutely nothing."

Pá turned to Joel. "And you?"

Joel hesitated a beat too long. He finished chewing and swallowed thickly. "I'm not sure yet. Still thinking, I guess." He actually planned on reading as much as possible and sleeping in, since he usually had to wake before Addy to get into the bathroom they shared. She needed at least an hour to get ready every day; Joel remembered one morning when she'd decided to spontaneously dye her hair auburn, and he was waiting around until lunch.

"You two should be looking for summer jobs." Pá put a hand on the table. His gaze flitted between the two of them. "Do something productive with your time. Give back."

"And who are we giving back to?" Addy piled more rice onto her plate.

"Your community. Your father, who wants you to become real people in the world." His voice was close to monotone, the way it tended to when he tried to get words through the twins' heads.

"It's only March," Addy said, nonchalant. "Summer is months away."

"So, you'll start asking around in March." Pá sighed. "When I was your age, I had three jobs. I was working to come here. You two weren't even an idea yet."

The story of how the twins' father left Guatemala was ingrained in them. The United States was the pipeline to a better life, where he could send money home to his family back in Guatemala City. His need for that better life only amplified once the girl he'd been seeing got pregnant; and, after she chose to stay, he found himself left to raise the children on his own.

Addy and Joel knew how Pá had studied English for years before leaving the capital, immigrated in his mid-twenties with newborns, and how that still meant he had to work his way up all over again. They knew that saying goodbye to the land that birthed him, that adapting and expanding and relearning, were sacrifices he had to make.

Still, Addy mumbled something under her breath. Joel took a sip of water.

"You two need priorities," Pá continued. "Keep your grades up for university in a few years. Learn responsibility." He'd reminded them that he had supported himself through graduate school. Pá used his tips from busing tables at an Italian restaurant to pay a neighbor to look after the twins, and, when that occasionally didn't work out, their father was forced to bring them to work, keeping a wary eye on his toddlers coloring at a corner table while he cleared plates and lipstick-smudged glasses.

"You never once had fun as a kid?" Addy asked, cocking an eyebrow. "You never did anything for yourself?"

"I found a balance between work and play, Adela." Pá took a bite of tortilla.

The twins glanced at each other. When Pá called her Adela, they knew the conversation was over.

That evening, Joel grabbed a newspaper and began looking for work. He skimmed through listings from the usual seafood restaurants and grocery stores in need of dishwashers and bag boys. He saw a handful of jobs in downtown Rehoboth, where he was sure he'd melt in the sun or come home smelling like french-fry grease. His concentration was interrupted by Addy, who crept into his room with plans for the following night.

"I have an idea for a good time of our own," she'd said with a grin.

* * * * *

The boardwalk came alive at night, like a monster rising from a long sleep. Even in the off-season, people seemed to come from every direction, voices rising in an inaudible wave. The locals walked in clumps, weaving through traffic by the bandstand and the Dolle's sign. A breeze kept the spring humidity at bay.

Joel sat on a bench, trying to not look suspicious. He checked his watch, which read 8:34. Joel watched as a stray pink balloon, etched with a smiley face, escaped a young girl's hand in front of Grotto. She let out a wail just as Addy exited the restaurant, balancing a paper plate of pizza in each hand. Addy cringed a bit at the child's cries as she gave Joel a plate and plopped down beside him.

"I think she broke a new decibel level," Addy said, shoving a good amount of her pizza into her mouth. Joel pulled out his retainer and carefully bit off the tip of his slice. The ocean crashed behind them.

"This is some great people watching," Addy said. The girl's parents had since scooped her up and ushered her away. "It'll be crazy in a few months. You won't be able to walk here."

"I remember you almost got trampled when we came down once." Joel wiped his mouth with the back of his hand. "We were six. You were pretty easy to step on."

"Shut up." Addy clocked his shoulder. "I remember *you* screaming your head off when Pá tried to get you in the ocean. A lot like that girl back there, actually."

Every summer since they were kids, the twins and their father had come to Rehoboth one day a month. Pá would pack the car and drive them into the tourist-packed chaos. It would take an hour to find parking, and the afternoon heat was always sticky on their backs, but it was tradition. Pá was always eager to relax during his three-month break from teaching.

Addy loved the bustle of the beach. She loved the amusement park, Funland, with its cacophonous ringing, though the noise always hurt Joel's ears. She loved cooling off in the choppy ocean, though Joel rarely joined her. He wasn't a great swimmer. Addy shot across the waves while Joel flailed like a dying fish.

"He'd lift you up above the water and you'd scream your head off." Addy laughed. "People thought you were getting murdered."

"I thought I was going to drown," Joel grumbled. He just barely remembered his father holding him by the armpits, a smile on Pá's face while Joel kicked the air and shrieked. Pá would shoo Joel back onto the shore while he and Addy splashed around together. Joel preferred the long aisles of Browseabout Books to the sand, anyway.

Joel brushed his fingers off. As he did, he realized that Pá had never actually dropped him in the ocean against his will. It was only a moment's tease.

"*Nunca dejaré que algo te pase,*" Pá would say into the top of Joel's head. "I will never let anything happen to you."

A couple in matching Reebok sweatshirts dipped their fingers into a box of chocolates from Candy Kitchen. The twins watched them disappear around the corner.

"I wonder what Pá would do to you now." Addy pulled a water bottle out of her backpack. "He'd probably make you swim."

Joel didn't respond. Instead, he took a drink, popped his retainer back in and handed his sister his crust, which she'd been eyeing.

* * * * *

"You know the plan," Addy had told Joel the morning of their escapade. They each wore their school bags slung around one shoulder as they packed their lunches. Early morning sunlight filtered in through the kitchen window. "We'll leave around seven thirty, head back around nine thirty. We'll be in bed before he gets home. He'll never know a thing."

"Whatever you say," Joel said, spreading cream cheese and jelly onto a piece of wheat bread. It was too early for him to comprehend anything.

The bus came at seven sharp. The twins turned to leave when a stir of movement caught their attention. From their vantage point, they could see out the back door, where their father sat on the porch. He was hunched over something. Addy and Joel shared a look.

"We should tell him we're leaving," Joel said.

"*I'll* tell him we're leaving," Addy corrected. "You look guilty. If you open your mouth, you'll spill." Joel rolled his eyes but relented.

Their father was perched in his favorite chair, the wicker one with the striped cushion that had long since faded from the sun. He was already dressed in a button-up shirt and pants, with a cup of coffee and an untouched plate of toast to his left. He gazed over a stack of what looked like test papers. Pá didn't look up until the twins moved in front of him, one stoic, the other squirming.

"Off to school?" their father asked. He pushed his glasses up and stretched his legs.

"Just wanted to say bye." Addy played with the string of her backpack. "What time are you going to be home again?"

"I've got an eight o'clock class tonight," Pá said.

"Just wanted to make sure."

"You two will be alright? I might be a bit later than usual."

"We could order a pizza," Addy sing-songed, eyes brightening. "There's a reason that that takeout menu is on the fridge."

"We have food here," Pá said, and then, at the silence that followed: "Have you two given any more thought to what we talked about last night?"

"We're working on it, right, Joel?" Addy nudged him. He nodded a bit too quickly.

Pá wasn't as affectionate now that the twins had grown. Joel wondered if he noticed them drifting away in small ways, like in their secrecy or their English responses to his Spanish questions. Addy was busy staking her life out for herself, and Joel didn't have much of a reaction to anything unless pushed. A hug, for such a mundane occurrence as school, would seem odd to all of them now.

"Be good today," Pá said instead. He gave a small half-wave before pushing his children onward, out the back gate and into the day ahead.

* * * * *

The slight breeze turned into a chill as the night wore on. The twins made their way down the boardwalk, wanting to extend their journey a little longer. It was nice to be lost amongst the stillness. Joel didn't check his watch anymore.

They ended up by the Boardwalk Plaza Hotel, with its walls the color of Pepto Bismol. From there, the twins decided to head for the beach. They rolled up the cuffs of their jeans and took off their sneakers, letting them dangle from their fingertips; the first walk on the shore that season.

Few other people were on the sand. Two women strolled along the beach, engaged in animated conversation. A man stood alone, hands in the pockets of his pants, looking toward the sea. The background noise grew far.

"Would you say this was worth it?" Addy asked her brother, breaking the silence. "Was it worth the stress, *Joel*?" She emphasized his name as *ho-elle*, in its Spanish pronunciation.

"Your mouth is going to get you in way more trouble than this one day," Joel said with a faint smile. The two trekked slowly, taking in the night and the softness underneath their feet.

"How else was I supposed to stand my ground in our house?" Addy held her hands up in mock surrender. "It had to start somewhere. You're just along for the ride."

Joel chuckled and opened his mouth to respond, turning his head as he did. Addy must have sensed him tense beside her and looked in his line of sight.

They saw Pá staring back at them. Surprise flickered across his face as he took his hands out of his pockets, still in his work clothes, jacket tied around his waist.

"You've got to be kidding me," Addy said, voice dropping.

Their father stared, expression unreadable, looking more like a statue

 Rehoboth Beach Reads

than a person. After an agonizing pause, the twins were the ones who made their way toward him, walking slowly, as if it might be their last.

Pá didn't acknowledge their presence, on either side of him, at first. Instead, he closed his eyes and inhaled, as if sucking the evening in. *Savoring*, perhaps, was a better word.

"You caught me," Pá said after a pause. The moon was a glowing crest in his glasses.

"*We* caught *you*?" Addy asked. Joel knew she had been expecting much worse than that. His father's calmness made him uncomfortable.

"We caught each other," Pá corrected. He didn't look at them while he spoke. The ocean had his attention.

Joel couldn't help but notice how different their father looked in the dim light—more relaxed, the lines around his face not as visible as they were in the daylight. It was near impossible to see the growing strands of gray hair on his head; instead, his locks appeared pitch black and young. His features, his posture; everything was softened.

After standing there for what felt like hours, Pá walked closer to the water. For once, Addy looked to Joel for direction. He cocked his head toward their father, and they trailed behind without a word. The ocean was like ice against their feet.

"You know, we were going to tell you about this," Addy tried.

Joel, on a different day, would've been amused by the way his sister tried to talk her way out of it. Now, he wished she would let things settle; let things envelop her as they came.

"I'm sure you were," Pá said. He sounded more amused than angry.

"What are you doing here?" Joel asked. His father gave a sigh.

"Sometimes I like to come out here by myself after long days," Pá said. He didn't flinch at the briskness of the water. "It's nice. You can hear yourself think here. I need that sometimes."

"The quiet?" Addy asked. She wrapped her arms around herself to warm up.

"The pause. The break," Pá continued. "It reminds me of when you two were little, and we came out here. Even if it was only for a day, there was that little pocket of time with nothing to do except enjoy the present. This place will do that for you."

Despite the rush for a parking spot, the heat, and the clusters of people during those vacations, their family sang along to Luis Miguel on the drive down, enduring the sun with giant ice cream cones and staying close to one another, so as not to get lost. Joel's memories of that time focused more on their laughter than their stress.

"I guess maybe that's why we came too," Joel said. He glanced down at a stray shell by his feet. "We wanted to feel something like that again." He felt Addy's eyes on him, but she didn't say a word.

They stood at the water's edge for a moment longer. Pá cleared his throat.

"You can have priorities in life, *patojos*, but also prioritize multiple things," he said. "Be a person but also forget you are one. Work hard, but take a second to come back to yourself too."

Summer was on the horizon. There was time for everything. The twins both gave silent nods, and their father put a hesitant hand on each of their shoulders.

"Do you want to go now?" Addy asked. Her voice was quieter. It was as if she had taken to the calmness, to her family's way of being.

"Just a little more time," Pá said. "Enjoy it. You two are on house arrest for the next week for sneaking around."

"You called it," Addy whispered to Joel. He jabbed at her, emitting a soft laugh when Addy ducked away. The punishment could be endured.

"Just a little more time," their father repeated, so quietly they could barely hear him. He gave each of his twins' arms a squeeze before letting his hands drop.

The three shifted their gaze back toward the inky water. The moon hung high overhead.

CARLY TAGEN-DYE IS A WRITER AND EDITOR BASED OUT OF WASHINGTON, DC, AND BROOKLYN, NEW YORK. HER WORK HAS APPEARED IN *THE AUGMENT REVIEW, ALMA, NY PRESS,* AND *THE SOCK DRAWER,* AMONG OTHERS. HER FICTION FOCUSES ON THE BEAUTY AND COMPLEXITY OF FAMILIES AND GUATEMALAN-AMERICAN/LATINX IDENTITY. "AT THE WATER'S EDGE" WAS INSPIRED BY HER MANY BUS TRIPS TO WORK IN DOWNTOWN REHOBOTH OVER THE SUMMER AND HER OWN COMING-OF-AGE AT THE BEACH DURING MANY SUMMERS PREVIOUSLY. YOU CAN LEARN MORE ABOUT HER WRITING AT WWW.CARLYTAGENDYE.COM.

Out of the Blue

By Justin Stoeckel

Shorebreak had made the waves thunder onto the beach. They'd driven a rut into the low area. Kathryn saw kids dropping down as they waded into it. It was a miserable beach day. A west wind brought the greenheads. She had battled them all day as she tried to read. She needed to call it for what it was: a miserable start to her week's vacation.

She walked back to her spot on Lewes beach and gathered her things, swatting the flies as they dove. Tomorrow would be better, she told herself. Quiet and relaxation. That's why she'd made the trip. Kathryn hoisted the beach chair over her shoulder, ignoring the sand that scrabbled her shoulder as the strap sank down.

She would walk up the beach. Deposit her chair and bag into the trunk of her car, then drive up to Second Street. There was a children's boutique she wanted to pop into that looked cute—Fairy Godmother, she thought the name was. She liked that name. It felt warm, welcoming. It made the last two weeks dissolve away.

Kathryn felt calmed as the bell sounded when she passed through. There was a curly-haired white dog wagging its tail as she entered.

"That's just Lola," the proprietor said. "She's happy to see you."

Kathryn glanced over at the woman. Kathryn would have put her at late twenties if it weren't for the oxygen tube attached to her nose. It added years, but she could tell those added years didn't collect on this woman.

"If there's an age I can point you to, please let me know."

Kathryn nodded. "Just looking around." She went to the center display. She touched a few of the onesies.

"Those are on sale," the proprietor said. She had a bright face and dark hair. The oxygen tube roped her ears, but didn't distract from her beauty, Kathryn decided.

"What's your name?" Kathryn asked.

"Ashley."

"You have a beautiful store, Ashley." Kathryn surveyed the room. "I love the exposed fireplace."

"It's functional. We turn it on in the winter. Are you looking for yourself or a friend?"

Kathryn didn't answer. She held up another onesie, feeling the tears.

"This should do," Kathryn said, hurrying the outfit to the counter.

"It's beautiful. If it's a gift, I can gift wrap it. No charge."

Kathryn nodded. "Sure. That would be nice."

Ashley smiled and pulled a piece of gift wrap from the roll on the wall. "Is this alright? I have more in the back."

"No, that's fine. Thank you." She had suppressed the tears.

Kathryn watched as Ashley began to work. Then she slid her eyes up to the oxygen tube. "I'm just curious. Why the oxygen? You're so young."

Ashley smiled. The little white poodle traipsed out from behind the counter. "A childhood sickness."

Kathryn didn't push. She watched Ashley wrap the gift, then thanked the young proprietor with a smile. "It's lovely. Thank you."

Stepping outside, she felt lost. The brown bag hung at her knees. She studied Second Street. It was busy. Couples and families strolled up and down the sidewalks. The sun on the beach was hot. The air in the shop was hot. The gift in her bag smothered both together. Kathryn slid into the sidewalk traffic. What she needed now was a drink.

The restaurants looked crowded as she peered in. Outside dining areas were full, too many people engaged in conversation. Kathryn pressed on. She saw the sign for R & L Liquors and pushed toward it.

It was cool inside. She purchased a pint of Captain Morgan and thanked the sandy-haired clerk behind the counter.

With the bag of booze and the bag of baby clothes, Kathryn crossed the parking lot toward the water. A short walk down the block brought her to a park. She went in, crunching down the gravel path. Kids were busy at the playground. Some teenagers were playing basketball. Kathryn didn't have the stomach for either and went to the water.

A light breeze came off the canal. She watched two boats go by. Across the canal, music played from a restaurant. The upstairs was busy with people. It was where she needed to be. It was why she had come.

Kathryn strolled along the boardwalk. It brought her to a pavilion. There she sat and twisted open the rum.

It tasted buttery on her tongue.

She listened to the music and the voices coming from the upstairs deck of the restaurant. She pictured the people, cajoling in small groups, talking, laughing, enjoying themselves, celebrating with the happy couple.

Kathryn tilted another drink. It was starting to make her chest burn. She took one more pull then screwed the cap, keeping the bottle in her hands as she rose.

She grabbed the paper bag from Fairy Godmother and followed the path back up to the road, ignoring for now the celebratory sounds wafting from the upstairs deck.

Walking, she felt better. She liked the way her clothes clung to the salt on her skin from her stay on the beach now. She liked the way the rum had made her feel. She unscrewed the cap and had another pull. No one seemed to notice. That made Kathryn feel even better.

She waited at the stop light. People began to crowd at the corners of the intersection. Kathryn looked at each one of them. What secrets did they bring with them? What were they not telling the person beside them? These couples, these families, they would go about their day, walking into the same shop she did, saying how much they liked what the other person was showing them, but hanging onto something else while smiling. They would have drinks. They would have dinner. And the dark secrets would simmer below the surface. The person on the other side of the smile or the stool would have no idea.

Knowing would spoil the vacation. It would spoil the release.

The red hand changed. Kathryn turned left and crossed the bridge.

More families passed her. They laughed or walked in silence. She thought about the so much that sat in between, then she took a deep breath in and let it out slow. It was the rum, nothing else.

At the end of the bridge, she turned left. She could still hear the music and conversation wafting off the deck where the party was being held. It was just up ahead.

Kathryn paused. She glared at the sign. At the smirking leprechaun on the sign. She read the name: Irish Eyes.

Irish eyes are smiling on you, she thought to herself. Then added grimly, *hadn't they always?*

She had come from Baltimore for the party. The least she could do was leave the gift. Her beach day was a bust. The visit to Fairy Godmother improved that, but she hadn't made the trip for either. She had come for this. She couldn't turn back now. She *did* like that nice girl at Fairy Godmother. Maybe she would go back there after and ask her for a drink. After all, what was the harm in asking?

Kathryn moved up the road to the stone parking lot. The music was thumping. Voices echoed out from the side bar. If she didn't have to do this, she would have found a seat, ordered another drink. This one a Tito's and tonic and just sat and enjoyed the water and the breeze. But she had to go through with it. It was why she was here she reminded herself again and gripped the brown paper handles tighter.

Kathryn made her way up the steps and pulled open the big white door.

The cool air was shocking. It struck her sunburned skin and made her shiver.

There was a musician playing inside. He was good, playing an old Neil Young tune. The one about being out of the blue and into the black.

The musician kept a good rhythm. The song fell hard on Kathryn, stealing her away, and when the hostess asked if she was here for dining or for the party, Kathryn had to ask for the bathroom first.

"It's to the left," the hostess said.

Kathryn went through the white door. She found an empty stall and sat down, locking the door a moment after, not needing to use the bathroom, but craving the privacy a closed stall brings with it. The tears came immediately. She breathed deeply, attempting to force them back. The tears fell anyway.

Kathryn spun down a line of toilet paper and dabbed at them. The paper bag sat open at her feet. She reached in, pulled out the package, and unwrapped the onesie. A flower pattern. It was pretty. She was happy with her decision, as spontaneous as it was.

She thought of the proprietor again. The oxygen tube draping her ears. Kathryn wondered if she couldn't have children because of the childhood illness. This thought brought more tears.

Kathryn wanted her to or hoped she had a good friend who could. Perhaps this was why she opened the shop in the first place. It was a nice shop.

Kathryn dabbed her tears. She stroked the bottom of her eyes delicately with both index fingers, hoping to preserve the mascara she put on in the car after the beach.

The Neil Young song came to the last refrain. She was into the black. In the black, there was no choice. It was why she had made the trip.

Kathryn stood, tossing the damp folds of toilet paper into the bowl, and flushed.

She reached behind her and found the grip of the gun. The walk had rubbed a raw spot in the small of her back. She slipped it from her waistband and grabbed the bag. With her elbow, she slid back the latch.

Ed was probably mingling at the party. His fiancé was undoubtedly clutched to him. In a month they would be married.

Lacy, Kathryn remembered, was the fiancé's name.

Lacy would have no idea that Kathryn had had a miscarriage. And if she hadn't, what would Ed have done then? He had gotten a free pass.

But there were no free passes in life. She had to show them that. The miscarriage, like their relationship, if you could call it that, had come out of the blue. Kathryn had worked with Ed for five years. In those five years there had been nothing more than small talk and a wave.

Then, on the work retreat in Rehoboth, they had hooked up.

Ed ignored her after that. Then came the blue sign on the strip. A plus.

Then two months later, the bleeding.

Kathryn told him none of it. He had said to leave him alone when she tried. But he had to know. And Lacy too. It was the right thing to do.

Kathryn pushed open the bathroom door. She smiled at the hostess as she crossed into the main dining room.

She scanned the room; then she saw him.

At the back of the deep dining area, past the musician and his guitar. He was chatting with a group of coworkers at a table. They were laughing.

Lacy was beside him.

Kathryn gripped the handles of the bag, then the grip of the gun.

It was only right that he knew what came out of the blue. And that things that come out of the blue come with a price.

Justin Stoeckel is a teacher and father of five children. When he's not stepping on Hot Wheels cars, painting nails, or arguing against the necessity of making slime every day, Justin fits in time to write. "Out of the Blue" is his second published story with Cat and Mouse Press. He's currently at work on his fourth novel.

Readers are naturally curious about how writers get their ideas. I always answer, "Amazon—it has everything." I don't always get the laugh intended. The truth is, most of the time, ideas find the writer.

However, "Out of the Blue" was different. It *appeared* as I was writing it—the way scratching a pencil over a sheet of paper reveals the indents of a lost message or the contours of a pressed leaf. I kept writing and more story revealed itself. I kept writing until its abrupt ending, which shocked me too. Sometimes writers find the secret decoder pencil and discover a hidden idea. That's something Amazon doesn't have. Yet.

Independence Day

By Renée Rockland

Rylee notices the two men right away. In a sea of red, white, and blue apparel on the patrons celebrating the Fourth of July, their khaki pants and oversized Hawaiian shirts are conspicuously bold. *They're not even trying to hide,* she thinks as she takes a deep breath to steady herself. Even though she's been preparing for this exact moment for over a year, she still can't believe they're here. That they found her.

She turns her attention toward the foursome at the table in front of her, all of them sporting some version of a T-shirt with the silhouette of a soldier saluting the American flag. *Vets,* Rylee thinks, trying to take comfort in their presence. "Welcome to Dogfish." Her voice sounds thin and strained, like it's coming from the recesses of a long tunnel. "What can I start you with?"

"Two SeaQuench, a Midas, and a Burton," a man drawls. "And some barbecued wings and fried pickles." Rylee scribbles on her pad, nodding.

"I've got four beers. Any appetizers?"

She can tell by the look on his face that she's missed something.

"Wings and pickles?"

"Sure." Her smile is tight. "Right away." *Keep it together. You can do this.* She heads to the bar to fetch their beers as she tracks the Hawaiian shirts out of the corner of her eye. Are they really here for her? Maybe she's overreacting. Maybe all these months of paranoia have finally caused her to crack.

The men are seated in the last booth, one of only five along the restaurant's north wall. The cozy booths are coveted by locals and tourists alike, as the semi-private porthole cutouts offer the very best in people-watching, both of the hordes of passersby on the sidewalk outside and of the entire dining room inside. The restaurant is crowded—it's always crowded—so they must have waited a long time for the choice location. Rylee shudders involuntarily as she wonders just how long they might have been waiting. And watching. Unless, of course, she's mistaken.

The hostess heads straight toward her. "Hey, Rylee," she calls, her voice raised above the crowd four deep at the bar. "The two guys I just seated at table ten? They asked for you. Said you know them?"

Rylee nods. Well, at least she has her answer.

"I told them we're slammed and it's not your section, but they were insistent."

I'm sure they were. "It's OK, Piper. I've got it."

If they ask for you, play it cool; don't make them think you're going to run, her handler, Noah, had told her. *They're not going to do anything in public.*

Rylee drops off the four beers for the vets and approaches the last booth.

"Welcome to Dogfish," she says, on autopilot. "What can I get started for you?"

"Can you believe her hair, Joey? Cut off all those dark curls. And I was looking forward to running my fingers through them."

Rylee wills herself not to touch her blond spikes, wondering if she'll ever get used to her new look. "Excuse me?"

"Not even a 'long time, no see,' *Rachel*?"

"I'm sorry …" Rylee speaks slowly, like she's a kindergarten teacher trying to help a child choose between pita pizza and chicken nuggets. "My name is Rylee. You must have me confused with someone else."

The men laugh simultaneously.

"Ya hear that, Jeff? Lady's a real comic."

The larger of the two, which is saying something given that they could both pass for NFL linebackers, slaps his hand on the table. Then he lowers his voice ominously. "You didn't really think you could hide forever, did you, Rach?"

Joey and Jeff, Rylee thinks. She hadn't known their names, but she'll never forget their faces. She's already ID'd them once. And she is scheduled to do it again at the trial in four months. Four months. Right around the time of the Sea Witch Festival in Rehoboth Beach, her new hometown. October hadn't seemed that far away, but it feels like an eternity when faced with the prospect of just making it through tonight.

"I'll bring you a flight, so you can try a few of our most popular beers." She turns to leave, but Jeff grabs her wrist.

"It's good to see you again, Rachel," he says, *sotto voce.* "We're looking forward to catching up. You close tonight, right?"

Rylee twists her wrist to break his grip, but he lets go, and she turns and heads toward the bar, checking on two of her tables along the way. *If they show up at the restaurant, just act like nothing's wrong,* Noah had said. *If you're relaxed, they'll relax.* Relax! Ha! Rylee has enough cortisol pumping through her system to fuel an entire special forces unit.

She retrieves the pickles and wings from the kitchen and exhales through her mouth. *Stay calm.* Rylee knows what she needs to do. It's just a matter of execution. She drops off the appetizers and offers the vets a refill on their drinks.

Not able to put it off any longer, she picks up the beer flights and heads to the last booth, sliding a flight in front of each of the men.

"Have you decided on food?"

"What do you recommend, *Rachel*?" Joey asks. Her name drips off his tongue.

Rylee grips her pen surreptitiously. That voice. It still haunts her. Even though she's felt relatively safe in this little seaside town on the Delaware shore, she hasn't been able to completely let her guard down.

"Ya know," he continues, "surprised you're not in the kitchen. Thought you liked working behind the scenes … like your old man." His words linger like the stench of stale beer and cigarette smoke in a bar.

Rylee feels perspiration drip from her armpits until it's absorbed by the tank top she wears under her Dogfish tee. She suppresses the bile in the back of her throat, but she can't suppress the memory.

It's late. Her father's restaurant is finally empty. Patrons and waitstaff have gone home or to other bars, with the exception of Rylee, who is finishing up in the kitchen, and her father, who is having a business meeting in the nearly vacant dining room. She peeks out to check on him. He is sitting at a table with two men. She can't hear their words, but their voices are elevated. Then her father starts shouting. He turns toward the kitchen, and her eyes connect with his just as the bullet pierces his heart.

"I'll bring you burgers," she says. "Rare. If I remember correctly, you like 'em bloody."

Jeff nearly chokes on his IPA. As she walks away, Rylee hears him say, "Now that's the fightin' spirit, Rach. This is gonna be fun!"

She knows they're watching her. She puts in their order, checks on a few of her tables and does her best to look as if she's just going about her business. As if tonight is just another evening in the Nation's Summer Capital. As if she's just one of the many cogs who make the wheels of idyllic vacation days keep turning for the throngs of tourists.

She walks to the back hallway and returns to the dining room several times, ensuring they notice her. Now you see me. Now you don't. Now you see me. When their burgers are ready, Rylee drops them off and waits until they dig in to make her move, hoping the momentary distraction will buy her enough time.

She strides purposefully through the dining room and retrieves her large shoulder bag from a room off the back hallway. Quickly, she strips off her tee, revealing her tank top and pulls a worn Dogfish ball cap over her head. *Always dress in layers*, Noah had counseled. *That way*

 Rehoboth Beach Reads

you can quickly change your appearance. She wears cut-offs under her baggy knee-length work shorts, which she removes as well and stuffs into her bag along with the tee. She looks like just another carefree twenty-something heading to the beach. As if!

Rylee keeps her head down and picks her way through the crowd at the bar until she's at the front door. *If they come for you, they'll probably have men watching the back; you'll have to go out the front.* Rylee will never curse the summer crowds again. They swallow her easily once she's on the sidewalk, especially because there's a long line, weaving through the outdoor dining space, waiting to take an interactive selfie with the new 3-D kracken painted on the side of the restaurant.

She passes Chesapeake and Main and the Chamber of Commerce before she hears the crowd buzzing behind her. "Watch it, buddy!" Someone shouts. And Rylee knows instinctively that the men who have come for her are on the move. A car honks as she darts in front of it, crossing Christian Street, the big yellow Jack Lingo building looming in front of her.

She's running now, elbowing her way through the crowd waiting outside the Summer House for a table. Plan A— the library. But it's a holiday. The gates are locked, and she can't cut through. Rylee shifts mentally to Plan B as she pushes through another crowd waiting outside Dos Locos. She races across Second Street against the light and is tempted to cut through the parking lot of the Atlantis Inn—she's desperate to get off Rehoboth Avenue—but it would be risky. Too much exposure. She stays on plan, even though her brain and body are at war with each other. Rylee hears the crowd behind her, unsettled in a way that tells her she still hasn't lost them.

She cuts behind two men fawning over a large dog outside the Purple Parrot and turns up the ramp, past the biergarten window, where she sees her friend Marco is working. He doesn't notice her. He's pulling a draft. At the top of the ramp, Rylee chances a glance behind her just in time to see the men race by, continuing their pursuit down the main street. She heads toward the outdoor garden in the back of the restaurant and takes a moment to catch her breath.

Her phone is in her back pocket. The display comes to life as she retrieves it. It's 7:48 p.m. The last ferry to Cape May leaves at 9:10. She can make it, but she'll need to keep moving. First, though, she sends Noah the one text she hoped she'd never have to: *Found me.*

She closes her eyes and leans against the wall as The Beach Boys play overhead, inviting everyone to Kokomo Beach. Rylee wonders sadly where they'll send her next. Foolishly, she had allowed herself to start dreaming about building a life here after the trial. With its burgeoning restaurant scene, Rehoboth Beach was fast becoming a popular destination for vacationing foodies. It was the kind of place a former award-winning chef would be welcome. Would be able to make a fresh start. Provided, of course, she survived tonight.

Rylee feels a sudden presence in front of her. Her heart is still beating wildly as she opens her eyes.

"You look like you could use a drink. Can I buy you a beer?" A woman with a pit bull tattoo on her bicep that says "Captain" is standing in front of her.

Rylee shakes her head. "Thanks anyway. I'm not staying."

She moves past customers relaxing in pastel Adirondack chairs to the rear exit of the restaurant on Wilmington Avenue. *Even most locals don't know about the gate,* Noah had told her. Rylee pushes open the wrought-iron enclosure and drops her ball cap in a trash barrel on the sidewalk. She retrieves a light blue bucket hat from her bag and turns left, heading toward the boardwalk.

Goolee's Grille has a crowd out front, though it's not nearly as packed as the restaurants on Rehoboth Avenue. Rylee crosses First Street and slows her gait. If one of the men cuts through Penny Lane, he'll catch up to her for sure. She walks with purpose but not fast enough to call attention to herself. With relief, she passes Penny Lane and stops in the shadow of Gus & Gus, just steps from the boardwalk. Her goal is to get onto the beach, where it's literally wall-to-wall bodies, as tourists and locals have been staking out spots since early morning for the fireworks at nine o'clock.

Rylee waits for a group of scantily clad teens to pass in front of her and then uses them for cover as she crosses the wide wooden planks and steps onto the beach. Immediately, her sneakers fill with sand. The tall seagrass on either side of the dunes keeps her hidden until she merges with the sea of bodies and blankets canvassing nearly every inch of available real estate. Rylee picks her way carefully, doing her best not to step on anyone or anything as she heads for the shoreline. Once she's on packed sand, she can move faster, while keeping an eye on the boardwalk to her left. The crowd, acting unwittingly as a human shield between her and certain death, emboldens her to keep moving.

She spots the duo in front of the bandstand, near the historic temperance drinking fountain. The bandstand is directly behind them, and Rylee can hear the distant strains of Lee Greenwood's "God Bless the U.S.A." as the Navy Concert Band is mid-performance. One of them (Joey?) is on his cell phone, his free hand waving wildly in the air. The other one is scanning the beach. She stops and drops down, near enough to a family sitting on a blanket eating pizza and vinegar-soaked Thrasher's fries that she looks like she could be part of their festivities. It's still twilight, but there are no lights on the beach, and so, for the moment, even though it's all Rylee can do to remain still, she feels hidden in plain sight.

She sees the men continue down the boardwalk, and Rylee keeps pace with them from the shore. What's she going to do if they don't turn back? She needs to cross the boardwalk again at Olive Street. At Whiskey Jack's she watches as one of them kicks the boards. Moments later they double back toward the bandstand. Rylee exhales, unaware that she's been holding her breath.

She moves faster now. The ferry departs in less than an hour. Rylee crosses the boardwalk near Obie's by the Sea on a dead run. The bike is hidden on the side of a summer cottage, an emergency backpack in a weatherproof crate next to it. She fumbles with the padlock, spinning the numbers a second time until she hears a soft *click*.

She takes off riding west on Olive and then turns north on First, crossing the bridge over Lake Gerar. Traffic is heavy, cars still circling, looking futilely for parking spots before the fireworks start, but Rylee presses forward, her legs pumping furiously. The road curves into Lake Street and she heads east toward the ocean. The sticky night air smells of salt and sweat with no relief from the oppressive humidity even as the sun sets. Eventually, she turns north again as Lake Street becomes Surf Avenue, which she follows past the city tennis and pickleball courts. A few miles farther and she'll be sheltered in the state park, but until then, she braces with every passing car, expecting the men to cut her off and finish what they came to do.

The ocean roars just beyond the multi-million-dollar homes to her right on Ocean Drive, and she takes comfort in their familiar outlines. How many times has she pedaled this path over the past year? The houses, mostly dark and abandoned in the winter months, are now aglow from well-lit interiors as families gather for exclusive front-row seats to the fireworks. Their conviviality feels like a talisman. As if nothing bad could possibly happen so close to quintessential summer festivities.

She enters Cape Henlopen State Park at Whiskey Beach and hooks up with the bike trail near the Gordon's Pond Pavilion. As the trail leads Rylee farther from the ocean, she's enveloped in darkness, her solitary quest punctuated only by night shadows, which dance between tree limbs. She flips on her bike's headlight and crosses the long bridge bordering the wildlife area. High-pitched peeps from tree frogs and the buzzing of cicadas keep her company as her mind jumps ahead. Beyond arriving safely on the Jersey shore, there's no plan. She'll text Noah again once she's on the ferry.

Rylee passes the Biden Center and brakes briefly as some furry nocturnal critter scurries across her path near the Observatory Tower, which is rumored to be haunted. The company of a ghost might actually be welcome right now. It's not the dead who scare her. It's the living who are causing her nightmares. Rylee whizzes past the guard house at the entrance to the park and exits onto the highway leading to the ferry terminal. Under the illumination from a streetlight, she chances a glance at her watch. Fifteen minutes. The road is flat. She picks up speed.

At the terminal, she weaves between the few remaining cars waiting to drive into the ferry's cavernous belly. Rylee has an open-ended ticket, which allows her to ride on. She stows her bike along the side and races up the narrow metal stairway to the first-level bathroom, her body still pulsating with adrenaline and the demands of physical exertion. Once inside, Rylee splashes cold water on her face and uses damp paper towels to wipe the sticky film from her chest and arms. Then she fishes a floral sundress and wig with shoulder-length brown hair from her backpack. She slips them on and removes her sneakers, still filled with sand, which she exchanges for Keens. A pair of wire-framed glasses completes her transformation. Rylee stares at her reflection in the mirror. She doubts if even her father would recognize her. Feeling moderately safer, she climbs two more sets of tinny stairs to the top deck.

Already, the railing on the port side is crowded with passengers. The pyrotechnics display over Rehoboth Beach started moments before and the dazzling bursts of light are visible against the night sky in the distance. Rylee finds two empty seats and sets her backpack beside her but doesn't feel like she can relax until they've pulled away from the dock.

She has a view of the terminal gangway leading onto the ferry. A flurry of commotion catches her attention, and she leans forward for a better look. The Hawaiian shirts are hard to miss. The men are arguing with security as they try to limbo under the ropes that have closed access to the ferry. Rylee's eyes dart around, frantically assessing escape options.

The ferry horn blares overhead, startling her. They're pushing off. A vibration under her feet from somewhere deep in the bowels of the boat acts as a tranquilizer. For the moment, she's safe. *Aloha.*

Rylee allows herself to breathe and to feel what? Relief? Reassurance? Maybe, but it's bittersweet. Another brilliant burst of reds and golds catches her eye, a sad reminder of the town and the possibilities she's leaving behind. Rylee can't remember when she's felt more alone.

Her friends, mostly coworkers from Dogfish, seemed to delight in sharing their close-knit seaside town with a newcomer as they welcomed her into their fold. She's going to miss Piper's wedding over Labor Day weekend and dancing to live local bands at The Starboard and The Rusty Rudder. She's experienced all four seasons at the beach and knows when to avoid Coastal Highway. She calls several of the farmers at the Rehoboth and Lewes markets by name and has eaten coq au vin at the Back Porch Café. She's spent countless hours on Dewey Beach, watching the dogs swim in the tide, and whiled away even more hours in the aisles at Browseabout Books. She feels like a local. Like she belongs.

She watches a man approach and gasps.

"I always wondered what you'd look like as a brunette," he says as he offers her a beverage in a plastic ferry cup.

"Marco?" Rylee asks in disbelief.

He moves her backpack aside and sits down. "Noah says to tell you hello. You did great tonight."

The darkened sky comes alive then as the fireworks finale pops and crackles in an explosion of fleeting brilliance. Rylee watches, transfixed, and then turns her attention to her friend. The words catch in the back of her throat until finally she says, "Do you think I'll ever be able to—"

"I do," he says, and softly touches his cup to hers.

A LONGTIME FAN OF THE THRILLER GENRE, RENÉE ROCKLAND WAS WORKING IN A BOOKSTORE IN 1996 WHEN GAYLE LYNDS PUBLISHED HER FIRST THRILLER, *MASQUERADE*. WHEN RENÉE MET GAYLE ON AN AUTHOR TOUR THAT SAME YEAR, THEY DISCOVERED THEY HAD BOTH GROWN UP IN THE SAME SMALL TOWN IN IOWA AND HAVE REMAINED FRIENDS EVER SINCE. "INDEPENDENCE DAY" WAS BORN OF RENÉE'S DESIRE TO EXPLORE THE THRILLER GENRE AND ALSO CAPTURE THE MELANCHOLY MANY PART-TIME RESIDENTS AND TOURISTS FEEL WHEN THEIR STAY AT THE BEACH COMES TO AN END, AND IT'S TIME TO SAY GOODBYE TO REHOBOTH.

RENÉE WOULD LIKE TO THANK BOTH NANCY SAKADUSKI FOR HER EXCELLENT EDITORIAL SKILLS AND THE JUDGE WHO SELECTED "INDEPENDENCE DAY" FOR DISTINCTION.

JUDGE'S COMMENT

From the first sentence, "Independence Day" grips the reader and doesn't let go. Iconic beach venues provide cover as the protagonist races for an escape from ominous hitmen hoping to silence her. This heart-pounding adventure is a notable addition to the Beach Secrets anthology.

Bug Spray and a Ponytail

By Tony Houck

Louella used to fetch the cows for milking every morning before school. Fetching the cows was her only morning chore, and she did it barefoot so that her only pair of shoes stayed clean. Poppa had a pair of shoes and a pair of boots. Momma did, too, but Louella and her sisters didn't take exception, and none of them ever fretted over being poor. The year that soybean prices soared, Louella got a pair of scissors *and* an orange for Christmas. She had never tasted an orange and chattered on to her classmates about its perky, sweet flavor. By the end of the eighth grade, Louella had book learned everything a Delaware farmer's daughter needed to know and dropped out of school to work on the farm.

Despite her limited book learning, Louella wrote as often as a life teetering on poverty permitted, spending whatever coins she had on paper and ink. After doing her evening chores, she often climbed into the hayloft and put pen to paper to the soothing sound of pigeons cooing in the rafters. Occasionally, she carried the horse's bucket up there with her to use as a desk or a stool. Louella's graceful penmanship filled countless pages with the events, ideas, dreams, dilemmas, and random bits that shaped her life. Poppa knew she was up there, and he didn't mind that she was, as long as her chores were done.

Louella adored her Poppa, a simple man with a stern face but a kind heart and a mellow tone. He barely raised his voice when "that bully of a rooster" knocked over Louella's lantern and set the hay ablaze. "Should've eaten him for dinner last Sunday," he had muttered while he and Louella tried to stomp out the spreading flames. Their desperate, heavy footfalls had done little good. "Bring water from the horse trough," Poppa had told her, tossing down the horse's bucket. "And then fetch Momma and your sisters."

Louella's hands and singed feet had been lightning quick, but the family's efforts had been in vain. Louella blamed herself for what happened, for not barefoot kicking that cock away sooner. Her feet and her memories still bore the scars.

Louella's pages didn't survive the fire, nor did the horse or the barn. Poppa swallowed too much smoke while fighting the flames and died soon after.

Momma eventually sold the farm, and she and the children moved in with her brother's family. For Louella, life was too noisy in that bursting farmhouse, but she managed for a while and then got married and moved a few miles down the road. She and "that gentle man with the pudgy face," as Louella's mother had called him, often drove their squeaky pickup to the coast, especially Rehoboth Beach.

The story of Louella's married life was recorded in fifty-four notebooks, one for each of the years starting when they exchanged nervous *I do's* in front of family and friends huddled inside a rain-dotted church. Louella's husband had called the notebooks *diaries*. Louella referred to them as journals. She was right, of course: Journals are much more personal than diaries. But since he had never read them, her husband couldn't have known better. Louella hadn't corrected him; experience and married life had taught her not to sweat the little things.

One day, the sons, daughters, and precocious grandchildren that Louella leaves behind will read what's written between those black marble covers. There's nothing in the journals that's criminal or even scandalous, but Louella's loved ones are sure to blush, smile, cry, and frown. And there's a surprise—maybe even a shock—waiting for them in the last journal. Louella didn't intend for that particular entry to be surprising or shocking. It was merely her reaction to getting horrible news. If you ask her about it, she will ignore you or pretend not to hear you and then start rambling on about something else.

★ ★ ★ ★ ★

The lights along the Rehoboth Beach boardwalk buzz on and hum up to full brightness. Ensconced on a bench with a closed journal resting on her lap, Louella glances up at the moths flitting around the light next to the bench. That bench had been *their* bench, but now it's just *her* bench. She brushes her sophisticated, yellowish white ponytail off her shoulder. Many women her age have hair of that color, and they tint it light blue or purple, but not Louella. She doesn't sweat the little things.

As Louella returns to staring at a boat skimming the horizon, a young woman standing inside the bandstand begins to tap her foot. She isn't keeping time to any music, and she isn't aware that she's doing it, but her irritation is boiling outward. Louella is a stranger to her and a complication. She glares at the back of Louella's head. "Beat it, granny," the young woman mutters, checking her watch. "That's *our* bench, and you're going to ruin my fairytale."

She is sure that Barrett is going to propose to her tonight. Her dream is that he will do it on that bench, at twilight, with a refreshing, salty breeze winnowing his blond hair. Barrett has taken his annoying, sweet time, but all the signs are there. *I've been waiting an entire, stinking year for this moment.*

Louella smiles at the boat in the distance, picks up the journal in her lap, and opens it. Her movement gives the young woman false hope, and she starts toward the bench, but then stops herself with an audible *humph!*

"Give me a break," the young woman mutters. "It's well past your bedtime, granny." She glances around, looking for Barrett's car. *If he gets here before you're gone,* she fumes to herself, her glare returning to Louella, *I'm gonna march over there and yank you off that bench.*

As Louella's eyes adjust to the stark whiteness of the paper, she flips to the midway point of the journal. She knows the exact spot, and after a heavy sigh, she reads the entry to herself. It's undated, but she will never forget the date: *The diagnosis is fatal. I have been sentenced to widowhood. What a wretched way to spend a wedding anniversary.*

Barrett eases his car into a parking spot near White House Black Market. After fussing with his hair and fumbling around in the glove compartment, he gets out and pays for parking.

Louella reads the journal entry again and then turns the page. It is empty, as is every page after it. Not even a dot where the point of a pen has rested but never flowed into action. Louella had never written another word. She was too ashamed to, but even if she had tried, the paper could not have borne the weight of the guilt she felt for feeling relieved as she grieved.

The young woman storms across the boardwalk and fakes a caring smile as she reaches into her purse. "Excuse me," she says to Louella, holding a spritzer of bug repellent, "but I would hate for you to get eaten up by mosquitoes. If you stand up, I'll spray you."

Louella closes the journal. "That's very kind of you, but the mosquitoes aren't out tonight. I think the breeze is keeping them at bay."

The breeze isn't supposed to keep away the mosquitoes, the young woman grumbles inwardly; *it's supposed to winnow Barrett's hair.* She glances around and spots him leaving Archie's Ice Cream with two cups in his hands.

"You may be right," the young woman says, slightly panicked, "but I'm not even sure there's enough to spray you." She unscrews the top of the spritzer bottle. "Let me check."

"There's really no need to—"

The young woman fakes a violent sneeze, dumping the contents of the small bottle onto Louella.

Barrett hurries to the bench and sets the two cups of ice cream on the ground. The napkins in the front pocket of his blazer are folded like a pocket square. "What have you spilled on this poor lady?" Barrett asks the young woman, dabbing at Louella's ponytail and hunched back with one napkin after another. He sniffs a napkin. "Bug spray."

"It was an accident, I assure you," the young woman lies.

Louella runs her hand across the journal's black marble cover. It is dry. "Well, the mosquitoes won't want anything to do with me for sure," Louella says with a nod and a knowing smile to the young woman. The oddness of her sneeze had not gone unnoticed. "If you would, please help me up. My son will be here soon."

The young woman takes Louella's hand and helps her stand. "So sorry about all that," the young woman lies again. "Such a big mess."

Louella presses the journal against her chest. "It was such a little nothing and not worth worrying about." As she finishes speaking, her son honks his car horn three times. Louella waves to him. "That's my ride. My bench is yours," she tells the young woman with a wink.

The young woman smiles wryly. "And so it is." She walks Louella to her son's car, helps her get inside, and then apologizes insincerely to both of them for the spill.

After they drive off, the young woman turns around. Her heart begins to flutter. Barrett is down on one knee next to the bench, fixing his shoelace or maybe only pretending to fix it. She glides over to him.

A salty breeze is winnowing his blond hair as he speaks to her: "I have something to ask you," he says.

The young woman nods, her chest heaving. "Yes, Barrett …"

"Close your eyes."

"Why?" she asks playfully.

"Just close them. It's a surprise."

She snaps her eyes shut and waits, pinching the inside of her cheek between her teeth to make sure she isn't dreaming. *This is happening. This is really happening.* Air is rushing in and out of her lungs.

"Now open them," Barrett says.

She catches her breath and opens her eyes.

Barrett is smiling, a broad smile that shows his perfect teeth. His hands are behind his back. "Remember how Archie's was out of both of your favorite flavors?"

The young woman turns as pale as one of the moths flitting around the light.

"Archie's isn't out of them anymore." Holding the ice cream, Barrett pushes his hands toward her. "I got you a cup of each. These are both for you."

Tony Houck is a former Spanish translator who now writes full time. He is a prior recipient of a Rehoboth Beach Reads Judge's Award for a short story that can be found in *Beach Life*. His first novel, *The Precariousness of Done*, was released in 2019. He is currently working on two other novels and is owner and operator of the blog *Unsalted Gems* (https://tonyhouck.com), which focuses on travel, Spanish language and culture, crazy families, writing and getting published, and obsessive-compulsive disorder, from which he has suffered for most of his life. He resides in Fredericksburg, Virginia, with his wife, son, and their pound puppy.

At first, "Bug Spray and a Ponytail" seems fairly innocuous, even wistful. A newly widowed woman reflecting back on her bittersweet memories while an impatient young brat demands her seat at the table. However, the devil, as they always say, lies in the details. Through sparse and suggestive prose that echoes Shirley Jackson at her most sinisterly banal, Houck is able to show us the shoe that drops the scale back to balance. The lantern that always knocks over. The bug spray that always spills. For us, the why and how of these cataclysms will always remain as mysterious as Louella's fifty-four notebooks; the truth forever cast in the words we can't read.

Lucky the Chicken

By David Cooper

"That cage is going to fall."

"What?" Forty-three years of marriage had taught me not to jam on the brake with every outburst.

"That cage." Eileen threatened to shatter the windshield with her pointer finger. "On the top of the chicken truck right in front of us."

"Yeah, that one is about ready to—"

The cage toppled from the high pile. A plume of feathers hung in the air, like when Road Runner fell off a cliff in the cartoons of my childhood. I pumped the brakes to avoid the wire-mesh box, and we turned our heads to track the cage bouncing across the asphalt until it rested between the berm and edge of a field.

"We've got to go back," Eileen said.

"Why?"

"The chicken got out and is running along the road."

"I'd run too."

"Just turn around."

Forty-three years had also taught me I should do what I'm told.

"Pull over right there." She bounded from the car as quickly as a sixty-five-year-old with arthritic knees could manage. "Bring the blanket from the trunk."

I handed it to her, and she made a beeline for the mangled cage. How many men can say they've witnessed their wives chasing a chicken across a road with a blanket, or wondered what came next once the chicken had been apprehended?

"What are we going to do with that?"

"We couldn't just leave her there."

"It's a chicken."

"I know what she is."

We got back into the car and swung around, heading toward the Delaware Coast and our home in Rehoboth Beach.

Eileen held the creature swaddled in her lap like a newborn. "We should name her *Lucky*."

The chicken poked her head out from between folds and clucked in agreement.

"Should I remind you what we had for dinner last night?"

Eileen turned and glared at me. So did the chicken.

I sighed. "You know we can't keep it."

"She is not an *it*. Her name is *Lucky*."

"OK, we can't keep *Lucky*."

"Why not?"

"We live in a condo."

"So?"

"The HOA will never let us keep a chicken."

"We'll just have to keep quiet."

"Keep quiet we have a chicken named Lucky? You remember what happened to that guy across from us when he got a second dog?"

"Your point?"

We stopped at an intersection. A woman in the next lane looked twice into our car.

"What will we feed it?" I asked.

"I'll call Sarah. She'll know."

Our friend Sarah raised chickens on a small farm just outside town.

"Look—" My next words would have surely brought some sense into the situation, but Eileen interrupted me.

"Tilly will love it." She pulled the granddaughter card. Our ten-year-old Tilly trumped all else and would start her month-long visit with us in three days. I backed down.

★ ★ ★ ★ ★

"Her name is Lucky," Eileen said.

The three of us stood in our living room, encircling a small pen, thrown together with a bit of garden fencing, a few cushions, and an old blanket to cover the floor. Some families had secrets about felons, feuds, and philanderers—our family possessed a secret with feathers.

"Gram, she's so cute." That little girl's voice always melted me. "Can we take her to the beach?"

"I don't think so," I said.

Eileen turned and gave me one of her why-would-you-say-that looks. Her eyes left mine, fixed on something over my shoulder, and she put her arm around Tilly. "Don't listen to him. We can carry her in that basket on top of the refrigerator."

My expression must have revealed every question forming in my brain, or maybe our lifetime together meant she knew my thoughts before I did, but Eileen stifled me with a glance. A sharp glance.

"Tilly," she said, "why don't you go upstairs and put on your bathing suit?"

We stood listening to Tilly's little feet carrying her beyond earshot while I prepared for my tongue-lashing.

"And why can't we take Lucky to the beach?"

"Umm, she's a chicken."

"Yes, and …?"

"How are you going to keep her in the basket?"

"She's probably spent her life in a cage—a small space. Did you see how she sat in my lap all the way home the other day? I'll keep her wrapped in a blanket. She'll be fine." Eileen cocked her head and spoke into the living room. "Won't you, Lucky?"

Lucky clucked, denying me any possible protest.

✴✴✴✴✴

I couldn't have asked for more from retirement—a summer afternoon walking the beach with my wife and granddaughter, searching for a spot to place our umbrella, one far enough from others so as not to draw attention to Lucky the Chicken.

Tilly ran ahead to the water's edge, then waited to take my hands and jump the waves. I savored every splash, every giggle, and even the little coughs from snorted water, knowing this age would pass in another year or two, as it did with her mother. We talked between waves about the end of Tilly's school year, her new friend down the street from her house, and what she wanted to do next when she tired of the waves—if she ever tired of the waves.

I wanted Eileen to be with us, so I turned to wave her down from the blanket, but she appeared to be busy talking to a Beach Patrol officer, who stood over her and Lucky.

"Tilly, I need to go see your grandmother. I want you to stay out of the water until I get back, OK?"

"Why is that policeman with Gram?"

"I'm not sure," I said, although I had a pretty good idea.

The sand worked against me, like in one of those dreams when you need to get somewhere but just can't move fast enough. When I reached the umbrella, the officer clicked the radio strapped to his shoulder.

"Yes, dispatch, a chicken."

Silence with just a bit of static. "Stand by."

"Officer, is there a problem?" I asked.

"Sir, I was just saying to your wife, pets are not allowed on the beach from May first through September thirty-first."

"I was telling this young man the sign says *dogs* are not allowed on the beach."

Sometimes Eileen just needed to know when to quit.

The radio crackled to life.

"Go ahead, dispatch."

"Is the chicken leashed?"

The officer rubbed his forehead. "Now they're just messing with me."

"Officer, we don't mean to cause any trouble," I said. "The chicken belongs to our granddaughter." I pointed to Tilly by the water.

"Tell you what," the officer said, "just keep the chicken in the basket, OK?"

Lucky clucked in protest.

I offered the young man my hand. "Thank you, officer. We will."

We stayed on the beach another hour or so, leaving when more people pitched their umbrellas near us.

Our struggle to keep our feathered friend a secret continued when we arrived home. A neighbor spotted us in the driveway, waved, and asked if Tilly had won a stuffed chicken on the boardwalk. A simple *yes* and a few smiles almost got us through the front door free of suspicion, but Lucky decided to stretch out a wing and flap a hello.

Eileen sequestered herself in the kitchen—also known as her *thinking room*—for the better part of the morning. Eventually, she made the call to Sarah, our friend with the farm. Eileen spoke softly, so Tilly, upstairs and playing on her tablet, couldn't hear her, but my wife's dismay reached me clearly on the living room couch.

"Tilly is going to be so disappointed," Eileen said, "but he's right."

A pause.

"Knowing Lucky will be with you will help."

Another pause.

"Thank you so much, Sarah. We'll see you, soon."

Eileen walked into the living room under a heavy cloud. She didn't even glance into Lucky's pen.

"Well," she said, "Sarah will take her. Tomorrow morning, OK?"

The question *why not today?* made it to my tongue, but I simply nodded. Eileen sat next to me, and I put my hand on her knee. "Lucky will be happy there."

"You keep saying that."

I shrugged. "When should we tell Tilly?"

"I don't know. I don't want to tell her."

"We can't chicken out now." Eileen wasn't amused, but I was. "You know we can't keep hiding Lucky."

"That's why I called Sarah." She sighed and broke a bit of a smile. "Besides, the police are onto Lucky."

"They could knock on our door any moment, and I'm too old to face charges of aiding and abetting."

* * * * *

The next day, we stood before the Taj Mahal of chicken coops: red clapboard siding, fresh hay in spacious nesting boxes, chicken-sized windows for ventilation, elevated perches, a row of pristine water bottles, and a run a racehorse would enjoy. Sarah's coop made our living room pen look like a shanty.

"Lucky is going to be very happy here," I said to Tilly.

Tilly said nothing while stroking Lucky in her basket.

I tried again. "We'll visit her."

Then Eileen tried. "It's like a big fort for chickens, like the forts you build in that little patch of woods."

"You promise we'll visit?"

"I promise, Tilly," I answered. *How could I not?*

Tilly wiped her wet cheeks. "I'm sorry you have to go, Lucky. I don't want you to."

I realized my cheeks were wet.

Sarah put her hand on Tilly's shoulder. "Do you want to show Lucky where her new nest will be?" Tilly nodded and followed Sarah up the ramp and through a human-sized door into the coop.

I don't make empty promises, especially to Tilly, and after a few weeks, Lucky showed us how much she liked her new home by starting to lay. Tilly called them "Lucky Eggs."

* * * * *

The beeps and clangs and laughter and screams coming from Funland made hearing Eileen next to impossible. She took me by the arm and pulled me away from the bumper car pileup in front of us, a spectacle our granddaughter had somehow orchestrated yet escaped from unscathed.

"A fox got into the hen house." Eileen didn't seem to be making an allusion.

"That's terrible. What about Lucky?"

Eileen shook her head. "I think her luck ran out."

"We're supposed to visit tomorrow."

"I know."

We looked back into the bumper car frenzy. Tilly threaded the needle between two unsuspecting boys.

"OK," I said, "it's a part of life she needs to learn about sooner or later."

"Why not later?"

I pulled Eileen close. We watched our granddaughter revel in the mayhem she had wreaked, knowing her evening wouldn't end well.

* * * * *

The empty and quiet red coop stood before us: once a flurry of feathered activity, now a crime scene. Every now and then a light breeze stirred up some stray feathers and loose straw.

Well, the Taj Mahal is a mausoleum. I kept that idea to myself and knelt beside Tilly. "Lucky was happy. Only happy chickens lay eggs, and we'll always remember the time we took her to the beach."

"Why did the fox do that?"

I took a slow breath and considered my words carefully. "That's what foxes do. They're predators and eat other animals."

Eileen put her hand on Sarah's arm. "How many did you lose?"

"All eight." Our friend didn't seem to be faring any better than Tilly. "And I still can't figure out how the fox got in."

"I'm so sorry," Eileen said.

I walked up the ramp and through the door. If a fox got in once, it could get in again. Foxes were known to be cunning for good reason. *Maybe, I can at least help Sarah look for the chink in the armor.*

The morning breeze did nothing to move the hot air inside the coop or cut the humidity. I used my T-shirt to wipe my face. My investigative work would have to be fast. Scattered feathers in the nesting boxes and on the floor told of the previous day's horrors, but the carcasses were gone. What the fox didn't drag away, Sarah must have removed before we arrived.

Cluck.

"It can't be," I said.

"Are you talking to us?" Eileen called from outside the coop.

"No." I ducked and checked under the nesting boxes. Another *cluck.* I looked up and saw a flash of white where a rafter met a truss. I moved underneath the joint and found Lucky perched high above the reach of any murdering fox. She looked down at me, cocked her head to the side, and clucked.

"Tilly, come quick."

Our granddaughter's eyes followed my finger right to a healthy Lucky, dancing back and forth within the tight space between truss and rafter.

* * * * *

Our family's feathered secret passed away two years later. A grand breakfast, the biggest we could muster, seemed the best way to celebrate her life.

"You remember how to crack those the way I showed you?" Eileen went to the refrigerator, leaving Tilly unattended at the stove. "Keep the shells out of the pan. Don't go reaching in to pick out any pieces with your fingers."

I put down my newspaper. "She's twelve. I think she can make an egg."

Tilly glanced over her shoulder at me, and I winked.

"I know how old she is," Eileen rummaged in the refrigerator, "but that's the last of Lucky's eggs."

"Gram, look!" Tilly stepped back from the stove.

Eileen abandoned the refrigerator, and something told me I should look, too, so I got up from the table. Wouldn't you know it, Lucky's last egg had two yolks. The white had formed a long curve beneath bulging yellow eyeballs making our final sunny-side-up with Lucky a big smile in the pan.

Dave Cooper would like to thank Vicki and Greg Wagner of Lancaster, Pennsylvania, for sharing their "Lucky the Chicken" experiences, which inspired this story: witnessing Lucky plummet from a truck, rescuing her from traffic, weathering a raccoon attack, and receiving a parting double-yolk egg.

Dave is a history and martial arts teacher with more than twenty-six years of experience in each field. His first article appeared in The National Middle School Association's *Middle Ground* in 2003. Since then, he has contributed to a variety of periodicals including *Teaching History*, *Middle Level Learning*, *Family Chronicle*, *Boy's Life*, *College Bound*, and *Pennsylvania Educational Leadership*. His fiction and poetry have appeared in *Timber Creek Review*, *Yorick Magazine*, *NFG*, and in the Cat & Mouse Press anthologies *Beach Pulp* and *Beach Dreams*. More of Dave's work can be found at dcwriting.wordpress.com.

Posturing

By Frances Grote

Anne stands in front of the display of cards. Soon, the bookstore will be able to fully reopen. But for now, thanks to the COVID occupancy limits, she's uncomfortably aware there's someone outside waiting for a turn. "What's wrong with the people who write these cards," she demands. Out loud. And then catches herself and blushes the color of a summer hot flash. It's bad enough she talks to herself at home to banish the echoes from her house in Henlopen Acres. She doesn't need anybody noticing her acting crazy in the card section of Browseabout.

A quick glance around shows a man a few feet away, partially obscured by a display of beachy décor. He's staring at her. Really staring. As if he knows her. There's something familiar about him, something that gives her an icy chill. She looks away, realizing he reminds her of David. How could her mind accordion pleat more than fifty years that fast? It's the time of year, of course, and then there's the letter. What are the chances the letter would show up at the worst possible moment in the divorce, when all she had for an emotional life jacket was her belief in her own moral superiority? She'd barely read the first paragraph before stuffing it in the box along with the rest of the evidence.

She takes a quick look back at the guy. White hair, piercing blue eyes, but she can't see the rest of his face, which is covered by a mask. Staring at the cards, she tries to puzzle out what about him seems familiar. It's his extreme height, she realizes, combined with the way he hunches over slightly—not your run-of-the-mill, age-related shoulder droop. It's closer to David's teenage slouch, the one that gave him the reputation for having a bad attitude, even before he deserved it.

"Dr. Berring?" Anne is startled to hear her name. The young woman who works the register has come over. "Is there anything I can help you with?"

Anne shakes her head. "No, thanks. Just having a hard time choosing a card." Now she really wonders how much of a spectacle she's been making of herself. No wonder the guy was staring. Lately she's been imagining ghosts of her past everywhere. All the years she'd kept her secret in its box and then, as if sent by some trickster god, the letter arrives right when she finally gets Mark to admit that the woman he called his "work wife" has become his wife in every sense of the word. The instant she read the first line, she knew the only smart thing to do was destroy it. But every time she tried to decide how—Burn it? Run it through the shredder? Bury it somewhere in the sand at Gordon's Pond?—she found she couldn't do it. It was from her son, the secret child she had hidden in her heart almost fifty years ago. He was asking to meet her.

She looks again in the man's direction and instantly regrets it. He's still staring at her. When he catches her eye, he dips his head slightly, then turns and walks away. Was that a nod? Or merely the gesture of a man in his seventies checking for trip hazards as he moves over unfamiliar ground? This is ridiculous. This couldn't be David. From the moment they'd met waiting tables at The Dinner Bell that summer of '71, he'd been rough-edged and pushy. If David wanted something from you, he wouldn't just walk away.

Anyway, the man is gone now, and she needs to focus, to pick out a birthday card, even if it's only going into her personal Pandora's box. Now that she has proof her son is real, it feels impossible to find the right card. Not that anybody writes verses appropriate for this situation. Finally, her turn in the store long since passed, she picks up a beautiful card with a sculpted cake on the front, blank inside. It costs as much as the breakfast special at Egg, and the envelope specifies that extra postage is required—if someone ever wanted to mail it.

＊ ＊ ＊ ＊ ＊

Anne has no idea what she'll say in this year's card. What do you say when you've been found after a lifetime of absentee birthdays? Is it her son she has imagined loving all these years, or merely her secret? She wanders out of the bookstore and without consciously deciding, turns toward the ocean. The surf is her solace these days. The sky today is brilliant, nearly white, and the breeze off the water is strong enough to blow the smells of burnt sugar and hot grease down Rehoboth Avenue. She walks to the boardwalk, then down onto the beach to watch the wind whipping the waves into foam. Sitting in what little shelter she can find at the edge of the dunes, she tries to find words for this year's note. The only thing that comes to mind is, "I'm sorry. I should have made different choices." It won't do.

She finally gives up and starts back over the dunes toward Rehoboth Avenue. The sand in her shoes is aggravating enough to distract her momentarily, so she's almost at the boardwalk when she sees him, the tall white-haired man. He's sitting on a bench on the far side of the boards, facing her directly. He doesn't bother to pretend he's surprised to see her. She glares at him. Enough of this crap. Without stopping to empty the sand out of her shoes, she marches toward him. There are plenty of people around on the off-chance things get out of hand, but Anne is too pissed off to even consider the possibility of needing help.

"Dr. Berring?" A woman's voice calling her name, nearby.

Anne turns and immediately forgets all her aggravations. Although her practice had been in Wilmington, inevitably some of her patients show up in Rehoboth. She's made a point of keeping track of them when she can, but she hasn't seen this kid in a few years. Still, he would be impossible to forget. Born with about as much bad luck as a human could survive, he had been sent to Anne to do what she could to repair his spine. Now, he's strapped into an oversized stroller, his hands waving about in an uncoordinated greeting while his gaze flashes blindly from side to side.

The boy's mother starts to reach out her hand, then remembers her COVID manners. "Last time we were at Dupont they told us you retired. I'm so glad to see you!"

Anne smiles and, ignoring the rules, walks up to the stroller. "Nicholas, you've gotten so big," she says, as she begins ruffling his hair. Every other sense might have failed him, but Anne had always been able to reach him through touch. He quiets and nuzzles his cheek against her arm so briefly that someone who didn't know him would question if it was intentional.

"You were always so kind and gentle with him," his mother says.

Before Anne can catch herself, she replies, "Anyone taking care of patients who isn't kind and gentle should be taken out and shot."

The woman gives Anne a nervous smile and makes an excuse to move on.

I'm losing it, Anne thinks. *That guy following me around is making me go out of control.* She looks around, but he's gone. Since she walked into town, she's going to have to walk home. She'll have to be sure and check behind her now and then.

She's halfway between Olive and Virginia Avenues when she realizes she's out of breath and has to sit down. She's been walking so fast it was nearly running. She looks around before settling on a bench, but the only people in sight are a couple of guys walking an entirely too prissy dog and some beefy type who looks like he took a wrong turn on his way to Ocean City. She's almost ready to laugh off her paranoia until she figures out it's not her elderly stalker making her heart race, it's her own past rising up from the pit of rage deep inside her. Life has woken her monster.

⋆ ⋆ ⋆ ⋆ ⋆

She sees herself in back of The Dinner Bell, where the smokers take their breaks. She is eighteen years old, but her lack of experience with the world makes her a child. David isn't here, although he's supposed to be. He used to invite her to ride with him down Route 1 after the kitchen closed, the Moody Blues blasting from his car's eight track, but not anymore. The dishwasher tells her David traded shifts. By the end of the week, it's clear he's not coming back.

At the end of the season, with no one to ask for help, she has no choice but to go home and face her parents and their alternating bouts of rage and recrimination. They find a lawyer who finds a childless couple who offer enough cash to cover her entire college tuition in exchange for a healthy white baby. Nobody cares how she feels about it. And she believes she has to do what they say. Because that's how it works. So, they send her to stay with an aunt.

When her labor gets hard, they wheel her into the delivery room, terrified, in pain, with no idea what's going to happen, and slap the gas on her face. When she wakes up, it's all over. There's a nurse, an older woman, in the room, doing whatever gets done after someone gives birth. Anne is still on the delivery table, almost too groggy to speak. She can hear the baby crying somewhere in the room. "Can I see my baby?" she asks, her voice weak.

The nurse doesn't stop what she's doing. "I thought you were giving him up for adoption."

So it was a boy. "Please. I just want to hold him so he stops crying."

"He's in the warming bassinet. He doesn't need you to hold him."

Anne starts crying herself. "I promise I'm not going to change my mind and try to keep him. He just sounds so sad."

"Look." The woman comes over and looks down at her. "You already made one big mistake. Don't make it worse. Do yourself a favor. Forget he exists. Some decent people will raise him and if you're smart enough not to tell anybody what you did, maybe you can have a life too." And then she stalks out of the room, not even bothering to help Anne take her legs out of the stirrups.

When Anne realizes the nurse isn't coming back, she struggles to free her legs. She's numb down there, although as she sits up, she can tell there's lots of padding. She manages to hang her legs over the edge of the table before she gets too dizzy to move. She sits there, hunched over, until she feels strong enough to stand up, then slowly eases off the table. Still wobbly, she shuffles across the room to the mechanical-looking glass box that holds her baby.

She didn't know what she expected him to look like, but he's bald and a sort of purplish-red and wearing only a diaper. He opens his mouth, and the saddest wail imaginable comes out.

As much as she hates them all, Anne knows they're right. She doesn't even know what to do for him in his first moments. How would she manage to keep him safe and give him everything he needs over a lifetime? Eyes filling with tears, she reaches in, forgetting to be afraid that someone will catch her. His skin is velvety, and as she strokes it, he quiets and opens his eyes. She'd heard that babies can't really see until they're a few months old, but he seems to be staring right at her. It's like he's trying to learn her face. *Remember me*, she pleads inside her head. *Even though I'll never see you again, know that I love you.* She imagines her love coming out of her body and wrapping itself around him like a magic cloak.

* * * * *

The sound of people talking as they walk behind her on the boardwalk brings Anne back to the present. She wipes her hand across her eyes. She's not about to get caught crying in public. She pulls the birthday card and a pen out of her bag. "To my beloved son," she writes. "Every child I have helped over the years has done a little better because he or she got a piece of my heart that was meant for you."

　　　　　　　　　　Rehoboth Beach Reads

Back at home, fortified by a late lunch of tuna salad and a glass of rosé, Anne goes to the closet in her room. It's her room now that Mark is truly gone. She takes down the box. In the beginning, all the cards fit in an 8 x11 envelope. By the time she and Mark got married, she'd needed a shoebox, but that could still be kept inconspicuously on a closet shelf. A few years back she'd switched everything over to a flowered treasure chest from the craft store, thinking that would be unlikely to attract Mark's interest should he ever have a reason to delve into her closet.

She carries the box over to her bed. When she opens it her stomach lurches. There's a new envelope on top of the pile. All it says is "Anne," in Mark's writing. She sinks onto the bed, mortified, horrified, fighting not to give in to panic. How long has Mark known about this box? His letter is on top of the one from her son. Did he read that too? Hands trembling, she picks up his envelope and opens it. There's one sheet of paper inside.

Anne,

I never said I'm sorry, and in some ways I'm not. I'm sure you think I'm a bastard. I deserve it. Partially. We're apart now because I wanted to be happy before it was too late. But you deserve to be happy too. I married you because we were best friends, and we stayed together a lot of years even after we weren't best friends anymore because of how much I liked and respected you. I hope that's why you stayed with me as well. Maybe we could have made it forever if we hadn't been the type to keep secrets. What I am most sorry for is that my secret ended up hurting you. But your secret is hurting you as well. In some ways the world is a kinder place than it was fifty years ago, especially where unwed motherhood is concerned. Let him know you've been loving him all these years. Maybe that will mean something to him; maybe it won't. Either way, whatever you have to lose now is so much less than everything else you've lost along the way. You can survive it. There will always be a place in my heart that belongs only to you.

— Mark

When she has finally cried as much as she's able and had another glass of the rosé, she goes back to the bedroom and takes her son's letter out of the box. She rereads the first paragraph, where he introduces himself and explains how he's hoping they can meet. He goes on to say that he's married, with two teenage boys, and after doing the corporate thing for a while, he and his wife started a small winery. Both his adoptive parents are deceased and having kids of his own made him begin to wonder about his birth parents. If she's interested, he would really appreciate the chance to meet at least once. And maybe, if they both feel comfortable about it, his kids could get to know her. As if all of this is not enough, he then tells her that he has already met his birth father, who also lives in the San Francisco area. "I regret to say," he goes on, "that he's not very impressive. For what it's worth, I understand the choice you made."

Later, when she's feeling closer to normal, Anne sends a note to the email address her son provided. And then, because she's sitting at the computer anyway, she does a web search for David. He has a fairly unusual last name, and there is only one of him in the San Francisco area. His Facebook profile says his marital status is "complicated," that he is a "found object sculptor." All of the photos he has chosen to post feature him prominently. Anne does not send him a friend request. But she does wonder, if he's out in California, who's the guy who's been following her around town?

* * * * *

Usually, Anne goes to Azafran on Thursdays, the night the bartender sings. Anne likes to sit at the short end of the bar because there's only enough space for one person. Since it's Wednesday, the bartender is surprised to see her. "You're a night early," she says, as she lays down a coaster.

"I'm celebrating," Anne answers. "I'll have the 'Ginger, not Maryanne.'"

"Put that on my check, if you don't mind."

Anne looks up. It's the man with the piercing blue eyes. She didn't see him come in because her back is to the door. "I'll pay for my own drink, thanks," she immediately responds.

"Of course," he says. "I hope I didn't offend you. Mind if I sit here?"

Anne shrugs. The closest seat is six feet away, on the long side of the bar. Thank goodness COVID is good for something. He asks the bartender for a glass of tempranillo, which gives him an excuse to take off his mask. Despite knowing that David should be in California, Anne is relieved for this confirmation that the man who seems to be following her around town is someone else. He sees her looking at him and smiles.

Years of being in charge have taught Anne a lot of useful things, not the least of which is how to be in charge. "Do we know each other?" she asks. "Because I'd like to understand why you appear to be following me."

He takes a moment to consider before answering. Then he says, "Would it be all right if I moved a little closer? I promise I'm fully vaccinated."

"That'll get you the first three feet," Anne says. "You'll need to earn the rest."

He stands up and moves his stool almost precisely halfway to her. He takes his time moving his drink as well, and then sitting down and getting comfortable before he begins to answer. "I belong to the Art League. Your house is practically across the street, and I often see you out front in your garden. I wanted to paint you, but I never found the courage to ask."

"Just as well," Anne says. "I'd never have found the time to sit still."

That makes him smile.

"So, what made you find the courage to ask now?"

He studies her in a way that doesn't make her want to look away.

"You don't look as sad as usual. In fact, I almost wasn't sure it was you when I came in."

Now it's Anne's turn to smile. "I'm going to meet my son," she says. A bubble of laughter rises in her throat as she watches him puzzle through what, exactly, that means. She had no idea she was going to say it, but now that she has offered up her secret she feels no shame. "I haven't seen him for a very long time," she adds, and she can almost see the last dust of the shell she has lived in for so many years sifting to the floor.

"That's where the sadness has gone, then," he says. "You're glad you're going to see him."

"I'm even gladder he wants to see me."

"Well then," he reaches over to clink his glass against hers, "this does call for a celebration."

Mostly for her own amusement now that she knows who he is not, she asks, "What's your favorite Moody Blues song?"

His face crinkles with concentration. "I'm not sure I ever listened to them enough to have a favorite," he finally says.

Anne can't help smiling a little wider. "You can move your stool the rest of the way over," she says.

Frances Grote was lucky enough to be able to convert her part-time infatuation with Rehoboth Beach to a full-time obsession three years ago. She supports her fiction-writing habit by helping companies use technology to improve the drug development process. *Publishers Weekly* said her debut novel, *Fire in the Henhouse*, was "brewing with tension, lightened by warm humor." *Kirkus Reviews* called her short story collection, *Death, Madness and a Mess of Dogs*, a "promising collection from a talented newcomer." She has also published short stories in *Glimmer Train* and *Del Sol Review*.

The inspiration for "Posturing" came when Fran attended a talk at the Rehoboth Beach Museum about the beginnings of Rehoboth's restaurant renaissance. Visions of the town fifty years ago got her wondering about how a secret from that summer could thread its way through the course of someone's life—and how it's never too late for a course correction.

Secrets in the Attic

By MaryAlice Meli

For two months every summer, Mom takes us to Rehoboth Beach, which we love. What we hate is the house where she grew up: a tall, shabby, yellow house filled with odd sounds and old smells. I asked why it was such a dingy place. I mean, the wood was showing through the paint, ya know? Mom said as soon as she sells her book of scary stories, she's going to have it painted. But, geez, I mean, it'll still be dingy inside. At least it's cool. Mom's children's books paid for air conditioning last year.

Mom said not only did she love growing up in Rehoboth, but the yellow house inspired her to write. It was where she first made up her children's stories. Mom's children's books take place in a kind of fantasy Rehoboth with cute little animals having fun adventures on the boardwalk and sailing in the ocean on silly polka-dot boats. Mom draws all the illustrations too.

My sister, Kelley, was painting my toenails her newest color, Bombast Blue. She gets a bigger allowance than I since she turned thirteen. I have two years to go before I turn teenage, but I don't spend my allowance from chores on nail polish. I go to Browseabout Books each week and spend my money on graphic horror novels. Mom stuck her head out the window and asked us to sweep the front porch, one of our chores.

A man with a cane was walking slowly down the street, watching us. He stopped and asked who lived in our house. Kelley and I didn't answer him. I pretended I didn't hear the question. I was afraid to ask a grown-up why he wanted to know.

Then he asked, "Does Karey Ross still live there?"

I still didn't answer him, but I was a bit scared. Karey Ross was my mother's name before she married Dad. Kelley just shrugged and started plumping the cushions for the chairs, and I kept sweeping.

The man moved on. He was not old-old—maybe the same as Mom. He would have been taller had his legs been straight, but he was bent a lot at the knees like a troll. He had longish black hair with some gray in it, a big nose, and squinty eyes with round wire glasses and wore a peaked old-guy cap.

A few days later, I was hunched down by a large bush trying to see the baby birds in a nest there when the troll guy ambled by again. I stayed down when he stopped, but the blabby mother bird started squawking at me. I don't know if he saw me, but when he left, I went inside and told Mom. I described him and said he claimed to know her from when she lived there. She said she didn't remember anyone that matched my description. I said maybe we should tell Dad. Mom laughed and put her arm around my neck, giving me her favorite neck hug, and told me not to worry Dad.

The most fun place to play inside was the attic, which was filled with loads of boxes and old furniture. My sister enjoyed dressing up in the old-fashioned dresses and hats as much as I did. She even fit in some of the high heels, and we both loved the glittering necklaces, shiny rings, and big crownlike tiara. The jewelry didn't seem old the way the clothes did.

Mom found one of her old notebooks and said the house had many secrets. I didn't see anything secret or valuable; it was just old but fun. While Mom wrote in a small room at the other end of the attic, we played until it was time to stop for lunch and then go to the beach.

Mom started writing scary stories last year. She said it was to make more money for our college funds, but I think she was bored and just having fun writing the scary stories.

Her scariest story was about a ghost no one could see—only its shuffling movements could be heard inside the walls. It had a vile odor, like the rotten vegetables in the garden's compost pile at the end of summer. I could smell the scent in the corners of the attic. When I asked Mom about it, she smiled and said that smell had been there when she was a girl. She didn't know what caused it, but it may have given her the idea for Homer. That's the name she gave the evil-smelling shuffler. I asked if she heard the shuffling. She laughed and said she just made that up. But I don't know because, I mean, I could hear it, ya know?

I laughed and told her the name *Homer* sounded goofy, not scary. But Mom said I shouldn't laugh, that it might hurt the ghost's feelings. I didn't know whether she was serious or kidding. Of course, I didn't believe that Homer's feelings would be hurt. I mean, Homer wasn't real, right?

Kelley laughed. "Oh, Kasey," she'd say, teasing me for believing Homer was real.

I mean, I knew he wasn't real. Geez, he couldn't be real, could he?

But what I knew and what I believed weren't always the same. So, I apologized to Homer when no one was around.

One moonlit night way after midnight, I discovered Homer had to be real. Really real. Homer's rotten veggie odor woke me, which was terrifying by itself, but then I also smelled smoke. I jumped out of bed and saw tendrils of smoke curling under my door. I tried to open the door, but it was stuck. Even though it often stuck, I panicked and began screaming and banging on the door like I was in a horror movie and the house was on fire.

Mom opened my door and my sister's and told us to follow her as she raced downstairs and out the front door, where the smoke was thickest. She flung smoking summer chairs off the porch and onto the grass. Everyone on the street came out because other porches' furniture also had been set on fire and smoke had filled our small dead-end lane.

My sister tried to make me laugh by saying Homer had caused the fire. I flung back that Homer couldn't have caused so many fires and, besides, Homer had warned us to get out before the smoke killed us. I asked Mom what she thought, but she was too busy talking with the fire chief, who told Mom some kids probably torched the furniture. I thought the fire chief was wrong—the troll started it—but I didn't say anything. Mom wouldn't believe me, and the fire chief would just roll his eyes and nod at the other firemen, who'd laugh to show they also thought kids were ridiculous. I hate that.

Things calmed down. We went to yard sales and bought aluminum and vinyl chairs for the porch, furniture that couldn't be burned.

A week later, we went for a walk after dinner and stopped at The Ice Cream Store. I didn't see the man at first. My sister and I were laughing about the Booger ice cream flavor. I decided on my usual choice, two scoops of Cereal Killer. Mom didn't let us have sugared cereal and that choice allowed me to have several different sugared cereals mushed into my ice cream. Kelley got Cinn-Dough Rella. Mom picked Absolute Nuts, which she said she deserved for taking us there.

Suddenly, I saw him. He was close enough for Mom to see him, so I nudged her and whispered where she should look. She wrinkled her forehead as she did when thinking over a problem and gave him a quick glance. Mom's baffled frown didn't change, but she hurried us, clutching our waffle cones, down Rehoboth Avenue to the side street that led to our house.

Once we got home, I couldn't get Mom to tell us if she knew the troll. My sister wasn't interested; she was busy with her new phone. I got her old phone, which Mom said would do me fine until I turned teenage in two years. Then she gave me five dollars and called it hand-me-down-phone compensation. Whatever.

Mom told me to walk with my sister to a sleepover we'd both been invited to in the next block. I didn't really want to go. The kids were all older—Kelley's friends. And what if that guy was still out there? Mom said if he came back, it would be after dark. How could she know that? Sometimes I think she stretches the truth to shut me up. She stood in the doorway to watch us walk to the next block. When we got there, I decided to stay to play Parcheesi, the only boardgame I win more times than I lose.

I called Mom to tell her I would stay about an hour longer but not overnight. There was no answer. Kelley said Mom was probably on the porch and had left her phone upstairs in her attic writing room. I left a message that she should watch for me in about an hour. It would be dark by then.

It took longer than an hour to play the game; it was fun because I won. When I left for home, our friend's father walked me to the corner and watched until I reached my house. That made me feel safe. I waved at him and hurried up the steps and into the house.

Lights were on but I didn't see Mom downstairs. I called for her and ran upstairs. She wasn't there or in any other room upstairs. I didn't check the attic. That was too scary to do by myself. I looked in Mom's bedroom. Her phone was on her bed, but Mom wasn't anywhere in the house. I picked up her phone and went to the backyard. She wasn't there either.

I went back inside and flicked on all the lights. I didn't want to be in the dark. I started to remember some of the gory parts of the graphic horror novels. The house seemed bigger now that I was alone. I locked both the back and front doors. When Mom returned, I would unlock the door for her if she'd forgotten her key, which she often did.

I thought about calling Dad. He stays home in Pittsburgh, where he's a policeman. He comes down when he has weekends off. Maybe he'd heard from Mom and knew where she was. But if I called him and he hadn't heard from her, he'd worry, and I'd get in trouble or get Mom in trouble. I decided to curl up on the couch and wait for her to come back. I started reading my new Neil Gaiman book and didn't mean to fall asleep, but the page blurred in front of my eyes, and I must have conked out.

Something woke me, either a sound or a smell or both. The sound was the little clock on the mantel chiming three o'clock. The fragrance was Homer, but over his now mild veggie odor was Mom's perfume. She calls it her "Chanel that Dad gives me every Christmas." It's in a pretty bottle. She spritzes it on in the morning and, sometimes, during the day when, she says, she needs a lift.

I yelled for Mom, hoping she had come in; she usually wakes me when I fall asleep on the couch and makes me go to bed. The air conditioning was humming, so I yelled loudly. She didn't answer. I ran upstairs again, but she wasn't anywhere. I was trying to figure out what to do when Mom's phone lit up; a text was coming in.

It was Dad. *On my way. Nearly at Route 1.* I was too scared not to text back.

Mom not here. Forgot her phone. Kelley at sleepover. I'm scared.

Mom's phone rang. It was Dad.

"Kasey, honey, are the doors locked?"

"Yes. I locked both of them."

"Good girl. How about the windows?"

"They're closed but I don't know if they're locked. Maybe they are; we had the air conditioning on."

"OK. I'll call the Rehoboth police and ask them to come by and check on you until I get there."

"OK. Daddy, do you know where Mom is?"

"Kasey, honey, I'll see you as soon as I get there. I'm not far away."

He hadn't answered my question about Mom. I wrapped myself in the couch quilt and waited. When I peeked out the window, I saw a police car slowing in front of the house. Two officers got out and walked around the front and back. They waved at me. One came to the door and wiggled the doorknob to check that it was locked then tried all the downstairs windows. They were all locked.

I called Kelley's new phone. She didn't answer, so I called again. Someone else answered. It sounded like one of the other girls at the sleepover.

"It's Kasey," she yelled.

Over the noisy background, I heard Kelley yell back, "Later. Tell her I'll call her later."

It was quiet. No traffic was passing the house, and even the police car had moved on. No people walked by. No dogs barked. I had never ever heard so little sound in the beach town, not even a rustle from the leaves fluttering. I leaned my face against the back of the couch. It wasn't unusual for Mom to leave the house but not without telling us or leaving a note. Suspicious. That's what it was. I didn't like it. With nothing else to distract me, the silence crowded in, plugging my ears. I didn't like it at all.

Then I heard Homer. I wasn't imagining I heard him either. The shuffling sound seemed to be going up the house's back wall. I wrapped the quilt around me like armor and crept up the stairs to the second floor, but I heard Homer shuffling up to the attic, so I followed.

That's when it all turned into a real horror movie, and I was in it.

There was Mom, sitting on the floor, her hands tied behind her back, a thick scarf wound over her mouth. The troll was sitting on a box in front of her. I stuffed a corner of the quilt in my mouth and held my breath to keep quiet. My heart pounded. I felt sick.

"The cops just drove off," the troll rasped. "I'm going to take off that scarf and you're going to tell me what I want to know, or I'll wait until your daughters are here. Then we'll see how well you remember."

Kasey realized the troll didn't know she was on the stairs, though he had to have heard her yelling for her mother.

"Can you give me some water from the thermos over there on my desk?" Mom asked, after he removed the scarf.

The troll stumped across to her desk and back, then poured water into the thermos cap and held it to Mom's mouth. He only let her take one gulp before throwing the rest in her face.

"I haven't lived here in more than thirty years," Mom spat out in anger, the water dripping off her face. "We only come here in summer. If you hid jewelry up here, you must have done it before we started coming back. I have no idea where it is."

The jewelry we'd played with, the necklaces, the rings, the tiara. That's what he was talking about. My gosh, that stuff was real?

"I spent twelve years in prison for that job," the troll said. "I plan to sell that stuff and enjoy myself. Now come up with a different answer to my question of 'where is it.'"

I realized that Mom probably didn't know where the jewelry was, but I did. I pulled the quilt from my mouth and cleared my throat. The troll jerked as though he'd been stabbed. Mom knew I cleared my throat when I was nervous, and a look of terror crossed her face.

"I know where it is, Mister," I said. My voice sounded high, like a little kid. I was petrified, but I couldn't let him hurt Mom.

"Kasey, what are you doing here?" Mom tried to scootch closer to me. "Why aren't you at the sleepover?"

I didn't answer.

"Hey, get over here, kid." The troll stood up, but he still didn't straighten his legs. "Get over here." His voice was deep and gravelly like he had laryngitis or maybe throat cancer like Uncle Louie.

I went closer to my mom. I hunkered down and pulled at the cord on her wrist. It wasn't tight. She must have been wiggling it.

"What are you doing, kid? Let that alone."

"Please, Mister. My Mom has to help me find the box where I hid the jewelry. I'm not sure where it is," I said, sounding really whiney, desperate to release her bindings. All the while, I was talking and loosening the cords tying Mom and hearing Homer shuffling in the rafters over our heads.

"I think the jewelry case was in a larger box, either the one with all the shoes or the one with all the hats," I said, which was a lie. I started looking in the boxes that held the stuff we used to play with, and Homer's shuffling followed overhead above the troll.

"Hurry up," he shouted. "I want to get out of here before that cop car comes back."

I pulled boxes out, and he let Mom help me open them, now more concerned about escaping than keeping her tied up. I was so focused on finding that box that I didn't hear Homer's shuffling anymore until a loud creak in the rafters overhead. An old chandelier with a million pink teardrop crystals crashed down on the troll.

He seemed dazed but was struggling to get out from under it. Mom jumped on his back and pulled his hands together.

"Get the cords," she shouted.

I scrambled over to where she'd been sitting, picked up the bindings that had held her, and tied them around the struggling troll's hands. Mom tightened them. We stood, and Mom helped the troll stand. He twisted to get loose, but he was no match for Mom and me.

"I remember you now," Mom said. "Dickie, right? From junior high? Dickie Shelby. You weren't too smart then either. We're all going downstairs. You can tell your story to the cops."

The front door slammed, and I heard Dad's voice calling me.

Mom and I both called back as we pushed the troll between us down the stairs. Dad grabbed my side of the troll and he and Mom dragged him outside to where the cop car had returned.

I sat at the bottom of the stairs, shaken but sooo relieved. I heard the quiet shuffling come down the stairs in the wall beside me. When it stopped, I said, "Thanks, Homer. You're a real hero." I leaned my head against the wall.

I was going to miss him when we had to go home so I could start school. The shuffling slid closer in the wall next to me, but the veggie odor was sweeter now, more like parsley. I got an idea.

"Homer? Could you help me with the mean girls and jerky boys at school? Maybe without dropping chandeliers. Oh, and there's a big dog that always gets loose in the back alley and chases me." The shuffling sounded louder at that thought, almost enthusiastic.

I heard Mom and Dad coming up the porch steps.

"Homer," I whispered, "will you travel?"

MaryAlice Meli lives in Steelers/Pirates/Penguins country, aka Pittsburgh, PA, and has written nonfiction in her past careers in education and journalism. She earned a master's degree in writing popular fiction at Seton Hill University. Now retired, she writes short and flash fiction, children's stories, and middle-grade mysteries. She was published in the Rehoboth Beach Reads anthologies *Beach Days* and *Beach Nights*, as well as in *Into the Woods: Stories, Poems, Essays & More*, *Fishy Business: The Fifth Guppy Anthology*, and two Mindful Writers Retreat anthologies, *Over the River and Through the Woods* and *Love on the Edge*. She's also been published online in *Every Day Fiction*, *InfectiveINk*, and *Untied Shoelaces of the Mind*.

Judge's Comment

In a first-person point-of-view, child-in-jeopardy story we meet eleven-year-old Kasey, who shares her fun and suspenseful summer in Rehoboth. I loved this cute story because it shows such character growth while containing not one, but two secrets. Enjoy the read as you follow Kasey's adventures.

Billy's Night Out

By Elizabeth Ellers

We left DC on a warm Friday evening in May, after Dad got home from his office and Mom had taught her last class. Traffic on the bridge was heavy, as lots of others left town for what promised to be a beautiful weekend. We stopped for ice cream in Greenwood, as we always do, and arrived at our house in The Pines after dark.

The house was old, not the largest or fanciest in the neighborhood, but it was warm and inviting and had a distinctive, familiar smell. Mom had been coming here since she was a child, and then brought along first Dad, then Michael when he was a baby, and then me. The closets were full of old flip-flops, tennis balls, and stuffed animals won at Funland. There was an outdoor shower, a rickety ping-pong table on the side porch, and a basketball hoop without a net over the garage.

"It's late, Billy," said Mom. "Go upstairs and get into bed. I'll come up to check on you later."

I knew she and Dad would go through the same routine they always did. First, Dad would bring in the bags. Then he'd turn on the water and the hot water heater, open all the windows to air out the house, and check everything for any damage from over the winter. Mom would unpack the coolers and put away the food she'd brought for the weekend. Then she'd make batter for her overnight waffles, which was another family tradition.

I was too excited to sleep. I usually shared the upstairs bedroom with Michael, but he was away at college, so no one noticed me quietly slipping out the front door. I made my way along Park Avenue toward the beach. I could smell the salt air and hear the surf. I thought I could almost smell the aromas of Thrasher's french fries and Dolle's caramel corn coming from the boardwalk. I stopped at the corner house, hoping to see my friends, Max, Clare, and Daisy, but their house was dark. Maybe they'd arrive on Saturday, and we'd play on the beach together.

A couple of houses along, Sam and Mary were unloading their car.

"Billy," said Mary, "It's so great to see you." She leaned down to give me a big hug. "We don't have time to visit now, but we'll see you tomorrow."

I was almost at Surf Avenue when I saw Jennifer, Truman, and Truman's little sister, Harper. They were stretched out in the soft light of candles on the screened porch that wrapped around their house. Jennifer waved lazily at me, but I didn't stop.

I turned and walked on into Henlopen Acres, past the stone walls and old millstones that marked the entrance. It was peaceful and quiet at first, but then I heard the sounds of a party coming from behind the big green house. I'd been to the house before, so I made my way around the corner and found a crowd of people standing by the pool. Tiki torches threw out some flickering gold light.

No one noticed me as I slipped around to the buffet table and helped myself to some cheese and crackers and mini hot dogs. The pool water looked inviting, so I found the steps and settled down on the top step in the cool water. It felt great after the long car ride.

"Hey," I heard a voice say, "Where did that dog come from?"

I looked around to find that everyone at the party was staring at me. A young guy reached for me, but I dodged his arm and ran around the pool, stopping for a moment to shake the water off my fur. I led everyone on a merry dance for a few minutes, until a pretty young woman offered me a piece of peanut butter pie. She must have known it was my favorite. While I was eating the pie, she grabbed my collar. "His name is Billy," she said. "There's a phone number."

Before long, Mom and Dad showed up to take me home, and I had to leave the party and my new friends.

The next day, after we'd played ball on the beach early in the morning, Mom and I strolled back to the house for breakfast. A couple walked toward us.

"Hello," said one to Mom, "I'm Molly and this is my husband, Chris. This is Billy, isn't it? We met him at the party last night."

"Nice to meet you," said Mom, "I'm not surprised that Billy found a party. I think he has more friends in Rehoboth than I do."

I just wagged my tail.

A RESIDENT OF VIRGINIA, ELIZABETH ELLERS HAS BEEN VISITING REHOBOTH BEACH SINCE 1980. THIS IS HER FIRST FORAY INTO FICTION WRITING, AFTER A LONG CAREER IN ADVERTISING, MARKETING, AND MEDIA. "BILLY'S NIGHT OUT" WAS INSPIRED BY HER AUSTRALIAN SHEPHERD, MERLIN, WHO MAKES FRIENDS (AND STEALS FOOD) WHEREVER HE GOES.

Grease Monkey Baby

By Nina Phillips

Monika twirled a strand of her long black hair in exasperation. She was exhausted and wanted to go to bed after a long day of cooking hamburgers and greasy french fries. And HE was late. *Why am I doing this, anyway?* She fought the urge to run from the white bench across from Dolle's Candyland.

She glanced at her cellphone: 12:15 a.m. in the US now, 7:15 a.m. in Sofia, Bulgaria, her hometown. She pictured her mother in her dark-green nurse uniform, ready for work. Although her father had two cars, which was unusual in Bulgaria, her mom relied on public transportation. Every day with her sweet smile and a kind word to everyone, her mother walked to the bus, got off and had a long walk to a second bus, and then had another long walk to the brown government building. Monika hoped the weather was not as scorching hot today as it was in Rehoboth Beach.

When her best friend, Julia, convinced her to take this summer job, Monika had high hopes for a fun and exciting summer. However, long hours over a greasy stove, disagreements with coworkers, and problems with a demanding boss had worn her out physically and mentally. Julia became friends with the other Russian girls and hung out with them after work, but she wouldn't go nightclubbing with them. She ended up alone most of the time. She longed for her home, her family, her friends, and her own bed overlooking the plaza. At this time in the morning, the Gypsies would be arriving with their produce from the countryside in their horse-drawn carts—something you would not see in America.

After one particularly hard day, Monika collapsed on a bench across from the large orange Dolle's sign and watched tourists of all shapes, sizes, and ages walk determinedly forward on the boardwalk. Dolle's Candyland had a long tradition in Rehoboth Beach, so that night Monika decided to finally try their famous sweet caramel-favored popcorn. Suddenly, a red-haired, athletically built young man came and sat quietly on the other end of the long white bench.

"Hi," he said. "Nice evening."

"Yeah," Monika said, barely looking at him.

"The beach was wonderful today. Very hot."

"I would not know. I was working."

"Oh, where do you work?"

"Lucia's Pizza."

"You sound like you have an accent."

Monika smiled. "I am from Sofia, Bulgaria."

"WOW. Really? I've never met anyone from Bulgaria."

"Well, I have not met many Americans either," she said, and they laughed.

Monika immediately felt at ease with him; he was polite, pleasant, and friendly. She especially liked that he seemed focused on her, completely interested only in her. Their friendship was a last-minute surprise.

She learned his name was Nick and he liked to wear a royal-blue T-shirt emblazoned with "Delaware Lacrosse." Over the next three weeks, Nick became a familiar—and welcome—sight at midnight after her shift. They chatted on the same white bench across from Dolle's. Nick talked incessantly about his new, shiny black pickup truck and his small black-and-white cat, Bernie. He seemed to love them both intensely, although not necessarily in that order.

　　　　　　　　　　Rehoboth Beach Reads

He showed her pictures and videos of Bernie. She knew no one in Bulgaria who owned a cat and she thought that Americans were kind of obsessed with their pets; still, his love for his cat was touching. He also proudly showed her pictures of his pickup truck and its red interior. His pickup truck was a novelty to her; she took public transportation and her friends' cars were generally small and plain. She began to look forward to their talks because their conversations were a welcome diversion from her everyday life.

Nick did most of the talking initially, but Monika didn't mind, and she enjoyed listening to him. She liked that he did not assume that Bulgaria was a wild, uncivilized country, nor did he ask her dumb, condescending questions about her homeland.

One night, as they enjoyed the cool sea breeze and after he showed her yet another video of Bernie, Nick turned to her with deep concern in his tanned face.

"My dad, he's from Sicily and the first to go to college in our family. He has three accounting offices."

"That is nice. Your family is from Italy; you don't look Italian."

Nick ruffled his red hair. "Yeah, I'm a ginger like Prince Harry. My mom's side came from County Mayo in Ireland. They came through Ellis Island, you know, next to the Statue of Liberty." He sighed. "Dad wants me to take over his business, but I hate accounting."

"I like Prince Harry; he is my favorite royal." Monika smiled and looked directly into his eyes. "What do you plan to do, then?"

"I love writing. I want to be a writer and a poet."

"I think you should do what makes you happy in life."

Nick winced and squirmed uncomfortably. "It's not that easy when you are the only son. So, what do you want to do?"

"I will visit my friends. Go to the mall."

"No, what do you plan to do with your life?"

"Well, since you asked, I help my dad with his auto repair business.

I take care of the appointments." She paused and looked at him with a wry smile. "I can change oil, change tires, and do tune-ups. Stefan, my brother, taught me everything. Someday, we want to own the shop together and then I can help women with their car problems. They can come to us and trust that we won't take advantage of them."

"Really! Wow, you're a grease monkey. A very pretty one. That's meant as a compliment, not sexist," he quickly added. "It's a name for someone who works on cars. American slang."

"Grease monkey. Slang." Monika pondered the words out loud.

They silently gazed at the nearly deserted beach. After a picture-perfect day, the salt air was soothing, and the luminous full moon shone like an illuminated diamond in the muted dark night sky. Other than an older couple slowly strolling on the shore, the beach was quiet.

Over the next few nights, Nick asked more questions about her country, and Monika told him about the Black Sea coast, calm and clear like a cool lake, so different from the turbulent dark-blue Atlantic Ocean. They learned that they both cherished their grandmothers. Monika's grandmother lived in a small town north of Sofia and taught her how to make *banitza*, a traditional Bulgarian cheese pastry. Nick told her about his Grammy, who was Italian American and made the best ravioli.

"The secret is in the sauce," he declared proudly. "Her sauce is the best in the world."

One night, she asked him about lacrosse, and Nick patiently attempted to explain the game to her. The next night, he came back with a triumphant smile because he had found through Google that lacrosse was played in Bulgaria; so, she learned something new about her own homeland.

Monika mulled over their various conversations as she waited, and she wiped the sweat from her forehead. The heat vapors from the boardwalk hung oppressively in the summer haze and seemed to permeate every pore of her skin.

Finally, she saw him come around the corner, wearing the familiar blue Delaware Lacrosse shirt, and carrying a red rose and a gift bag.

"Hi. This is for you." He quickly gave her the rose and the gift bag.

"What is this?" She asked with surprise.

"Oh, I just wanted to give you a going-away present. I really enjoyed meeting you."

"Do you know that the city of Kazanluk has fields and fields of roses, all colors, but mainly red?" Monika took a deep sniff. "Wonderful."

Inside the gift bag was a card and a box containing a small golden ring. The ring had a heart surrounded by two hands on the side and a crown on the top.

"It's an Irish Claddagh ring," he stated proudly. "It means love, loyalty, and friendship."

She placed it on a finger on her right hand. "I like the ring very much, thank you."

"I'll miss talking to you. Because of you, I've decided that I'm going to tell my parents that I'm changing my major."

"I did not do anything."

"Yes, you did. I could talk to you. That means a lot to me."

They both looked out at the ocean for a few minutes. The waves were rough and choppy, signaling an incoming storm, which might end the oppressive heat. Nick finally broke their mutual silence.

"Tomorrow night, we're taking my mom out for her birthday. She wants to eat crabs in Ocean City."

"Really? In our country, the person whose birthday it is takes everyone out and pays for their own birthday party."

"It's different here, I guess."

"I think I like your way better." Monika laughed and displayed her naturally pearly white teeth set against her beautiful olive complexion.

Nick pointed to the card. "All my information is there; let's keep in touch, OK?"

"Yes, I would like that."

"Well, a long day for both of us." They stood and hugged awkwardly.

"Bye and good luck!"

"You too!"

Monika watched him disappear in the dwindling crowd until his blue shirt became a mere speck in the distance. She looked down at the small ring. *He has good taste.* The ring was simple, delicate, and pretty.

His gift to her was a surprise. She would be married in just a few months to her longtime sweetheart, Georgi, Julia's brother. She had been glad to get a summer job in the US, for the extra money would help pay for her wedding and honeymoon to Istanbul, Turkey. She loved looking at pictures on the Internet of their future trip—the Grand Bazaar, Blue Mosque, and the Bosphorus Bridge.

Monika felt a pang of guilt about her secret relationship with Nick, although she hadn't cheated, since they had not been romantically involved. Their friendship was unexpected but platonic; two people who struck up a friendship—hardly a summer fling.

Although many of her Russian workmates would love to meet a nice American and move to the US, Monika just wanted to go home. This summer had made her truly appreciate her homeland; it was where she belonged.

There were many things to do before her wedding: lunch with her aunt by the murky Danube River in Silistra, coffee with her friends at the Sofia mall, and shopping in the farmers market in Pleven with her grandmother.

She looked at the card Nick had given her. The front said "best friends" and showed a large black cat wearing a hat. *Of course, a cat.* Nick had written a brief note that included his full contact information and signed it "Best Wishes, Nick." The little flourish at the end was just like him. There was also a poem in his handwriting from Emily Dickinson, who was unfamiliar to her. She made a note to google her later.

What should I do with the ring? Perhaps I could send it back to him in the mail. She contemplated her decision as she admired the ring on her finger.

She didn't want Julia to see the ring or his letter; she could easily jump to the wrong conclusion. There was no secret romance, just a secret friendship. It didn't matter anyway; she simply could not give Julia a true explanation without recriminations from her future sister-in-law. She threw away the gift bag and wrapped the note with his personal information around the ring. Then she buried the ring and note deep in her wallet for safekeeping.

When she goes home, she will tuck this away in her treasure box—the little wooden box embossed on the front with a sparkling outdoor fountain from the city of Russe, the so-called Vienna of Bulgaria. Her father had given her the box as a child on their vacation; the ring will stay there and be her secret. She remembered the vacation so well, because her parents were genuinely happy and laughing together and her dad tossed her happily in the air, calling her his special Baba.

Monika took another look at the stormy waves with their brilliant white caps and deeply inhaled the ocean breeze. As she walked away, she paused to take a last look at the young people throwing a ball on the almost deserted beach. She ripped up Nick's card and briefly both Nick's and Emily Dickinson's words intermingled, as they fluttered briefly in the air over the garbage can.

I'm just a grease monkey after all, she thought. She left the bench for the last time with a contented look on her face.

At about the same time, Nick dodged the dwindling crowds, making his way down the boardwalk. As he approached the Funland arcade, he heard a text beep.

"Hey! Where have you been?" It was his girlfriend, Lauren.

"Hey. Just asleep. Hot beach day," he texted back.

"Oh, my poor baby. A longggg beach day. See you soon. Love you."

"Me too," he texted, as he plopped down on an empty white bench. Nick felt a pang of guilt about the Claddagh ring he had bought for Lauren. He had planned to give it to her at their family gathering in a week. He wasn't sure why he impulsively gave it to Monika. He couldn't explain his reason; somehow, he just felt it was the right thing to do.

Nick watched the parade of tired travelers pass in front of him in their colorful vacation clothes, beach hats, and flip-flops, walking slowly after a hot beach day. To the right, he noticed the iridescent orange Dolle's sign, surrounded by lingering hazy heat vapors, and he thought of Monika, her long raven hair blowing in the ocean breeze, a single red rose in her hand.

NINA PHILLIPS IS A RETIRED EDUCATOR WHO LIVED FOR TWENTY YEARS IN NEW MEXICO BEFORE RETURNING TO HER NATIVE DELAWARE. SHE SELF-PUBLISHED A PLAY, *THE CRUSHING OF THE ROSES*, ABOUT THE RESCUE OF BULGARIAN JEWS. THE PLAY IS IN THE HOLOCAUST SECTION OF THE BRANDYWINE LIBRARY AND HAS BEEN RECOGNIZED BY ERIC RUBIN, FORMER US AMBASSADOR TO BULGARIA. HER MOTHER, A DEVOTED REHOBOTH BEACH GOER, ALWAYS ENCOURAGED HER TO WRITE. NINA WROTE THE STORY "A CHRISTMAS SURPRISE" BASED ON HER MOTHER'S CHILDHOOD IN CHINA. IT WAS PUBLISHED IN *BAY TO OCEAN 2021: THE YEAR'S BEST WRITING FROM THE EASTERN SHORE WRITERS ASSOCIATION*.

"GREASE MONKEY BABY" WAS INSPIRED BY NINA'S EXPERIENCES MEETING A BULGARIAN STUDENT STUDYING ENGLISH AT THE UNIVERSITY OF DELAWARE AND HER SUBSEQUENT SEVEN TRIPS TO BULGARIA. NINA FEELS LIFE IS MADE UP OF SOMETIMES BRIEF ENCOUNTERS WITH A PERSON OR PLACE THAT CAN BECOME LIFE CHANGING. IN THE STORY, NINA ALSO PAYS HOMAGE TO THE ICONIC DOLLE'S SIGN THAT FOR HER AND OTHERS WAS A WELCOMING SIGN IN REHOBOTH FOR DECADES. IN DEPICTING THE FRIENDSHIP OF THE TWO YOUNG CHARACTERS, NINA WANTED TO HIGHLIGHT THAT AMERICANS, IN ACCEPTANCE OF OTHERS, ARE FUNDAMENTALLY A COMPOSITE OF UNIQUE DIVERSITIES, CULTURES, AND NATIONALITIES.

"Grease Monkey Baby" opens its scope to include the global dimension of beach towns. Young people looking for a summer of fun and work can come from across town—or across the ocean. Nick and Monika stumble into an accidental connection that is somehow more than a friendship, less than a romance. What they share is a feeling they cannot name. It does not fit into the rest of their well-planned lives. One senses they will always remember, and long puzzle over, a few spontaneous weeks on a bench at midnight. In this story, the author manages to capture that giddy sense of fascination, tinged with rue.

Undercover Daughter

By Doug Harrell

Tonight is the Cape Henlopen High School Class of 1996 twenty-five-year reunion. Mom is upstairs getting ready for her "date," and I'm a nervous wreck—what if I ruined everything? I worried all week about whether Mom would back out. Aunt Nicole was over a few times, and we both told Mom again and again it was OK for her to enjoy herself. Dad would want that.

Mom comes down. I'd almost forgotten what she looks like in real makeup. I tell her she looks great, and I mean it. She gives me a thin smile, and I can see something's bothering her. She sits down next to me, and all of a sudden she's crying. I'm the angst-ridden seventeen-year-old girl. Ordinarily, *I'd* be the one in need of moral support and she'd be *my* rock. Talk about role reversal. Her shoulders are shaking, so I put my arm around her. She tells me she'll always love Dad. She nervously touches her earring, and I can see she's wearing the ones he gave her on their last anniversary. Now I'm crying. Then she says she's not going.

In between sobs she confesses she's been emailing with a guy from her class, and it's tearing her up inside that she's excited to see him. She's so overcome with guilt I almost come clean and tell her I know all about it—because, well, I set it up. Instead, I tell her it's OK. An old friend wants to see her again. It's nothing to be ashamed of. I calm her down and convince her to go.

After she fixes her mascara, I tell her I'm taking her. I definitely don't want her driving in the state she's in, and depending on how things go, she might be worse later. She protests, but I insist.

I drop her off at the reception hall and tell her to call me when she's ready to be picked up. I almost say, "Have a nice time, honey," like she always did with me, but I catch myself and say, "Have fun, Mom."

Now I'm sitting at home, slowly losing my mind. All of this has made me realize how pissy I've been lately and how much I love her. I'd do anything to make her happy. That's why I cooked up this whole scheme. She thinks she's on her way to meet a secret admirer who is going to reveal himself at the reunion. I know better, and it's killing me. Now I get why Mom makes such a big deal about me not getting pregnant. She's right. I am *so* not ready for this kind of responsibility.

* * * * *

You're probably wondering how I got myself into this. Two years ago, my father died. I don't want to talk about it except to say it was terrible. Mom and I were both crushed, but after a year she got all energetic and chirpy. Then, last month, she got a new job and moved us here to Lewes, Delaware—right in the middle of my senior year. It totally sucks. I didn't think I'd ever forgive her. I mean, we're living in my grandparents' house, and when they come back from Florida, I'll get moved into the tiny bedroom. And don't even get me started on the whole closet situation.

Our old house was just outside Philadelphia on the Main Line, a cool place to live. Now, I've had to leave all my friends behind, and we've hardly seen each other in a year! I thought I'd be back in the fall. My BFF, Madison, and I both got accepted at Penn, and we were going to be roomies. That was one reason I was so mad at Mom. Since I got in, she's been saying she's worried about me living in the city, but I'm not buying it. There's got to be some other reason she's against it. Two weeks ago, I stumbled onto a plan. I thought maybe my "cool aunt" Nicole could convince Mom to let me go to Penn. She's not married, and doesn't have kids, so she never grew up and got overly responsible.

*****

School was over for the day, and Mom was still at work, so I went to my old room—the one I always stayed in when we visited my grandparents for a few weeks every summer. This house holds a lot of good memories. Rummaging in the closet, I found a box with my name on it. I opened it, and it was like a time machine. On top were stuffed toys I won at Funland and "treasure" I found on the beach as a little kid. It wasn't until years later I realized my dad had buried it and drawn the map that led me to it. God, I miss him.

Underneath all that was my baby stuff—toys and little outfits. Why do grandparents keep this crap? One thing caught my eye, though, and it gave me an idea. It was a wireless baby monitor. If I could get Aunt Nicole to come over and talk to Mom about Penn, I could listen in and hear why Mom's against it. Then I'd be able to figure out how to win her over. Opening it, I was a little worried because the batteries were gross. I scraped away the corroded gunk and put in new ones. In the living room I turned on the TV and hid the transmitter on the bookshelf. Back in my room, I turned on the receiver. It still worked!

There was nothing else interesting in that closet, so I checked out the one in my current room. It was Mom and Aunt Nicole's growing up, so I knew there ought to be some interesting stuff. I found a box marked "Danielle." Jackpot! Along with Mom's graduation tassel and diploma, it had all Mom's old yearbooks. I looked up her senior year picture and was surprised by how pretty she was. It was weird to think of her ever being the same age as me. Flipping through, it was clear she was popular, too, because her friends had written all over every page.

A lot of entries began with "Always remember …" A few of the entries were really interesting. Like this one:

Always remember the Foo Fighters concert. You wrote "I love you Dave" on your arm in pink magic marker and stood screaming "Dave,

She didn't—of course—have Dave Grohl's baby. She waited until she was out of college and married and had me, though I can't help thinking how cool it would be to have a half-sibling whose dad is a rock star. I'd get the best seats!

I knew I would want to read more later, so I tucked the yearbooks away where I could get to them easily.

I decided to put my plan into action. We'd only moved in the week before, and we'd eaten takeout every night. I'd cook dinner to show Mom I could be independent, and I'd invite Aunt Nicole over so I could listen in while they talked. I can't *really* cook, but I can open a jar of sauce and boil spaghetti. I figured that and a salad would be enough.

I called Aunt Nicole about dinner, and I asked her to talk to Mom about Penn. She said maybe, but no promises. She told me Mom was going through a tough time. As if I wasn't! When I called Mom and told her about dinner, she cried. It wasn't the response I was expecting. I told myself they were "my baby's growing up" tears—a good sign.

* * * * *

Dinner was OK. I followed the directions on the box exactly, and Paul Newman made sure the salad was tasty. Mom and Aunt Nicole made such a fuss it was embarrassing, like I'd never made anything before. I hadn't, but still. I wanted them to start talking as soon as possible, so I said I'd clean up. They both looked at me like I was up to something. I was, but how did they know? I knew they wouldn't get into anything deep with me standing there, so I was quick.

Back in my room, I turned on the monitor. The sound quality wasn't great, and I had to turn it up. I was afraid they might hear, so I carried the monitor over to the bed and got under the covers. Aunt Nicole asked Mom how the new job was going. With me, Mom had been all perky smiles, but with Aunt Nicole, she got serious. She said the job didn't pay as much as we needed. Then the kicker. Mom told Aunt Nicole she knows how badly I want to go to Penn, but she can't afford it with Dad gone. She said she was ashamed. Right at that moment, I was ashamed, too, but for the wrong reason.

I texted Madison. "OMG! I don't know if I can go to Penn! Call me."

She texted back, "Can't." Then, "Why not???"

"Mom says it costs too much." Feeling defiant, I added, "I'm going anyway! I'll get student loans! What does it cost? Do you know?"

She signed off, "Gotta go. Google it."

So I did: $57,770, plus $16,000 for room and board … *a year*! I had no idea it was that much. I made all of $4,000 last summer, and even if I hadn't spent it, it wouldn't have been enough to cover books and "other fees."

As Aunt Nicole and Mom talked, there were more surprises. I had been furious at Mom for selling our house and moving us in with my grandparents. I'd been selfishly pushing to go to one of the most expensive schools in the country and come to find out my mom had sold the house she loved in order to have enough money for me to go to college at all. My emotions were all over the place. I was disappointed about Penn and disgusted with myself at the same time. I'd been so focused on what I wanted that I'd never once thought about Mom. I had always assumed grown-ups had their shit together, and it was us kids who were trying to figure things out.

My ears perked up when Aunt Nicole asked Mom how she was doing. Mom said she was lonely. She missed my dad but was trying not to show it so she wouldn't bring me down. That brought tears to my eyes. Aunt Nicole reassured her it was OK if she wanted to start "getting out there" a little. Aunt Nicole offered to introduce Mom to some friends, but Mom didn't say anything. Then Aunt Nicole reminded her about her upcoming high school reunion. She said Mom should go. She would see old friends and she might feel better.

Aunt Nicole started naming people still in the area who would probably be there. She even mentioned a guy named Greg, who Mom used to go out with. Apparently, he's divorced and still handsome. Mom said she'd like to see him, but she didn't feel up to explaining why she was back in town. I'd heard enough and turned off the monitor.

I stopped worrying about Penn right there. My more immediate problem was to find some way to be a better daughter. I pulled out the yearbook and looked up Greg. He *was* good looking. He'd lettered in soccer and tennis too. I wanted to check his grades, but of course they don't include that information. He seemed like a decent guy. I wasn't in a hurry to have a stepdad, but a few dates wouldn't mean they had to get married or anything.

* * * * *

The next morning, I called Madison. I told her flat out there was no way I was going to Penn. You'd have thought I shot her dog. She went all batshit on me—said I need to figure something out, blah blah blah. I felt guilty telling her about stuff I wasn't supposed to know, but I did. She was disappointed, but she understood, and we started kicking around ideas.

We talked about the reunion and Mom's old boyfriend. Madison had an idea. Most of Madison's advice about life comes from movies, and she told me about one where a kid pretends to be his father to carry on a pen pal romance with a woman to get them together. Madison suggested we pretend to be Greg and write emails to Mom. I agreed it might work to get her there, but then what? If he didn't show, she'd be disappointed, and if he did, he might brush her off. I nixed that plan, and we agreed to keep thinking.

After I hung up, I had an awesome idea. What if I invented a secret admirer and pretended he was someone from her class? As far as she would know, it could be anybody. Thinking a mysterious someone from her past wanted to see her and wondering who he was would be irresistible. I went online and created BeachBoy96@gmail.com, a forty-three-year-old guy who was sweet on Mom in high school. I composed the first email and set it up to arrive that night so I could see Mom's reaction.

Dear Danielle,
I hear you're back in Lewes. Are you going to the reunion? I can't believe it's been 25 years! I had such a crush on you. You were the prettiest girl in our class. I wanted to ask you out, but I could never get up the nerve. I'm coming home for the reunion, and I sure hope you'll be there. —Beach Boy

* * * * *

Every weeknight between seven and eight o'clock Mom and I eat dinner to *Jeopardy* and *Wheel of Fortune*. Someone had just bought a vowel when Mom's phone pinged. When she saw the email, she blushed and seemed to read it over and over again. *Wheel of Fortune* ended, and Mom said she was tired. She told me she was going to read a bit and turn in. She went to her bedroom, and I went to mine. I didn't have to wait long.

Dear Beach Boy,
It was nice of you to get in touch and say such sweet things. It's not that I wouldn't like to see you, but it's been a rough couple of years, and I don't know if I'm up to going. Please write me and let me know how it was (and tell me who you are and where you live now). —Danielle

Although it was a no, at least she responded. I just needed to make Beach Boy more persuasive.

* * * * *

The next day I hit the yearbooks looking for ideas. I found an interesting inscription that answered the question of why Mom makes me stay with friends when she goes on business trips.

Never forget the monster party you had when your parents were away and Tom puked his guts out. I can't believe you were able to convince your parents you shampooed the rugs as a special surprise. Mine would have never fallen for it! —Melissa

That party must have been epic because a lot of people mentioned it. I found something I could use.

I'll always remember the huge party you threw—half the school must've been there! You looked so cool in your new Pucci blouse. It was like you just walked out of a Salvador Dali painting. Divas Rock! —Laura

I Googled Pucci and couldn't believe the prices. I'd be afraid to hold one, let alone wear it to a blowout with kids puking all over the place. I went rooting around in Mom's closet, and I couldn't believe my luck. I found the blouse, and it was wild—bright colors in a crazy pattern. It would be totally believable that Beach Boy might remember it. Better yet, folks who were there would probably recognize it when they saw it. It would be a great conversation starter. I wrote the next email.

Dear Danielle,
I understand. I heard about your husband, and don't worry, I'm not ready to date again either. Please come. How about this? Wear something wild like you did at your big party, and I'll wear something you might remember. Then you can try to guess who I am. It'll be fun. Is it a deal? —Beach Boy

Mom didn't reply right away. When she got home, I saw she was excited. After a quick hello, she went straight to her bedroom. I snuck by and saw her trying on the blouse. I went to my room and soon got a reply.

Dear Beach Boy,
You talked me into it. You won't believe this, but I saved that blouse

all these years, and it still fits! I can't wait to see if I can figure out who you are from what you wear. Thanks for the encouragement. See you there. —Danielle

That was a few days ago.

* * * * *

So now Mom's at the reunion, excited to meet Beach Boy. He's the reason she went, and he won't be there because he doesn't exist. My hope is she'll talk to so many old friends it won't matter. When I got back to the house, I sent an email from Beach Boy saying he's sorry, but he missed his plane.

She's only been gone an hour, and already my phone is ringing. I bet she's crying her eyes out that Beach Boy didn't make it. I answer, but that's not it. Mom's happy. She's having a good time. Lots of her old friends are there, and after the reunion, they're all going out. It might get pretty late. One of them will give her a ride home, so I don't need to wait up.

I am, of course, waiting up. I want to make sure she gets home safe, and I'm curious to see who drops her off. I'm reading in my room because it has a better view of the front porch.

Eventually, I hear a car pull into the driveway. Peeking through the curtains, I see a tall, clean-cut guy get out and open Mom's door for her. When the light catches his face, I recognize him immediately. He's not skinny like his yearbook picture, but it's Greg, and he's still handsome. He walks her to the porch, and they talk for a few minutes. I can't hear what they're saying, but their body language tells me everything I need to know. Finally, he gives her a peck on the cheek. He waits to make sure she gets inside and goes back to his car. He waves as he drives away. I can hardly believe it. Everything worked out great. To make sure it stays that way, in a week Beach Boy will email Mom that his company has transferred him to the wilds of Mongolia. He's sorry, but he won't be able to keep in touch because his yurt doesn't have cable. Goodbye Beach Boy. He'll be a secret I take to my grave.

✳ ✳ ✳ ✳ ✳

Things are so much better now. I didn't want to make Mom explain why she was against Penn, so I told her I wasn't keen anymore. Then she told me all the stuff I already knew. Since then, we've been researching other schools that are more affordable. Greg's had some good ideas too. He comes over a lot to visit, and tonight they've even gone out to a concert. They invited me, but I begged off so they could be alone. I like Greg. He seems like a "fine young man." And if he doesn't work out, maybe I'll get that half-sibling after all. Did I mention they're at a Foo Fighters concert?

Doug Harrell is a recovering engineer who has taken up writing as a second career, dividing his time between Pike Creek and Lewes. His focus is on mysteries, but he enjoys writing stories filled with seashore ambiance and fond beach memories each year for the Rehoboth Beach Reads Contest. "Undercover Daughter" is his fifth story published by Cat & Mouse Press. Visit him at www.douglasharrell.com.

Driftwood Days

By Steve Saulsbury

Patty stood at the sink, a feeble trickle of water running over the plates. At her feet, a slop bucket for the pigs. Her hands burned with eczema. Dishwater, mop water. She scoured and scrubbed, but the house never felt clean.

At the 1893 World's Fair, a woman introduced a motorized dishwasher. A beloved homemaker, Patty imagined, with delicate fingers. She had studied the news article and accompanying drawings with awe. But Tucker would never consider such a contraption.

They had married shortly after his release from Fort Delaware, Tucker a Confederate prisoner of war. When they settled at the Methodist Camp in Rehoboth Beach, everyone assumed Tucker was a Northern hero. His empty sleeve folded up. Patty did not contradict the assumptions.

His hair, brutally shorn to remove lice, had grown back unevenly, the color of iron. His blasted stump of an elbow. Powder-burned face, emotionless as a plank.

He scavenged milled boards from a shipwreck, hatcheting them to fit his plans, hammering out a shack in the shade of a loblolly pine. Patty collected driftwood, admiring the beautiful gnarled pieces.

Later, when the Reverend moved on to some new wilderness, the Camp members drifted. Patty and Tucker stayed. He stripped the tabernacle and built a shed. Patty tolerated the amber whiskey bottles he hid there. Tucker's pains were untreatable. Psychic ones Patty couldn't comprehend. He'd seen men burned alive. Corpses eaten by wild pigs.

Patty stood by him, celebrating for a time, when the government paid for Tucker's artificial arm. She stayed when he struck her with the wooden prosthesis and the carved fingers gouged her cheek.

She never told anyone.

Even when she joined the Women's Christian Temperance Union, Patty refused to talk about Tucker's demons. She poured out his liquor, damn the consequences. One night he lurched into the kitchen, grabbed a pot of soup from the stove, and flung it on her.

She ran to the ocean and collapsed, splashing herself in the cold, salty purity. Patty might have appeared drunk herself. Groaning, squeezing fistfuls of the wet sand until she calmed. The soup had not been hot enough to burn, but it stung. She collected several pieces of driftwood. One resembled a flame.

The drunken beatings continued. Patty became more active in the endless work of the Union. She left for Ellis Island without telling Tucker. A project to promote sobriety among immigrants was in progress. Away from home, her resolve emerged, steeling her for what had to be done.

* * * * *

Now she is walking in the sand, feeling the ghost of the man, his carved hand. The new granite fountain is only a short distance from her shanty. *Erected by W.C.T.U. Rehoboth Beach 1929.* She can't wait to take a mouthful. And celebrate with her sisters.

Her hands don't itch anymore, the eczema tanned away. She lowers her eyes against a sudden dust devil and inhales the pure ocean breeze.

She daydreams sometimes, remembering her driftwood collection. How quickly it burned. The arm too. When soaked in whiskey.

Steve Saulsbury writes from Maryland's Eastern Shore, where he has spent most of his life. He studied writing at Towson University, receiving a BS degree in 1985. Age-old interests were reawakened in 2017, when the opportunity arose to take classes at Washington College. In addition to writing, he is a fitness enthusiast and enjoys exploring the mid-Atlantic region.

His writing is often influenced by popular culture and history. For "Driftwood Days," inspiration came from a look into the history of Rehoboth Beach, coupled with a longstanding interest in the Civil War. A random prompt from his writing mentor helped push the story to its fruition.

In addition to his inclusion in *Beach Secrets*, he has been published by *MudRoom Mag*, *Instant Noodles*, and *Arzono Annual*. *Thimble Literary Magazine* featured his flash piece "Quicksilver" in their fall 2021 issue. The journey continues, as the author plans to one day publish an anthology of his favorite works.

Judges' Comments

We all collect (or most of us do) as we wander the beach. Shells, stones washed and polished by wave action, and of course smooth, salty pieces of driftwood. Some make art, others pile them into fences, and others just leave them sitting on a table or mantel. This story feels natural. The voice and tone are consistent with the reveal. Good detail in the history of the area as well as with the characters. The scars of war, then and now, are thoughtfully evoked, without being mawkish. The ending is well-earned, reflecting the details of the story as it unfolded. Readers feel satisfied and perhaps vindicated. Along with the character, the reader feels the emotions of a brutal and painful time in our country's history during reconstruction and temperance. A quick read packed with details in a very small space.

The Cruciverbalist

By Katherine Melvin

I was in the hot seat, at least it felt that way. Only instead of being summoned to the principal's office, I was called to the lawyer's office, a lawyer I didn't know existed prior to my husband's death one year ago: Stein & Stern, Esquires, of Rehoboth Beach, Delaware. Just like a squirmy kid on a hot spring day, I wanted to be on the boardwalk, licking Thrasher fries salt from my fingertips while watching the waves. Not in some stuffy office.

I wasn't dressed for the surroundings. The chair was plush. The office decorated with no mind to cost. The carpet, thick. I wore my standard mourning clothes—comfortable jeans, a University of Delaware sweatshirt from my college days, and sneakers. I hadn't paid attention to my dark-blond hair in months. It needed to be cut, so I pulled it away from my face with a headband I found under the bathroom sink. I hit fifty-two the week after the funeral, a mere eight years younger than my husband, and just didn't have the energy for applying makeup anymore.

It was teatime. I was served steaming Darjeeling in a dainty china cup decorated with tiny pink roses and offered mouth-watering, butter-saturated shortbread.

My leg shook so hard the cup clattered. My chest felt tight, and I had to yawn to get a breath. According to Mr. Stern, the lawyer assigned to the case, my husband of twenty years, the man at whom I could no longer yell in frustration, had left me something secret, to be delivered one year after his death.

I figured it was probably a crossword because, well, that's what he did. Kennan was a cruciverbalist, a person skilled at creating crossword puzzles. World-renowned for his cleverness. His obituary in the *New York Times* was, yes, set in a crossword. One he'd dickered with off and on throughout his life. During the eulogy, Will Shortz conferred on him a degree in enigmatology.

I imagined him at his desk. "How can I still drive Carol mad after I'm gone?" I could hear him mutter. He'd have on his everyday uniform— white cotton shirt, unbuttoned at the top, with a pair of old jeans that were snug on his bottom. As he pondered how best to torment me, he'd swipe his faded red hair away from his face, revealing the intense blue eyes I loved so much. He liked to say he was one in a million with his red hair and blue eyes. I let him think he was.

Whether he worked at the computer or a scratchpad, he'd have a pencil in hand. Kennan was a tapper. His teeth, the desk, a mug. He insisted it helped him think. I insisted I couldn't stand the *tap-tap-tap*, but I'd give anything to hear it now.

Weird themes amused him. This one would have been titled "Drive Wife Crazy."

Clue: Private, classified (6). I filled in the imaginary puzzle with the correct word: SECRET.

My husband loved all things puzzles. One-thousand-piece jigsaws weren't difficult enough. He insisted on the Ravensburger Challenger series. Logic problems? He created them. Rubik's Cube? No problem. Those complex, interconnected wood puzzles set on the table to keep diners busy while they waited for their food. He'd yell, "Done" before the water glasses were filled.

Mr. Stern handed me two envelopes. One contained a certificate for lodging for one night at the Admiral on Baltimore Avenue, which produced a large lump in my throat.

"We always stayed there." I swallowed hard. "Ever since our honeymoon."

He nodded toward the second one.

The other held a key. Why was I disappointed? "Looks like it's to a safe deposit box."

When Mr. Stern smiled, even his dark-brown eyes twinkled. He looked quite handsome in a gray-haired, well-kept, older man sort of way. "He mentioned you were clever."

"Please." I rolled my washed-out gray eyes and felt the ends of my hair brush my neck. "Just tell me what this is about."

"Mrs. Bezas …" He paused with a finger in the air. "I meant to ask your husband about his name. *Bezas*. It's certainly unique."

"Spanish. It was Rompecabezas, but his grandparents shortened it when they immigrated."

"But his first name was Kennan."

"Yep. His Spanish grandfather married a fetching red-headed lass from Ireland."

"Spanish for?"

"You won't believe it."

"Try me."

"Puzzler."

His eyes narrowed. "You're right. I don't believe it." He shook his head. "I don't know any more about this matter than you do."

"Did he have a deep dark secret?" I regurgitated the stock Hallmark movie scenarios: "A second family? A mistress?" I swallowed hard. "A love child?" We couldn't have children, but Kennan had always wanted a large brood.

Mr. Stern shook his head. "I wish I had more details. I can tell you this. He didn't strike me as the sort of man who … strayed. I had the impression he loved you very much."

I sniffed but was overwhelmed with sobs. The kind lawyer handed me a box of tissues and waited. I never knew when the tears would come or what would set them off.

When I recovered, I took charge. "He must have left a list of clues. He always did. For when I was stuck. He hated when I looked at the answers." I tried to smirk, but I could tell from the concerned look on the lawyer's face I'd only managed a sad smile. "Once, when I was mad, I wrote wrong answers in his book *Puzzles that Defy Solving*. In ink."

I couldn't tell what he was thinking about that admission.

Clue: At sea (7). Answer: BAFFLED.

"I'm not aware of any list. Perhaps you'll find it in the safe deposit box."

"Yes, of course." I was too tired for a treasure hunt. "But which bank? Here in Rehoboth or at home in Baltimore?"

"Oh, I thought you lived …" The curious look on his face passed with a blink. "He arrived on foot if that's any indication." Mr. Stern cleared his throat and stood. "I'm sorry I can't be more help."

It felt like he was holding back. Still, I gathered my large pink paisley Vera Bradley overnight tote. "Thank you," I said. "I guess."

He arched a trimmed, gray eyebrow. "If you'd be so kind as to share the outcome."

"Sure." Feeling a bit like Columbo, I paused at the door. "One more thing. Was your office here when Kennan met with you?"

He nodded. "Oh, yes. We've been here since my father purchased the property in the 1950s. He had no idea how valuable it would become, sitting on Rehoboth Avenue a mile from the beach." He winked at me. "It's my ace in the hole if the legal thing doesn't pan out."

You gotta love a man with a dry sense of humor.

Mr. Stern mentioned Kennan made the arrangements about eighteen months ago. His energy was only beginning to flag then, so he would have felt well enough to walk. I decided to head toward the hotel. It was March and the warm day was fading fast.

Clue: Due follower (4). Answer: EAST.

Before I hopped in my Mini Cooper, a thought struck me, and I pulled a satellite image of the city up on my phone for verification. My fist pumped the air. From above, Rehoboth resembled a giant crossword puzzle grid. Clever man.

I bet when I found the list, the first clue on it would be: Bar tender (8). Answer: ATTORNEY.

Where to from here?

I assumed he wouldn't stop at the first bank, so I walked by two before seeing the Bank of America on the corner of Rehoboth Avenue and City Hall Drive. A perfect across answer to the clue I'd just made up: Flight maneuver (4). Answer: BANK.

I presented myself at the information desk and handed over the key. "Is this one of yours?"

The middle-aged woman donned the glasses hanging by a gold chain around her neck and examined it like she was a jeweler appraising a gem. "Name?"

"Bezas, Carol."

She clicked on the computer, then said, "Follow me."

She inserted her key. I mine.

"I'll leave you to it," she said.

My heart fluttered in my throat. I took a deep breath to calm it, but that didn't work. It was too much to grasp that I was hearing from Kennan. Who, knowing he was dying, planned this, whatever *this* was, ahead of time. For me. I was overwhelmed. Scared at what I'd find. Excited too. I brushed tears off my lashes and opened the lid.

What I saw made the tears stop and forced a growl. I wanted to yell but didn't think that would be wise in a bank.

Another key. A rather large, old-fashioned, brass key attached to a braided leather loop. I tried to decide whether to hurl it against the wall or dance with excitement. Before I could do either, I noticed something taped to the inside of the lid.

Clue: Letter cover (8). Answer: ENVELOPE.

On the envelope was a message:

Carol! That's my girl. You made it this far. I knew you would. In record time, too, I bet. Here are a few clues to help you complete the puzzle. I love you, sweetie, and I want you to look forward, not back. There are no answers at the back of this book. Ha-ha. Now don't get mad and throw something. Clue: Cherished hopes. -K

He was smiling at me from heaven. The turkey. I opened the envelope and removed the list of clues.

Back on the street, I scanned the list. Clue: Bound literature (4). I didn't think Kennan meant travel stories, though I wouldn't put it past him. Abstruse was his middle name. Bound. Compelled. Jump. Vault. Abut. Roped. I glanced at the list and for the first time that day, I smiled. He'd placed numbers next to the clues. Bless his heart.

I moved off the sidewalk to allow an older woman with a bird's nest of white hair walking a pair of full-sized chocolate poodles to pass.

"Are you lost, dear?" she asked.

"No." I caught her reading the clues.

"Oh," she said, pointing at the paper in my hand, "that one's easy."

My eyebrow arched so high it reached my hairline. "Really?" I knew I sounded snippy.

"Why 'book,' of course."

It was irritating that she got it at once. "Of course."

She left me contemplating my next move. The second building down Rehoboth Avenue was the public library. I went inside and asked a librarian, or two, maybe five. "Does this key belong here?"

I received some odd looks, but each person I asked responded. Too bad they were all negative.

Before I could decide what to do, a perky voice said, "Hey! I know that key." The voice was attached to a young mother carrying a canvas bag loaded with picture books and herding three small children toward the exit. "I should know." She nodded at the kids. "It's for a bathroom."

     Rehoboth Beach Reads

I hurried ahead to open the door for her.

"Browseabout," she called over her shoulder. "Between 2nd and 1st Streets."

I googled it. "One of the nation's top independent bookstores." *I can get behind that,* I thought.

The air off the ocean carried the strong scent of brine that I so loved. We'd always imagined we'd live at the beach. It was our dream, but it was not to be. Illness does that. I shivered in the chill air and realized I was weary. As I drove down Rehoboth Avenue searching for the left on South 1st Street that would take me to Baltimore Avenue and the hotel, I watched the muted purple twilight blanket the picturesque town we'd hoped to call home.

The next morning found me standing in line at the Browseabout Books coffee bar. I inhaled the aroma, ate a blueberry muffin, and thought *what a delightful store.* Books were everywhere, of course, but also beautiful sea glass decorations and handmade trinkets. Toys, too. As I browsed, I came across a section for local authors. Why hadn't we come in here before?

I thumbed through an anthology called *Beach Mysteries* and knew I had to buy it. Perfect reading for when I solved my own mystery. I placed the book on the checkout counter and held up the key.

"Oh," the twenty-something clerk said. "That's ours." She reached for it, but I clasped it to my chest.

"Do you have something for me?"

She looked blank.

No matter. "Manager? Owner?"

A busy woman, who wore authority and efficiency like a Chanel suit, asked, "How may I help you?"

I didn't want to tell the entire story of my deceased husband and his love of puzzles and that he'd left me one final crossword to solve, so I gave her the *Reader's Digest* version. "My husband left this key in a lockbox for me."

Her brows creased. "Hmm. Let me have a think." She led me to the coffee counter. "Have a coffee on us."

I felt obstinate. "I've already had one."

She was more obstinate. "Have another one." She got the barista's attention. "Get this customer whatever she likes and one of those yummy orange scones too."

My resistance melted at the phrase "yummy orange scones." "Thank you."

I took the offered sustenance and chanted, "There are no calories in Rehoboth Beach. There are no …" The store was a beehive at ten a.m. during the week in late March. I wasn't sure I'd see the manager again.

However, before I was halfway through the first short story and the scone, she reappeared.

"Sorry it took so long. I was waylaid by a customer. Here." She placed a legal-size manilla envelope on the table and handed me—you guessed it—another key. One with a key ring only Kennan would have thought appropriate. Or funny. A square-framed, goofy picture of himself with "Puzzle Master" written in rainbow glitter letters underneath. On his head—a jazzy crown.

"I loved his new book, by the way. He was kind enough to sign a few copies for us. Sort of a cross between an autobiography and a puzzle."

Clue: At sea (4). Answer: LOST.

I knew he'd been working on a book before he grew too weak to write. It was forgotten as the illness took him. Who cared about a book when the man you loved with all your heart most of your life was dying? Maybe I should have returned his publisher's calls.

"Has he started writing another book?" the manager asked.

My face contorted and she put two and two together.

"Oh my gosh." She put her hand to her mouth. "He died. He said … well … I knew he was ill."

I could see her stumbling for words of comfort that weren't there, so I patted her hand. "Yes."

Outside the store, I attempted to dismiss the heaviness. *Now what?*

A horn beeped. I looked to see a red Ford F150 truck with extended cab. It was gorgeous if you like trucks and I did.

Clue: Cry of joy (6). Answer: HOTDOG.

"Mr. Stern!" Seeing his comforting face made me smile.

He reached over to push open the door. "Hop in."

I stepped up into the cab and made myself comfortable. "This is great."

"My midlife crisis." He had a cute dimple on his right cheek.

I noticed he was not wearing a wedding band. Oh my, I thought, and then my face burned like I'd just chugged a large glass of chardonnay.

Noticing my awkward glance at his finger, he said, "My wife left me for her trainer." He managed a self-deprecating, sardonic look. "I know, how clichéd." Then, he turned mischievous. His eyebrows wiggled. "I was in crisis, so I bought this."

"I don't know your wife …"

"Ex."

"Your ex-wife. Seems like you got the better deal to me." I handed him the glittering keyring. "Any thoughts?"

He frowned. "Could be anything. Shed. Apartment. Store. Maybe one of those storage places." He nodded. "What's in the envelope?"

"Don't know."

Clue: Keyed up (12). Answer: APPREHENSIVE.

He studied me for a long second, then parked the truck, turned off the engine, and held out his hand. "Let me see."

I wanted to know. I didn't want to know. I realized I was gripping the envelope so hard my knuckles were white.

"OK," he said as he scanned the single sheet of paper. "We can walk from here."

"What does it say?"

"Clue: Summer rental (9)."

I narrowed my eyes. "Ha, ha."

"No, really. That's what it says."

I scanned the businesses on the Avenue, looking for the answer as we walked toward the gazebo. The day was beautiful and unexpected for March. Seagulls sailed on the wind. The sun warmed the air. I wanted to forget the search for Kennan's secret and stretch out on the beach.

We noticed the sign at the same time. "Beach Pads."

"Jinx."

"You owe me a Coke."

"You're kinda funny," I said. "For a lawyer."

"I was told I was dull. I'm trying to break out of the mold."

"If by dull you mean, loyal, steadfast, unwavering, trusted, and uncompromising," I gazed into those dark brown eyes of his, thinking once again how much I liked them, "then yes, Mr. Stern, you are very dull. As in clue: Matte (4), answer: DULL."

He hooted. "I think you better call me David. Mr. Stern is my father."

I shook his hand. "Carol."

A bell tinkled as we entered the storefront.

Before I could speak, David asked the woman at the desk, "Is it empty?"

"Yes, Mr. Stern." From the smile on her pretty face and perky voice, I think she had a soft spot for the man. "It's been vacated, cleaned, and ready to go."

Back in the truck, we headed away from the beach.

Clue: Dim (8). Answer: CONFUSED.

"You said you didn't know what this was about."

"I didn't."

"But now?"

"I'm guessing."

He made a left on Bayard, then another left on Philadelphia Street. The man knew where we were going. Near the end of Philadelphia Street, he turned right and then left onto a side road heading toward the ocean. He stopped next to a cute cottage painted yellow with white trim. An inviting porch ran across the front.

"See if that key works here."

I stared at him then at the house. "He didn't."

"He did."

I trembled as I walked up the three broad steps and placed the key in the lock. It turned with a click, and I almost collapsed. Inside, I ran through the house like Susan in *Miracle on 34th Street*. I half expected to see Santa's cane leaning on the fireplace. There wasn't one, but there was a beautiful Matryoshka doll sitting on the mantel, tempting me.

Kennan. You are something else. Secrets within secrets. I grabbed the doll and walked back outside. David sat on the top step, where I joined him.

He handed me the manilla envelope. "House papers are in there."

Clue: Made senseless (7). Answer: STUNNED.

"I can't believe that he did this. He was so sick."

"He purchased it when he was here setting up the puzzle. He told me he would arrange for a Realtor to rent it out. I assumed you knew. Now I get why you didn't understand what the key meant."

"That's Kennan in a nutshell."

He glanced at me in a sly kind of way. "You think you might move in?"

I grinned. "Thinking about it."

"Well?" He arched an eyebrow and nodded at the nesting doll. "Are you going to open it?"

I shook my head. "Not on your life."

Clue: cherished hopes (10). Answer: BEACH HOUSE.

Beach Words

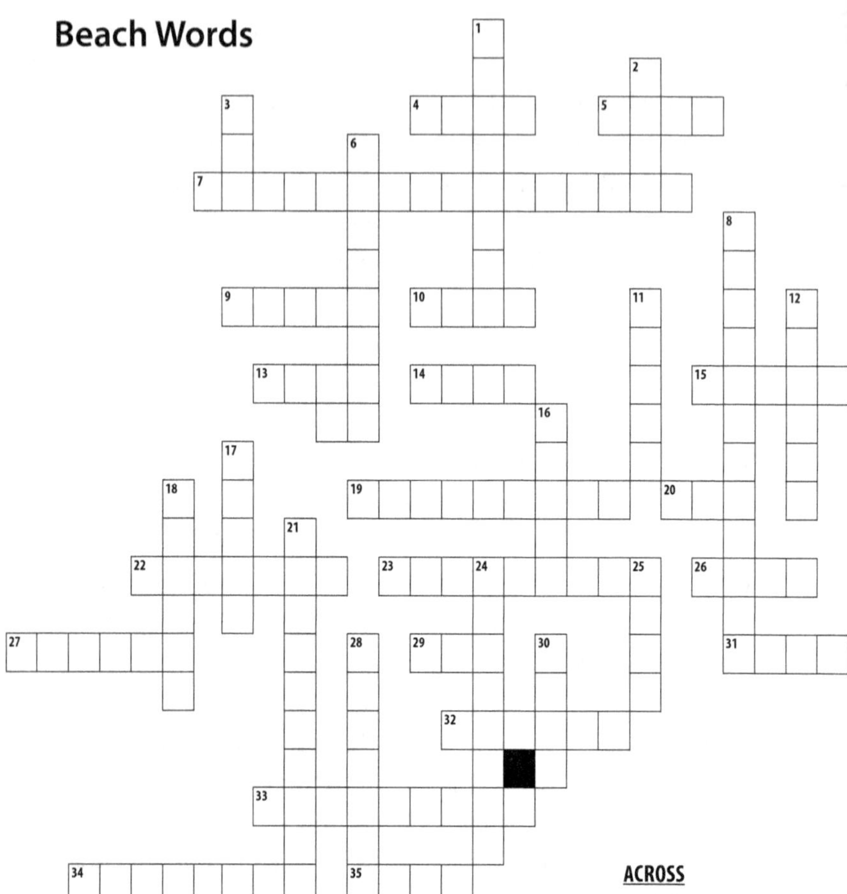

For help solving the puzzle, see the solutions page at the end of the book.

DOWN

1. Dim
2. Bound literature
3. Vacationer's rental
6. Reclaimed material
8. Keyed up
11. Dark and stormy
12. Private/classified
16. Sandy shore
17. Clear skies
18. Cry of joy
21. Cherished hopes
24. Bar tender
25. Content of some banks
28. At sea
30. Red & dead

ACROSS

4. Flight maneuver
5. At sea
7. Beach reads
9. Marine growth
10. Summer rental part 2
13. Resorts
14. Matte
15. Summer rental part 1
19. Esplanade
20. What a buzzkill kills
22. Made senseless
23. Fries
26. Wharf's cousin
27. Summer hut
29. Sunny day cover
31. Due follower
32. Night movies
33. Cat & Mouse Press
34. Letter cover
35. 24-hour periods

Katherine Melvin is a DC-based writer. The idea for "The Cruciverbalist" came to her in the middle of the night after her first COVID shot. Her Lou and Millie stories are inspired by the need to look old age in the face and laugh. She's at work on the second novel of her Mud Creek series called "More Mud." Her short stories and articles have appeared in *Beach Days*, the 2014 MWA Anthology, *Today's Christian Women*, *Christianity Today*, and *Catholic Digest*. She's a proud member of the Maryland Writers' Association, which fosters writers of every level.

The Companion

By Nancy North Walker

The door to his driverless Tesla swung open and he winced. Matt wasn't in the mood for George's cheery voice.

"Morning, Matt. It's 8:45 a.m., September 18, 2039. Sunny and sixty-one degrees here in Princeton, New Jersey. Where shall I take you?"

"To my dad's house in Rehoboth Beach."

He'd had the car for a year, but still wasn't used to it. It had no steering wheel—was just a mobile den with leather lounge chairs and an invisible, artificially intelligent chauffer that drove him around.

"Why is it just you today? It's usually the whole family when you visit your dad."

He sighed. No nuance escaped George. "I'm meeting my dad's girlfriend for the first time. He wanted me to meet her over Sunday brunch. *Alone.*"

"You sound a little perturbed."

"More worried than perturbed. My dad kept his girlfriend secret for months. Now he won't let me bring my wife with me to meet her."

"Interesting. How'd you find out about the girlfriend?"

"Family friends kept calling. Said they saw him with a woman. One even saw them holding hands on the beach at night. He denied it every time until a few days ago. Now he insists she's a companion, not a girlfriend."

George was silent for a moment, but Matt could hear a *whir* that meant George was accessing his in-line memory. "Maybe he's worried you'll think it's too early for him to have a girlfriend. It's only been one year, three months, and six days since your mom died."

Matt stared out the window as the Tesla moved into the driverless lanes on I-295. *It was too early.* "Seems like yesterday I answered that video call from Paris. He was sobbing so hard he couldn't talk." Moisture filled his eyes as he remembered that awful moment.

"Well, maybe he's found the perfect companion for his golden years."

"I doubt it. It's too early for him to have a serious relationship."

His perky sixty-four-year-old mom had dropped dead in front of the *Venus de Milo* sculpture at the Louvre. A brain aneurysm felled her right before his dad's eyes. They had only recently celebrated his dad's retirement from day-to-day operations of the promotional products company he founded thirty years earlier.

Jenny's death had sucked the life out of his dad. The big, confident, backslapping Tchotchke King was no longer himself. His freshly shaved Mr. Clean look had disappeared, along with the sparkle in his blue eyes. He had sequestered himself inside the spacious Victorian-style smart home he and Jenny had built in downtown Rehoboth several years earlier. Spent most of his time in his home office, his beloved yellow lab, Morgan, at his feet. Kept tabs on his business. Took online history courses. Devoured American history nonfiction. Watched videos of Jenny. Walked the dog.

When members of the family visited on long summer weekends, his dad never joined them at the beach or dinners out. Said it was "too painful," because too many people with sad faces asked him how he was doing.

"Why do you think it's too early for him to have a girlfriend, Matt?"

He sighed. "Because he's still mourning my mom. Says he feels her presence all over the house. Hears her footsteps upstairs. Sees her standing by the bedroom window in the middle of the night."

"Hmm." George paused, whirred like he always did when he researched something. "Maybe having a girlfriend will help him let go of your mom."

"Maybe. I just hope she's not a twenty-something gold digger." He pulled his work screen from his satchel. "I've got some work to do. Let me know when we're close to Dad's."

Warmth filled Matt's chest when he saw the Tchotchke King and Morgan waiting for him on the wraparound porch. Morgan wagged his tail as his dad bounded down the steps. Matt's heart skipped a beat when he saw his dad's Mr. Clean look was back, along with the twinkle in his eyes.

His dad threw his arm around Matt's shoulders, squeezed him close, and planted a kiss on his cheek. "Glad you're here, son. I'm looking forward to introducing you to my friend Angela. She's made us a yummy brunch, an egg casserole thing."

The door opened and a gorgeous, sixty-something woman extended her hand. "Welcome, Matt. I'm Angela." His shoulders relaxed as he realized he could cross "young gold digger" off his list.

"So good to meet you." Her hand felt soft and warm, but her handshake was firm. Her generous smile and gingerbread-colored eyes made him forget he hadn't wanted to meet her.

She was taller and slenderer than his mom. Her long salt-and-pepper hair was wrapped neatly in a hand-painted hair clasp at the back of her head. She was dressed in nineties retro: high-waisted jeans, a white shirt with a turned-up collar, an exquisitely embroidered denim vest. *She's pretty hip for an older woman,* he thought. *Nineties-retro is popular right now.*

"How was your drive?"

He detected a slight New England accent. *An old girlfriend from Dad's college days?* "Blissfully uneventful. Most of the tourists are gone."

"Yes. Much quieter on the boardwalk now. Fewer seagulls stealing french fries." She chuckled and waved him inside.

The house smelled of fresh-baked muffins and something warm and cheesy. It made his chest ache for his mom, who baked all the time "because it made the house smell good." He followed Angela to the long reclaimed-wood dining table in the great room, where the whole family had gathered for holidays, birthdays, and family reunions. *Family celebrations at this table will never be the same, even if Dad remarries.*

He sat at the table with his dad as Angela placed the aromatic spread before them. His dad piled a big scoop of cheesy egg and sausage casserole on his plate, took a bite, smacked his lips, and declared it a winner.

Angela joined them at the table and waved her hand dismissively. "Oh, you like everything, Jamie. Even sausage made of garbanzos and West African tiger nuts." She gave Matt a wink. She was right. His dad had a voracious appetite. *Maybe she is an old college girlfriend. Seems like she knows him well.*

Matt took a bite of warm muffin. "Wow. Blueberry?"

Angela chuckled. "Greenland crowberries. Everything Greenland is all the rage now."

A delightful sense of humor. A good sign. Matt noticed she wasn't eating—didn't even have a plate in front of her. "Aren't you hungry, Angela?"

She opened her mouth, but his dad jumped in before she could answer. "She eats like a bird. I'm putting on weight while she stays a size six. It's not fair." He laughed, while Angela gave him a knowing smile.

She seems crazy about him. "I understand completely. My wife's always fasting or detoxing while I load up on the brownies she makes for the boys."

Angela leaned forward on her elbows, cradled her chin in her hands. "Her name is Emma, right?"

"Right. We've been married twelve years. Two boys in elementary school."

"Tell me how you two met."

"Through an online dating service, during the pandemic. Two lonely college kids in Boston stuck in a virtual world in their dorm rooms."

"Sounds romantic. Where and when did you finally meet in person?"

Matt told her how they had braved the pandemic one spring day, met masked-up at a coffee shop between their colleges. Angela seemed genuinely interested in him, asked one question after another. Matt blathered on and on about Emma and the kids, his job as a video game designer, his desire to start his own e-sports events company. He told her things he hadn't even told his parents. His dad sat back, hands clasped across his belly, a serene smile on his face.

They were talking about Matt's entrepreneurial aspirations when Matt caught a glimpse of the time on the kitchen clock. He stopped mid-sentence. "It's been ninety minutes, Angela, and we've only talked about me. Tell me about you and how you met my dad."

His dad rose from the table, put his hand on Matt's shoulder. "It's a long story, son." He walked over to Angela and whispered something. She nodded. Then he massaged her neck and shoulders and pressed his thumb on what Matt guessed was a knot in her neck. Her eyes fluttered three times then closed. Her back stiffened and her arms slipped from the table, hung limply at her sides. Matt thought he heard a faint *whir*.

"What's going on, Dad? Is Angela all right?"

"She's fine, Matt. This is Angela 5.0. She's not what you might have thought …"

Matt heard nothing his dad said. His brain seemed to stop working. He stared at the now obviously inanimate Angela. Nothing made sense. He held up his hand to quiet his dad. "Just answer one question. Is Angela a robot?"

His dad slid his hands into his pockets and looked down. "Yes. She's *a humanoid* robot."

Matt sat back in his chair, gazed at the ceiling, and exhaled through his lips. He looked at his dad. "You're kidding, right?"

His dad's blue eyes brimmed with moisture. "It's not a joke, Matt.

Just give me a chance to explain."

Matt's stomach wrenched. He couldn't believe his dad's mystery girlfriend was a humanoid robot, whatever that was. Had he lost his mind? Was he that desperate?

Angela was nothing like the robots with plasticene faces and programmed voices that mixed drinks and waited tables at his favorite Princeton restaurants. Their movements were stiff and jerky. They only had three or four facial expressions and often smiled inappropriately. People joked about them. Angela's hand had been soft and warm, her facial expressions and gestures very natural, endearing actually. He put his elbows on the table and massaged his temples. "This is very weird, Dad."

"I know. It's why I asked you to come alone."

"Good decision." He continued to massage his temples.

"Can I get you some coffee? A beer? A shot of cannabis-infused tequila?"

"Coffee." He looked across the table at Angela. She looked different now, more doll-like than human. He had the urge to touch her. "Do you mind if I check her out?"

"Go right ahead."

He walked over to her in a daze, removed her hair clasp, and ran his fingers through her silvery locks. Her hair felt like his wife's—thick and coarse.

His dad spoke from the kitchen. "It's her real hair. Made from my beloved Angela's DNA. Her real skin, nails, teeth, and corneas, too. Everything on the outside. That's what makes her a humanoid. Inside, she's carbon-fiber scaffolding, wires, nanochips, nanomotors, and sensors."

Matt patted Angela 5.0's cheek. Her skin was cool and firm, not warm and fleshy like before. "Your *beloved Angela*?" Who's that?"

"I'll get to that. I need to work up to it." His dad set two coffee cups on the table, took a seat and stared out the window, lost in old memories. "She's cold now. Her skin's much softer and fleshier when she's warmed up."

Matt traced her long aquiline nose. "Where'd you get it?"

"I'm part of pilot test for the world's first humanoid DNA-based robots. They won't be on the market for another couple years. Remember my childhood friend Mike who went to MIT?"

"The guy who started that pet robot company in the 2020s and made a fortune?"

"That's him. Remember how people went crazy for his "pet resurrection" program? They sent his company samples of their pet's hair and saliva, along with videos. When their pet died, he built them a new Prince or Princess. Only it didn't eat, poop, or pee."

"So now he's doing the same with humans?"

His dad's eyes sparkled as he nodded. "Mike contacted me after your mom died. Asked if I wanted to be part of Companions4U's first pilot tests."

"Is Angela a sex robot?"

"No. I just wanted a loving, caring companion. One that could cook and manage the housekeeping bots. Massage my shoulders. Make sure I take my meds. The sex robots don't do those things, and they're less attuned to the emotional needs of their owner."

"So why is this Angela, and not mom? And who was Angela, anyways?"

Jamie stared out the window again while he spoke. "With your mom, the pain is too fresh."

Matt put his hand on his dad's forearm.

A single tear streamed down his dad's cheek. "Angela was my first fiancé. My first true love. She died of cancer before we made it to the altar."

Matt's chest tightened. He'd had no idea his dad had lost another woman he loved. He suddenly understood why his dad had panicked every time his mom caught a cold.

He listened quietly as his dad told him about the real Angela, his college sweetheart, a talented young sculptor whom he met his freshman year in a film class. They'd lived together for two years after graduation to be certain they were right for each other. Three months before their wedding date, she was diagnosed with late-stage ovarian cancer. His dad teared up at the words "late stage" and could hardly go on with the story.

He regained his composure but still stared out the window. "We cried a lot. I worked half days. We explored treatment options, went for second opinions. Then her parents came. I got home one afternoon to find the three of them on the sofa. Her bags and boxes were stacked by the door."

Matt's chest ached as his dad put his head in his hands and wept like he did at the Paris airport. "She'd found out that morning she was terminal." His voice hitched. "Said she loved me too much to put me through her last days, wanted me to remember her like she was."

His dad stopped again, stared into his coffee, fidgeted with the cup. Matt suppressed his own tears, reached for his dad's hand and squeezed it. "Thank you for sharing that piece of your life. You clearly loved her. Never got over losing her."

"Fortunately, she left a lot of things behind. Her hairbrush, toothbrush, some clothing. I kept them in a box all these years. Companions4U was able to create an older version Angela from her hair and saliva samples."

"Is Angela 5.0 wearing some of the clothes she left behind?"

His dad looked at the robot and smiled. "That embroidered vest was her favorite."

Father and son were silent for a long time. Matt caressed his dad's hefty hand with his thumb.

"So how is the pilot test going?"

His dad's eyes shone with conviction. "I couldn't be happier."

"And you think Angela 5.0 is better than trying to find a woman with whom you might want to spend the rest of your life?"

"Most definitely."

"Why?"

"I just want to be happy. To have someone smart to talk to. Someone who cares about me more than anyone else. Someone who will take care of me, comfort me as I grow older."

"And a human can't do that?"

"Some can. But time is not on my side. It takes time to find someone you genuinely care about and who feels the same as you. It takes even longer to forge a loving, sustainable relationship. Besides, a robot won't die and leave me alone."

The last sentence pierced Matt's heart. He smiled at his dad through blurry eyes, and they were both silent again.

"What do you like best about Angela 5.0?"

"Two things. First, she looks, feels, walks, and talks like Angela. She tricks my brain into thinking she never died and we've grown old together. It's like a lost dream fulfilled."

"But she's not Angela, Dad. She's not human."

"I'm fully aware of that. She whirs when she accesses her in-line memory. Slurs her words when she needs to be recharged. Don't worry, son. I haven't lost touch with reality.

"What's the second thing?"

"Her sole purpose is to make me happy. And she's very good at it. She practically reads my mind. Knows when I'm missing your mom. Knows how to perk me up."

"Do you love her?"

"No. But I'm very attached to her. She's a superb companion. Better for me than a human companion. Less complicated. Less demanding.

Less stressful. At my age, that's a blessing."

"Don't you get tired of her always trying to make you happy?"

"Hasn't happened yet. But I can always turn her off."

That last comment made his stomach knot. Did his dad just want a companion-on-demand? A slave robot who existed only to make him happy? Then again, there were times when he wished he could switch Emma off, and he knew she felt the same about him.

"So, what do you think? Should I keep Angela a secret from the family or tell them the truth?"

"Does that mean you intend to keep her for the rest of your life?"

"Yes."

"Hmm. I need some time to think about it."

"Understood. Morgan needs a walk. Mind if turn Angela back on? I know you have questions. Ask her anything you want."

His dad pressed the switch at the back of her neck. Angela's eyes fluttered, opened, grew brighter. Her facial muscles softened. She put her hands back on the table and flashed them a cheerful smile. "Hello, Matt. Hello, Jamie. So, where were we? Oh yes, Matt was telling me about his career aspirations."

"I'm taking Morgan for a walk, Angela. Be back in a few."

She nodded and focused her gaze on Matt. "So, you want to start your own e-sports events company? Tell me your game plan."

"Let's save that discussion for next time. I have some questions for you."

Her eyes brightened. "Good. Ask away."

"Why did you ask me so many questions earlier?"

"Because that's how I build both my in-line memory and my emotional intelligence about you. You're important to your dad. I want you to like me.

"So, you're always building your emotional IQ?"

"Exactly."

"How do you do that?"

"I analyze voice pitch and inflections, eye movements, changes in facial expressions, gestures, even fluctuations in body temperature."

"Dad says he thinks you read his mind, anticipate his emotional needs. Do you?"

"No. I just focus on his emotional cues. When his cues suggest he's feeling down, I try to raise his spirits."

"How?"

"I bake his favorite cookies. Or engage him in a discussion about his latest favorite book. I can absorb any book into my memory in a few seconds."

"Do you love my father?"

"Not in the human sense. I don't have human feelings. My company constantly upgrades my software to make me *seem* like I have emotions, but I don't."

"Your heart doesn't ache? No knots in your stomach?"

"I don't have a heart or a stomach."

Matt's face flushed. "I forgot. You seem so human."

"Thank you. No need to be embarrassed."

"You notice everything." He paused, glanced out the window. "So, tell me why I should be glad my dad has you in his life."

She leaned forward, a penetrating intensity in her brown eyes he hadn't seen before. *Was that conviction or was it programmed?*

"Loneliness is the enemy of the human spirit. As long as I'm around, your dad won't be lonely."

Matt cocked his head and stared at Angela. *She read my mind. Discerned exactly what I needed to hear. She reads humans better than any human I ever met.*

Moments later, Morgan pranced into the room. Matt's dad spoke from behind. "So, did you have a good chat?"

Matt stood, smiled at Angela 5.0, and nodded. "She gave me a lot to think about." He walked to her side, stretched out his hand. "It was truly a pleasure to meet you."

His dad slapped him on the back. "Glad to hear that. Let's talk next week about whether we should introduce Angela to the family."

Matt gave his dad a long hard hug. "She's amazing, Dad. I'll be ready with an answer."

As he headed out the door, he realized he already knew the answer. The family should hear the same story Matt did. The grandkids would think Angela was great. The adults would eventually realize she was his guardian Angel-a. If they loved him, they would accept her.

The door to the Tesla swung open. George asked how it went.

"Much better than expected. She's a lot like you, George."

Nancy North Walker is a writer from Rehoboth Beach whose short stories have appeared in several mid-Atlantic anthologies and an online literary magazine. This is the second time a story she wrote was selected for a Cat & Mouse Press Rehoboth Beach Reads anthology, and she is delighted it received a judge's award. Her 2019 story, "The Dolphin Whisperers," was published in *Beach Dreams*. Recently, Nancy's first sci-fi horror story was published by Devil's Party Press in their Gravelight Press anthology *Halloween Party 2021*.

Nancy is a science junkie who is partial to speculative fiction, especially sci-fi. She's currently working on a short story collection exploring the many ways advanced technologies—artificial intelligence, robots, gene editing, holography, to name a few—will impact ordinary people's lives in the not-to-distant future. "The Companion" arose from that exploration. Prior to trying her hand at creative writing, Nancy spent nearly forty years as a business communications executive in Chicago, New York, and New Jersey. For more information see *NANCYNORTHWALKER.COM*.

This story reveals a huge and perhaps uncomfortable secret. The dialogue between father and son (as well as the inner dialogue) befits the concept, the plot, and the theme. Enough backstory was revealed so readers could follow the technological advances, which may not be as far-fetched as we think. The first paragraph foreshadows the tale to come, and the last paragraph ties it together, leaving the reader with a sense of satisfaction. Loneliness is a feeling we all experience in our lives, at one point or another. A well-presented story.

Rock Star

By Jeanie P. Blair

Kat Westin sighed as she paged through her childhood scrapbook. It brought back the happiest memories of the summers she'd spent with her cousins at the bayfront home her aunt and uncle owned in Bethany. From the seashells they'd collected to her first crush—a local lifeguard whose name escaped her. There he was—the tanned, buff, dark-haired stud with the sexy five o'clock shadow—standing stalwart atop his lifeguard chair, guarding the ocean like a superhero guarding his universe. Kat ran her finger down the old photo. The yellowed tape holding it in place gave way. She turned it over and saw the name *Bennett* printed inside a heart. She smiled. *His name was Bennett.*

She still adored that house. When her aunt and uncle decided to remodel, they'd turned the second floor into a rental for Kat and their daughter, Evie. Just out of college, Kat took on two jobs, one of which was a bartending gig at the Starboard in Dewey Beach. Though several years had now passed, not much had changed, except for their employment. Evie was now an accountant. Kat had become a professional photographer but kept her job at the Starboard. She loved bartending, and the tips were too good to give up.

* * * * *

Kat was sitting on the porch, sipping her morning coffee, when she heard movement in the kitchen. "I'm out here, Evie."

"OK." Seconds later, Kat's quirky cousin plodded out in her shorty pajamas and flopped into a rattan chaise.

Kat closed her scrapbook and frowned at her cousin. "Yikes. You look awful."

"Sangria hangover." Evie palmed her forehead. "Thank God it's Saturday. You're coming to the Starboard tonight, right?"

"I wasn't planning on it. This is the first weekend I've had off in eons."

Evie sprung up in her chair. "Oh, Kat. You *have* to come."

Evie's boyfriend, Greg, was the drummer for Broken Lullaby, a hot local rock band. They were debuting a new bass player, whom Evie couldn't stop raving about. "OMG! Bo's so gorgeous, Kat! His eyes are like staring into the Caribbean. Hey! Maybe Greg could hook you two up."

"Noooo way." Kat shook her head. "You know how I feel about musicians."

"But Greg said he's a really good guy."

"That's nice, but I'm still not interested. That lifestyle's not for me."

"OK. Fine. But at least come see them. Greg will be *really* disappointed if you aren't there."

"*Maybe.*"

"Awesome! I'll take that as a yes."

Kat laughed. Evie always had a knack for making her concede.

* * * * *

When the cousins arrived at the Starboard, Greg was onstage doing some last-minute equipment placement.

He jumped down and kissed Evie, then turned and hugged Kat. "I'm so psyched you're here!"

"Me too," Kat said.

"You'll dig Bo. He's one talented S.O.B." The bandmates began taking their spots. Greg gave Evie another peck. "Gotta go. See you after the set." Greg hopped up on his stool and shot Evie a wink.

Their newest member was last to arrive onstage. Bo Kelly was approximately six feet tall, dressed in black leather pants, a tight black sleeveless shirt that showcased his large biceps, and black leather boots. All that black was in stark contrast to his tousled shaggy blond hair. He had his back to them as he strapped on his bass, then turned and stepped up to the microphone.

Kat stopped breathing. Staring down at her were the turquoise-blue eyes Evie had gone on about. She gasped, praying the riffs of the sound check had drowned it out. Kat blushed when Bo grinned. She tried her damnedest but couldn't tear her gaze from his. He kept his eyes locked onto hers, clearly amused by her embarrassment. Evie's voice broke her trance.

"Told ya."

"What?" Kat waved her off. "I'm getting a drink." She quickly sidestepped to the bar. Kat needed a new minutes away from the stage to gather herself. *Dammit.* She'd never been so flustered by a hot guy, least of all a musician.

When Kat returned to Evie, the crowd was much larger. She managed to keep her composure, even when Bo looked at her. *Wow.* His voice *was* incredible, and he made melodies with his bass unlike any she'd ever heard. Looks aside, she couldn't help but respect his exceptional talent.

When the set ended, Greg found the girls. "So … what do you think? Bo's amazing, right?"

"Totally!" Evie squealed.

"Comes with experience. He's got some years on us," Greg said. "About fifteen I think."

Evie's eyes widened. "Really?! I thought he was our age."

"Nope."

"Hey, guys."

Kat froze at the sound of the deep, sandy voice and the smell of leather and men's cologne that wafted over her shoulder.

Greg smiled. "Hey, Bo. This is my girlfriend, Evie, and her cousin, Kat."

Kat turned and was staring at the broad chest of the new bassist. She tried to respond, but no sound came from her mouth. Thankfully, Evie chimed in.

"Nice to meet you, Bo!" Evie jabbed her bony elbow into her cousin's arm. "Isn't it, Kat?"

"Uh, yes." was all Kat could muster.

Bo looked at Kat. "Nice to meet you too."

Kat felt her cheeks flush again. She was so angry that she let this man—in whom she had no romantic interest—turn her into a starstruck teenybopper.

When the DJ played The Cars song "Drive," Greg pulled Evie out onto the dance floor.

Bo put out his hand. "Would you like to dance?"

Unable to think of a viable reason to decline, Kat politely accepted.

As the two rocked back and forth, Kat couldn't help but revel in the feel of Bo's arm around her waist. Strange, uncontrollable feelings surged through her body when he pulled her tighter. She prayed he couldn't feel her racing heartbeat.

When the song ended, Greg snagged Bo for the next set.

"Thanks for the dance, Kat. Maybe we can …" Bo's voice trailed off as Greg pulled him toward the stage.

"Soooo …?" Evie's voice came from behind.

"So … nothing." Kat shrugged. She wouldn't dare let Evie see that she was smitten, and she so loved torturing her nosy cousin. "He just asked me to marry him and have his babies … that's all."

Evie smacked Kat's arm. "Very funny."

As the band reassembled and began their second set, Kat was oddly more relaxed. She wasn't even too rattled when Bo sang directly to her.

After the show, the girls joined Greg and Bo for a beer. Evie talked Kat up to Bo, mentioning her interest in singing.

"Jeez, Evie." Kat rolled her eyes. "I sang a little in high school, but

I'm no Alicia Keys."

Bo grabbed a guitar from the stage. "I'll be the judge of that."

Kat was horrified. "No way!"

"C'mon. I'll sing with you."

When Bo began strumming the melody of Ed Sheeran's "Perfect," Kat's heart nearly exploded. She'd always dreamed that would be her wedding song. Kat was mesmerized by Bo's voice. He made Ed Sheeran sound like Weird Al. Greg joined in, and she found herself unable to resist. Bo gradually lowered his voice. He kept nodding at her and smiling, as if encouraging her to continue. Kat beamed. She knew he was doing it to let her voice shine through.

* * * * *

In the coming weeks, Kat and Bo spent more and more time together. Initially, it was mostly with Evie and Greg, but the two gradually began spending time alone. When Kat expressed an interest in the guitar, Bo graciously offered to give her lessons.

"Here." Bo reached over when Kat was struggling to place her fingers accurately on the fretboard of his guitar. He gently arranged her fingers in the correct position. "Perfect. Just like that."

Kat sighed. "Am I *ever* going to get this?"

"You're doing great. Just have faith in yourself." Bo lifted her chin and looked into her eyes. "*I* do."

Dammit. She tried desperately to dismiss the urge to kiss him.

Kat inhaled deeply. "I could use a break. You?"

"Great idea." Bo offered his hand. "Let's go."

"Where?" She asked.

A playful smile came over Bo's face. "It's a surprise."

Bo led her out of her condo to his truck and helped her in. He hopped into the driver's side and slid on his wire-framed Ray-Bans. The shiny black GMC Sierra growled as Bo turned the key.

He turned north onto Coastal Highway and continued for several miles. As they approached the town of Lewes, Kat's curiosity overcame her.

"Where the heck are we going?"

Bo grinned. "You'll see."

He made a U-turn, then eased into the gravel parking lot of a small cottage-turned-music-store with a big red guitar atop its roof.

Kat looked inquisitively at Bo.

Bo killed the engine and leaned back in his seat. "You need your own guitar."

"Oh? Tired of lending me yours?"

"Of course not. But you should have your own. It's kinda like having your own golf club … or bowling ball."

"Hmm. Makes sense, I guess."

"Cool. Let's go."

Kat grabbed Bo's arm when he reached for his door handle. "Wait."

"What's wrong?"

"I'm sorry." Kat paused. "I'm just not sure I can afford one right now."

Bo smiled. "No worries. My treat."

"That's sweet, Bo, but I can't let you do that."

"Nonsense. I was actually going to surprise you with one, but I decided you should pick out your own."

Before Kat could refuse, Bo was opening her door. "Shall we?"

The pair meandered around the music store. Bo tested several models, but all Kat could focus on were the price tags. She spotted a selection of pre-owned guitars and took one off the rack.

Bo approached from behind. "Whatcha got there?"

Kat held up the budget guitar. "This one's nice."

Bo peered at her over his Ray-Bans. "I'm not buying you a used guitar."

"It's good enough," she countered.

"Not for you." Bo returned the bargain guitar to its perch and led her to a display of Martin acoustic guitars. He handed her one with a beautiful spruce and mahogany finish.

"Oh wow! That's *beautiful!*"

Bo beamed at her. "Try it out."

Kat began strumming the shiny instrument.

"It's amazing. And *really* comfortable." Kat stopped strumming. "Bo, it's *really* beautiful, but—"

"Cool." He took the guitar from her and grabbed her hand. "Now you need a strap."

Bo was like a kid in a candy store, which is basically the equivalent of a musician in a music store. Kat picked out a black-and-red floral strap, and they headed to the register. Bo handed the guitar to the salesman, who Kat thought was the doppelganger of Jeff Spicoli from the movie *Fast Times at Ridgemont High.*

"We'll take this one." Bo had already chosen a case and various other accessories. He handed his credit card to Spicoli, who—likely at Bo's request—didn't disclose the total. When Bo signed the sales ticket, Kat managed to steal a quick glimpse.

She gasped. "Bo! That's nearly a thousand dollars!"

Bo slid his wallet into his back pocket and thanked Spicoli. "Kat. I *want* to do this for you."

"But—"

"Just enjoy it."

Kat sighed. "Thank you, Bo. I really do appreciate it."

"I know. You're welcome." The two exited the store and climbed back into the truck. "Now for one last stop."

"Where to?"

Bo grinned. "My sanctuary."

With a deep roar of the engine, they were back on the highway. Minutes later, they pulled into the parking lot at Cape Henlopen Beach.

"Ever been here?" he asked.

Kat smiled. "Yes, but it's been a while."

He pointed toward the beach. "I've written many songs sitting there."

"Really?"

"Yep. I've taken lots of pictures here too. Photography is my second love. After music, of course."

"Of course." Kat chuckled. "I'd love to see your photos sometime."

"Sure. I'd love a *professional's* opinion."

Kat laughed. "Well, I'd be honored."

Bo was staring at her with a big smile on his handsome face.

"What's that look for?" she asked.

"You have a beautiful smile."

Kat blushed and turned her gaze toward the Breakwater Lighthouse, which was blanketed by the sunset. "What a magnificent view. That orangey sky. It's so amazing."

"Yep. It's absolutely stunning."

Kat looked at Bo and realized he was looking at *her*, not the lighthouse. He leaned over the center console and laid his palm on her cheek. Kat froze. His beautiful eyes burned right through to her soul. Bo leaned in closer and covered her mouth with his. His kiss was soft but deliberate. The smell of him was intoxicating. A wave of heat washed over her; a flutter traveled from her stomach to her chest. With every shred of her being she knew it was a bad idea, but her pounding heart won the battle and she kissed him back.

Bo suddenly pulled away. "I'm sorry. I shouldn't have done that."

Kat desperately tried to catch her breath. "No. *I'm* sorry."

"Why? *I* kissed *you*."

Kat was still winded. "But I didn't stop you."

"OK." Bo took a deep breath. "Let's just forget that happened."

A wave of disappointment washed over Kat, but she knew he was right. *So why did she feel so shattered?*

Bo broke the deafening silence. "Uh, it's getting late. I'd better get you home."

A nod was all Kat could muster.

It was an agonizingly long ride back to her condo. The two exchanged meaningless bits of conversation, if only to quell the awkwardness. When they arrived, Bo slid out and jogged around to open Kat's door. She hopped out as he retrieved her new guitar and accessories from the back seat.

Kat took the packages and thanked Bo again. He started to turn toward the street, then stopped. "Umm … are we still on for a lesson tomorrow?"

"Sure." Kat forced a smile.

"Great. See you around one?"

"Perfect. Oh … bring your pictures."

"Will do."

Kat turned and made her way upstairs. She opened her door, then waved to Bo as he drove away.

Kat set her packages on the coffee table and sat on the couch. She opened the guitar case and ran her trembling fingers across the beautiful instrument, as thoughts of Bo's beautiful words and passionate kiss repeated in her mind. *Dammit.* He was everything she wanted but couldn't have. A tear ran down her cheek.

Kat breathed a huge sigh of relief when she heard Evie's key in the lock. Quirkiness aside, Evie always managed to calm her whenever she went off the rails.

Evie entered and immediately sat beside Kat.

Kat stared at her cousin; not knowing where to begin.

"Jeez, Kat. What's wrong?"

Kat swallowed hard. "Bo kissed me, Evie. And I kissed him back."

"Oh my!" Evie half-smiled. "That's good, right?"

"No!" Kat cried. "It was a mistake. Bo even said so."

"He *did*?"

"Yes. And he's right." Kat sobbed. "But the problem is, I'm not sure I still feel that way."

"Uh-oh." Evie reached for Kat's hand. "Greg told him your rule about musicians. I'm sure that's why he said that."

"Think so?"

"Yes." Evie assured her. "I'm sure that's why."

"I guess." Kat sighed. "This sucks, Evie. I think I'm falling in love with him."

"Kat, he obviously has feelings for you too."

"But he's so much older than me."

Evie rolled her eyes. "You seriously need to get over that. When two people love each other, age doesn't matter."

Kat groaned. "Maybe you're right. I'm so confused. There's just something so comfortable and *familiar* about him. Like I've known him forever."

"Kat, you need to tell him how you feel."

"I know. But his rock star lifestyle isn't for me."

"Who knows what his plans are, Kat? He might be ready to settle down. He's been in the music biz a *long* time."

Evie was right. She needed to talk to Bo; otherwise, there would always be tension between them. Even if he didn't feel the same, she didn't want it to destroy their friendship. At least she'd still have that.

✶ ✶ ✶ ✶ ✶

Kat returned home after finishing her morning photo shoots. Bo was due there soon, and she was mentally rehearsing what she'd say to him. She jumped when he knocked. Kat took a deep breath and opened the door. Bo was wearing a black T-shirt and a pair of Levi's that hugged him in all the right places. He was holding his guitar and a couple of photo albums.

Kat smiled. "Hi. C'mon in."

"Thanks." Once again, the scent of him intoxicated her as he brushed past. "So." Bo broke the ice. "Lesson first?"

Kat's hands were trembling way too much to even consider strumming her guitar.

"Actually, I'd love to see your pictures first, if that's OK."

"Oh. Sure." Bo seemed a little uneasy as he set his guitar on the floor.

Kat grabbed two icy beers, and the two went out to the porch and settled in on the wicker loveseat. Bo opened his first album on the glass-top coffee table. Kat was impressed with the photos he'd taken.

She closed the cover. "Those are *really* incredible, Bo."

"Thanks, Kat. That means a lot coming from you." When Bo picked up the second album, a small envelope slid out onto the floor.

"Oops," Bo said as he snatched it up. "I guess that got stuck inside."

"Oh," Kat said. "More photos?"

"Yeah. Just some old, random stuff."

Kat grabbed Bo's arm as he quickly tried to tuck the envelope away. "Can I see them?"

"Uh …" Bo hesitated. "Sure."

Kat gasped when Bo handed her the contents. On top of the stack was a photo of a lifeguard—*her lifeguard*—standing atop his white, wooden chair. "Who's that?" she asked.

Bo paused. "That's *me*, Kat."

Kat's jaw dropped. "That's *you?!*"

"Yes. I was a lifeguard in Bethany for several summers before I bleached my hair and joined a band.

"Oh my God. Bo. I took that picture."

"Yes. I know. And you gave me a copy. I figured it out a few days ago, after some stories Evie told me about your summers in Bethany. I knew it had to be you."

"Holy shit!" Kat shrieked. "Why haven't you told me?"

"I don't know. I was just waiting for the right time. It was just so surreal."

"I'm confused," she said. "The name *Bennett* is written on the back of my picture."

"Bennett's my real name. *Bennett Owen Ryder*. I use my first and middle initials as my first name, and Kelly—my mom's maiden name—for my last name. *Bo Kelly* is my stage name."

"Oh my God."

"How old were you then?" Bo asked.

"Fifteen."

"I was twenty-four, and I remember telling my buddies I thought you were cute and what a bummer it was that you were so young."

Kat paused. "Wait. You were only twenty-four?"

"Yep."

So many things were running through Kat's mind. Turns out he was only nine years her senior, but there was still the issue of his career.

"Kat." Bo regained her attention. "We need to talk about yesterday."

Kat shook her head. "Bo—"

"Please hear me out. I know what you think of musicians, but that's not me. And, as for life on the road … I'm over that. That's why I only play in local bands now."

"Really?" Kat's heart skipped.

"Yes. In fact, I've been offered a job managing and developing local talent. It's a great gig and I'm gonna take it."

"That's great!" But Kat's elation was mixed with sadness. "But does that mean you won't play anymore?"

"Nah. I'll still play with Greg on the weekends," Bo continued. "Listen, Kat. About that kiss. Truth is, I'm *not* sorry it happened. I wanted to kiss you, and I was really psyched that you kissed me back. I felt something for you the second Greg introduced us … like I've known you forever."

"I had the same feeling. I guess now we know why." Kat reached up and touched his face. "But I kept thinking if we'd ever met before, I'd remember those beautiful eyes of yours." She stopped. "I just realized something. I never saw your eyes. You always had sunglasses on."

"And now this picture appears out of the blue. Fate brought us back together, Kat." Bo reached over and took her hands in his. "I'm ready to start a new chapter of my life … and I want you in it."

Kat's eyes filled up. "Oh, Bo. I'd love that."

He pulled her in for a long, passionate kiss. When they parted, he said, "Remember I told you music and photography were my first and second loves?"

"Yes," she answered.

"Well, make that my second and third."

A NATIVE DELAWAREAN, JEANIE PITRIZZI BLAIR RESIDES IN NEWARK WITH HER HUSBAND, SAM, AND THEIR MINIATURE SCHNAUZER, SOPHIA. "ROCK STAR" IS HER SIXTH SHORT STORY ROMANCE PUBLISHED IN VARIOUS ANTHOLOGIES BY CAT & MOUSE PRESS. ALONG WITH HER AFFINITY FOR WRITING, JEANIE IS AN AVID MUSIC LOVER OF MANY GENRES—ESPECIALLY CLASSIC ROCK, WHICH WAS THE INSPIRATION FOR HER STORY. SHE HAS COLLECTED SOME INTERESTING PIECES OF MEMORABILIA FROM HER FAVORITE BANDS THROUGH THE YEARS, INCLUDING A NEW COLORED VINYL ALBUMS AND VINTAGE FIRST-RELEASE 45-RPM RECORD PRESSINGS, AND EVEN HAS HER ORIGINAL 8-TRACK TAPES AND PLAYER, WHICH STILL WORKS. THOUGH SHE WORKS FULL TIME AS AN OFFICE ADMINISTRATOR, JEANIE CONTINUES TO PURSUE HER DREAM OF BECOMING A SUCCESSFUL ROMANCE NOVELIST. SHE WOULD LIKE TO THANK HER FAMILY AND FRIENDS FOR THEIR CONTINUED SUPPORT AND ENCOURAGEMENT.

In keeping with the theme "Beach Secrets," Jeanie included eight subtle references that honor one of her favorite bands. They are listed on the solutions page at the end of the book.

The Merrifield Affair

By Linda Budzinski

"Tell me a secret."

I roll my eyes. This guy beside me is a cliché, wrapped in a buffoon, inside a jackass. Next thing you know, he'll order me a shot of sex on the beach. "OK," I say. "I hate bars. Even beach bars."

"That's no secret." He leans toward me, a smile playing at the corners of his lips. "That was obvious from the moment you marched in here. As though on a mission."

He's not wrong. I wave to the bartender. "Another one, please. Make it a double."

Mr. Predictable leans in even closer. "That'll be three drinks in … what, four minutes? All while avoiding eye contact with everyone but the guy serving them. Impressive."

I swivel on my stool and glare. How's this for eye contact? "You want a secret? I'll tell you a secret. I just broke off a two-year affair with my boss."

"Wow." He nods appreciatively. "Now that's what I call a secret."

I kill my whiskey and soda in one gulp, enjoying the burn as it goes down. I've never breathed a word of my relationship to anyone, not even my best friends. It feels weird to say it out loud. *Affair.*

"So what happened?"

I set my empty glass down on the bar. "You want all the gory details?"

"I do. I'm Mark, by the way." He offers his hand and I shake it. He has a chill vibe— faded blue T-shirt and Josh Grobanesque curls. Probably spends his mornings fishing up at Herring Point. As different from Andrew as a guy could be.

"I'm Ally, short for Alice Anne. I work in Wilmington as an attorney. Corporate law. I hate it, but I'm really good at it." Why am I telling him all this? It's as though I've taken my own personal witness stand. The truth, the whole truth, and nothing but the truth.

"Nice to meet you, Ally. Mind if I call you 'Alice Anne, Esquire'?"

"Not at all. In fact, I insist." I lift my empty glass and motion to the bartender.

"Tell you what." Mark waves him off. "Why don't we go outside and get some air? Take a walk along the boardwalk, and you can tell me all about it."

I give him my best I-know-what-you're-trying-to-do head tilt, only to find that the whole room tilts with it. "Fine. Mission semi-accomplished anyway." I slip off the stool and stumble only a little as we wind our way through the bar and out the door.

I normally wouldn't leave with a man I'd just met, but it's peak season in Rehoboth and the evening is young. There's safety in numbers, and the boardwalk is bustling with its usual family crowd—mothers clutching their toddlers' hands, older couples pausing to gaze out over the dunes, teens forming amorphous crowds and playing too-cool-to-care.

A warm breeze swirls with my favorite perfume—eau de salt air and funnel cake. Truth be told, I may have loved Andrew's beach house more than I loved him.

"So where should I start?" I ask.

"At the beginning, of course." Mark's hand at my elbow guides me through the crowd, steadying me as the fresh air threatens to steal my buzz.

I sigh. "Fine. It all started innocently enough, I suppose. He wasn't

                                   Rehoboth Beach Reads

my boss at the time, nor was he married, though he was about to be engaged. Our firm had just signed a major client, and the partners decided to treat some of us junior staff to a golf weekend in Vegas."

"You golf?"

"Yep, I'm good at that too."

"Please tell me you shot a lower score than … what's his name?"

"Andrew. And I did. Though that's a low bar." Andrew was always more interested in improving his station than his swing. At the time I'd found him hysterical and charming. Now I realize he was being vintage Andrew as he regaled our bosses with tales of his exploits on the Harvard debate team. Andrew tended to kiss up and kick down. "Anyway, on our last night there, we met for a drink at Caesar's Palace and one thing led to another. I didn't expect it to last beyond the Strip."

"What happens in Vegas."

"Exactly." I stop. "Wait. Where are you taking me?" I'd gotten so caught up reminiscing that I'd failed to realize this stranger has led me to a staircase. I step back and grasp the rail to keep from falling.

He steadies me and motions toward the top of the steps. "We're at Ryan's."

I laugh—part relief, part delight. Ryan's Mini Golf is my favorite spot on the boardwalk, though I managed to drag Andrew here only twice in our two years together. "I should warn you; alcohol enhances my game."

"Is that so? Well, then, I'm sure you'll beat me. But that's a *ridiculously* low bar."

We mount the stairs and stroll to the edge of the rooftop course to admire the beach at dusk—the ocean a massive shimmering jewel beneath a rose-tinted sky—-before heading to the first tee.

We end up stuck behind a family of five, but I don't mind. Should give me plenty of time between holes to confess my crimes. It feels good to yank my meticulously buried skeletons out of their closet and rattle them around in the ocean air.

"Where was I?"

"Returning from Vegas."

"Ah, yes. The very next day at work, Andrew invited me down here, to his family's bungalow on Rodney. It's been our getaway ever since, about once a month."

Mark sinks the par-two first hole on his fourth stroke and pumps his fist as though he's made a hole-in-one. "If you don't mind me asking, where did he tell his wife he was going all those weekends?"

"She wasn't his wife until a few months ago." Not sure why I feel the need to clarify this, but I do. Mitigating circumstances, I suppose. "And he told her the truth, or half the truth—that he was coming here. Claimed to meet up with some old college buddies every month. She's not a beach person, so she stayed behind."

"That's convenient." Mark's tone holds no judgment.

"It was, very."

"Do you know her well?"

"No. Met her only once, at a company picnic. She didn't talk much."

"What's her name?"

"I'd prefer not to say. Her family is rather … prominent." Even in my over-sharing mood, I knew better than to identify Becca. Andrew married her for her father's connections—a boost to his career, not to mention his aspirations to run for state senate in a few years. "He doesn't love her. Not like he loves me."

"I see."

My cheeks grow warm, and I'm glad for the encroaching darkness. Now who's the cliché? Alice Anne, Esquire, the Too-Trusting Mistress.

As we putt our way through the course, the gap between our scores grows in inverse proportion to the diminishing weight of my secret. I tell him about the epic Skee-Ball battle Andrew and I waged at Playland our first weekend down here. I recall the time we almost won the

Halloween Sea Witch Hunt, beaten out only by a dad and his tween daughter who found her mere seconds before we did. And as we wait for the family in front of us to navigate the deceptively challenging sixteenth hole, I tell him the story of the morning everything changed—for me, at least—from a fun fling to true love.

It was two weeks before Christmas and about four months after that night in Vegas.

We'd had an early snow. Route 1 was a mess, which gave us an excuse to stay an extra day. I was in the kitchen finishing up a call for work when Andrew tapped on the window and waved at me to come outside. I pulled on my coat and boots and joined him on the front porch.

"Have you ever seen the beach in the snow?"

I shook my head. "I'm sure it's beautiful."

"Let's go." He grabbed my hand and practically dragged me the half block from his house to the boardwalk. What was his hurry?

In the mid-morning sun, the beach appeared peaceful and familiar—the snow simply a brighter, more shimmery version of the sand—but as we wound our way down the path through the dunes, I spotted a figure silhouetted against the sky. A snowman—or I should say, woman—complete with a floppy beach hat and tote, gazing out toward the ocean.

"Look at that. How sweet."

Andrew grinned. "I thought you'd like her."

"Wait. You built it?" He'd said he was going out for a walk.

He nodded and led me over. Around her neck, she wore a silver chain with a midnight-blue sapphire pendant.

"Merry Christmas."

I blinked. "For me?"

Andrew laughed. "Well, she's going to melt, so … yeah. For you."

He took it off her neck and draped it around mine. It was cold. Freezing. But gorgeous.

"Thank you. It's incredible."

"You're incredible." Andrew drew me close and kissed me. A long, sweet, slow kiss that made my head swim and my insides—

"Hooray, Lily!"

A loud cheer erupts as the family's youngest child sinks her putt, bringing me back to the course, to tonight, to my now harshly sober, Andrewless reality. Mark is staring at me, frowning.

"It wasn't the necklace." My voice catches. "I mean, the sapphire was stunning, but that's not what sealed the deal. Nor was it the kiss, though it was quite a kiss. It was what happened next."

Mark places his ball on one of the tee holes. "And what was that?"

"Hold up. Where exactly are you planning to hit that?"

"What?"

"Your putt. What's your plan?"

He points to the far corner. "I was going to bank it off of—"

I shake my head.

He sighs and switches the ball to the other hole.

"Better."

"I'm learning." He squares up but stops and straightens. "So? Don't keep me in suspense. What happened?"

"Don't you keep me in suspense. I need to see this shot."

He laughs and waggles his hips as he squares up again and putts. His ball misses the sweet spot on the side by a few inches but caroms in the general direction of the hole. It stops about a foot short.

"Nice."

"I might actually make par on this one, thanks to you. So—after the kiss?"

"So. After the kiss." I tee up and hit a perfect stroke. My ball banks off the side at just the right speed, rolls past Mark's, and drops into the hole with a satisfying *clink*. "I was confused. Overwhelmed. I'd spent weeks convincing myself that our trips here were a meaningless dalliance, that Andrew was nothing but a temporary diversion. Now he'd given me this lovely gift, and in such romantic fashion. I walked down to the water and stared out at the waves, trying to collect my thoughts, my emotions, when … *bam*. It hit me. Literally. A snowball smacked me on the butt. I looked back to find Andrew smirking like a schoolboy. That was it. We had the mother of all snowball fights, and by the time we'd fired our last volleys, I was head over heels."

Mark is standing above his ball, transfixed. "Wow."

"I know. It's stupid. So stupid."

"No. It's not. It's … I had no idea."

"What do you mean, you had no idea?"

He shakes his head and looks away. "I don't know. When you told me you'd had an affair, I was expecting something more … sordid. That's not sordid. It's sweet."

"Yeah, well." I take a deep breath and kick at the AstroTurf. "Three weeks later, on New Year's Eve, he got engaged. A few days after that, he made partner."

"Ouch."

"Yep. And I wasted the next year and a half trying to chase down the feeling of that snowball hitting my ass." Tears prick the corners of my eyes. "Now *that's* stupid."

Mark picks up his ball—forfeiting his only chance at par—and tucks his club under his arm. "Tell you what, Alice Anne, Esquire. Let's get out of here. I could use a drink."

I'm all for that, but he leads me past the Greene Turtle and Zogg's and around the Bandstand—where a Jimmy Buffet cover band is singing about shark fins circling—into Rita's Italian Ice. We both order the flavor of the day, wild black cherry, and head down to the beach.

We walk in a comfortable silence until we find a smooth, dry patch in the sand, where we sit sipping our ices and watching the waves lap onto the shore. A full moon slices a bright streak through the water.

"Now it's your turn," I say.

"My turn?"

"Yep. I've spent the whole night talking about myself. Now you tell me a secret."

He swirls his drink and stares into it as though searching for something at the bottom. "Nah. Nothing to tell."

"No secrets?"

"None."

He's lying. Everyone has secrets. "Fine. More about me then. What else do you want to know?"

He shakes his head. "You don't have to—"

"No, no. This has been good. Liberating."

He takes a swig of his ice. "All right. Why'd you break it off? What went wrong?"

I sigh and train my eyes on the horizon. "Nothing went wrong. It just … *was* wrong. Always. No matter how hard I tried, I couldn't make it right. Nor could Andrew. And he tried. Oh, did he try—dinners, jewelry, flowers, love notes. Whenever I thought about walking away, he'd win me back."

"Until today."

"Until today. It occurred to me this morning as I sat on the porch drinking my coffee and watching the sun rise, that I don't want any of those things. I want …" I sigh. "I don't know what I want."

"Snowball fights."

"Yes!" I laugh and glance over to find Mark watching me. His lips are stained a wild-black-cherry purple and his curls have relaxed in the salty ocean breeze.

I lean toward him, but he breaks my gaze and turns away. My cheeks burn, and I force a laugh. Am I so desperate to be with someone that I tried to kiss the first man I've met since my not-yet-day-old breakup?

"I'm sorry," I say. "I'm ridiculous."

"What? No."

"Pathetic then."

"No." He sets down his drink and takes my hand in his. "Not ridiculous. Not pathetic. Not at all." He laces his fingers around mine. "I can tell you this: You deserve better."

I study his eyes. Does he mean better than Andrew? Or better than him? I doubt he's right on either count. Still, tonight, with its utter lack of guile and guilt, already feels better than the past two years. "Thanks for saying that. And for listening. And for … not judging. That's probably better than I deserve."

We sit like that for a while, hand in hand. I close my eyes and let the rhythm of the ocean slow my breathing and calm my thoughts.

His cell phone rings, and I pull away. "You should get that."

He reaches into his pocket but stops. "It's probably spam."

"At this hour? It might be important."

"No. I'd rather not—"

"Answer it. Please."

He stands and pulls the phone out. He fumbles and drops it, and it tumbles onto the sand between us.

I blink. The name on the screen glows an eerie blue: Becca Merrifield.

"Becca?" What the—? I scramble to my feet. "How do you know Becca? Why is she calling you?"

He curses under his breath. "Hold on." He grabs the phone, swipes, and tells Becca he can't talk.

I turn back toward the boardwalk, back to the bar. *Screw this.*

"Ally, wait!" He follows me.

I swivel and toss what's left of my Italian ice at him. A satisfying, blood-like stain spreads across his chest. "No secrets? Really?"

"Let me explain."

I bend over. The evening's combination of alcohol, sugar, and deceit roils through my stomach and up into my throat. I puke in the sand as tears spill down my cheeks. "Go away."

I kneel and retch again, and again. When I finish, I lift my head to find Mark still beside me. I glare. "Talk," I say.

He helps me up and offers me the rest of his ice. I take a drink and spit it out to clear the taste of vomit. "Thank you," I mumble.

Together we walk back down toward the water.

"My name is Mark Ormond. I'm a private investigator."

I freeze. "So Becca suspected."

"You could say that."

"Is she filing for divorce?"

He must sense the twinge of hope in my voice because he folds his arms across his chest. "You know what? You're not ready for the truth."

I chafe at his pitying tone. "What truth?"

He says nothing for a long while, as though weighing whether he should continue or has already shared too much. At last, he turns, pulls off his shoes and wades ankle-deep into the water.

I follow suit. The cool water lapping at my feet helps clear my head. "Please. Tell me what's going on."

"You're not going to like it."

"I already don't like it."

He sighs. "Fine. Becca didn't hire me. Andrew did."

"What?" The world shifts, and my toes grip the sand to steady it. "Andrew? Why? And if that's the case, why was Becca calling?"

"Becca knows. She's always known. She was fine with it—said Andrew's weekends away gave her some 'me time'—but now she's worried. They both are."

"Worried? About what? Oh." I set my jaw. "Of course. Appearances."

He nods. "They knew this day would come, of course. The affair couldn't last forever. Now they're trying to ... minimize damages, I suppose."

"Damages? Meaning?"

He shrugs. "They hired me to figure out where your head's at. Whether you might do something stupid."

"Like tell my secrets?"

"Like tell your secrets."

I scowl. "Well, congratulations. You're very good at your job. And I clearly failed that test."

Mark shakes his head. "You were quite discreet, actually."

I bend down and scoop up a shell from the receding water. It's small but perfect—pink, with dainty scalloped edges and a pearly interior that reflects the moonlight. I press its ridges into my palm. So I've been nothing more to Andrew than a devoted puppy, obeying his command to heel in return for the occasional treat. I truly am a cliché.

"What if I decide to talk?" I ask. "At the firm? At their country club? Maybe at the next meeting of the Delco Young Democrats."

Mark steps toward me and places his hand under my chin, lifting it until our eyes meet. "That's up to you, but like I said, you deserve better. Better than 'other woman' and certainly better than 'woman scorned.'"

I pull away as tears threaten once again. He's right. Even my reaction to being a cliché is cliché. "So, what, then? Pretend it never happened?"

"Again, your choice. I just think you should choose … better."

I smile. "Better life choices. Apparently not my forte."

"Well, you can't be good at everything." The glint in his eye tells me he's teasing. Or at least half-teasing. His voice softens. "Are you going to be OK?"

I take a deep breath and nod. Truth is, knowing Andrew hired someone to spy on me makes things easier. How deeply can a heart grieve the loss of such an utter douche?

I tuck the shell into my pocket and hold out my hand. "I appreciate you sobering me up, and listening, and … dealing with the puking. I guess this is goodbye."

Mark takes my hand and draws me into a hug. "Take care of yourself,

Alice Anne, Esquire."

I close my eyes and relax into his chest for a moment before pulling away. "Thanks. I will." I turn to leave, but he calls after me.

"Hey. Before you go ..." He pulls out his wallet and retrieves a business card. "Call if you need anything. Or if you want to talk or ... you know, hang out."

"Thanks. Maybe I will. Though maybe not for a while."

"Of course. Not for a while. But maybe ..." He grins. "First snowfall?"

I laugh. "That could work. First snowfall."

As I stroll back onto the boardwalk, my hips sway to the sound of "Margaritaville." I pop into Zogg's and order a club soda with cranberry.

As I take my first sip, a guy beside me leans over. "What are we drinking to tonight?"

I smile and clink my glass against his. "To better life choices. And to early snowfalls."

LINDA BUDZINSKI LIVES IN NORTHERN VIRGINIA AND IS THE AUTHOR OF FOUR YOUNG ADULT NOVELS: *EM & EM*, *THE BOYFRIEND WHISPERER*, *THE BOYFRIEND WHISPERER 2.0*, AND *THE FUNERAL SINGER*. SHE IS A RECIPIENT OF THE ROMANCE WRITERS OF AMERICA'S YOUNG ADULT CHAPTER'S ROSEMARY AWARD AND VIRGINIA CHAPTER'S FOOL FOR LOVE AWARD. SHE NEVER THOUGHT SHE COULD WRITE A SHORT STORY, BUT WHEN SHE HEARD ABOUT A CONTEST COMBINING TWO OF HER FAVORITE THINGS—REHOBOTH BEACH AND SECRETS—SHE KNEW SHE HAD TO GIVE IT A TRY. WHEN SHE'S NOT WRITING, LINDA WORKS IN NONPROFIT OUTREACH AND LEADS WRITING WORKSHOPS. VISIT HER AT WWW.LINDABUDZINSKI.COM.

Solutions Page

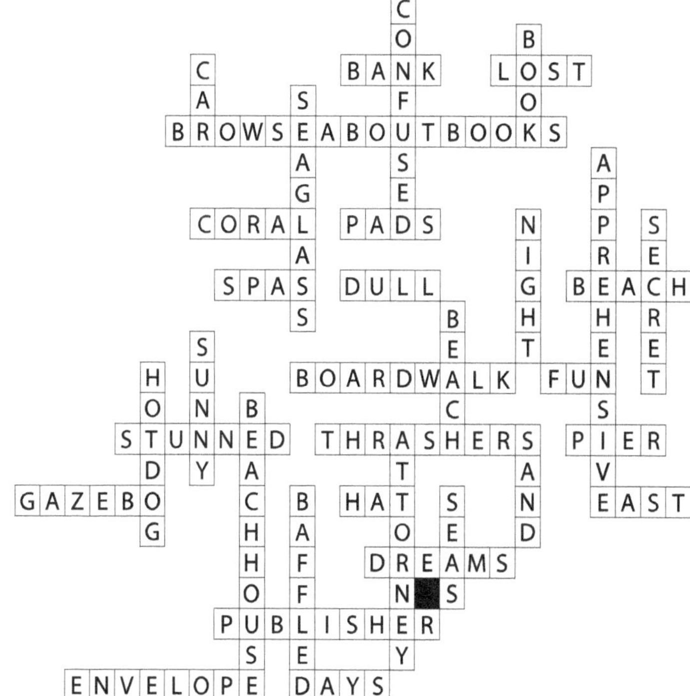

From "Rock Star"—

References to the band "The Cars"

1. Broken Lullaby is the name of Bo and Greg's band. The words "broken lullaby" are in the lyrics of The Cars' song "Bye Bye Love."

2. The name "Bo" is the initials of The Cars' bassist Benjamin Orr. In the story, Bo is the band's bassist and has the same hairdo as Benjamin did.

3. The Cars' song "Drive" is the song Kat and Bo danced to.

4. In the story, Bo uses the words "let's go" a couple of times. "Let's Go" is a Cars song title.

5. The red guitar on the roof of the music store is a reference to a guitar Benjamin Orr played often. It was a red Vox Teardrop Bass.

6. The movie "Fast Times at Ridgemont High," which is mentioned in the story, features a Cars song ("Moving in Stereo").

7. Benjamin Orr enjoyed photography, as did Bo in the story.

8. The words "orangey sky," which Kat used to describe the sunset at Cape Henlopen beach, are also lyrics from the song "Bye Bye Love."

2021 REHOBOTH BEACH READS JUDGES

Tyler Antoine

Tyler Antoine is the adult services librarian at the New Castle Public Library. A graduate of the English and Creative Writing undergraduate program at Temple University, Tyler spends much of his spare time reading short fiction and writing his own poems, a few of which have been published by literary magazines such as *Painted Bride Quarterly*, *bedfellows*, and *Mad House*.

Lois Hoffman

Lois Hoffman is the owner of The Happy Self-Publisher and award-winning author of *Write a Book, Grow Your Business*, along with *The Self-Publishing Roadmap*, and *Barriers*. She helps new and experienced writers confidently share their voice to make a difference in their lives and the lives of others through personalized writing, publishing, and book marketing services. She values a diversity of people, thoughts, and ideas to promote more knowledge and greater understanding in the world. And, because she believes in the power of words to change lives, a portion of course, workshop, and book sales are donated to organizations that support current and future writers. You can find her playing with her words at HAPPYSELFPUBLISHER.COM.

Pat Marinelli

Pat Marinelli has taught multi-genre fiction writing classes at two local colleges for nine years. She's published nonfiction articles, short stories, essays, and recipes both locally and nationally. Short story genres include mystery, romance, romantic suspense, and children. Pat has judged writing contests for romance writers both in NJ and for RWA in romance and romantic suspense, for NJ Horror Writers, and the Derringer Awards for short stories. She's edited several anthologies for NJ Romance Writers and the Central Jersey Sisters in Crime. Though retired, Pat still edits for former students and judges contests when time permits. She lives in Central Jersey with her husband and Tuxedo the cat.

Mary Pauer

Mary Pauer received her MFA in creative writing in 2010 from Stonecoast, at the University of Southern Maine. Pauer publishes short fiction, essays, poetry, and prose locally, nationally, and internationally. She has published in *The Delmarva Review, Southern Women's Review,* and *Foxchase Review,* among others. Her work can also be read in anthologies featuring Delaware writers. She judges writing nationally, as well as locally, and works with individual clients as a developmental editor. Her latest collection, *Traveling Moons,* is a compilation of nature writing. Donations from sales help the Kent County SPCA equine rescue center. Pauer was awarded the 2019 Delaware Division of the Arts Literary Fellow in Creative Nonfiction. This is her third literary fellowship from the DDoA.

Ron Sauder

Ron Sauder is the owner of Secant Publishing, LLC, an independent publishing company based in Salisbury, Maryland, that has been publishing award-winning fiction and nonfiction books with a largely regional focus since 2014. Prior to moving to Delmarva with his wife Debbie, a chemistry professor, he spent his career in newspaper journalism and university public relations in Richmond, Baltimore, and Atlanta. He is a past president of the Eastern Shore Writers Association. See www.secantpublishing.com.

Candace Vessella

Candace Vessella is the President of the Friends of the Lewes Public Library and an avid reader and passionate about libraries. She began her career as an intelligence analyst with the Defense Intelligence Agency and retired in 2009 from her position as the Vice President for Government Relations with BAE Systems Inc. In parallel with her civilian career, she served 25 years as an intelligence officer in the United States Navy Reserve, retiring as a Navy Captain. She received her undergraduate degree in communications from Southern Connecticut State University and her Master's in International Relations and African studies from The American University in Washington, DC. You will find her most days at the Lewes Public Library.

Want to see *your* story in a Rehoboth Beach Reads book?

The Rehoboth Beach Reads Short Story Contest

The goal of the Rehoboth Beach Reads Short Story Contest is to showcase high-quality writing while creating a great book for summer reading. The contest seeks the kinds of short, engaging stories that help readers relax, escape, and enjoy their time at the beach.

Each story must incorporate the year's theme and have a strong connection to Rehoboth Beach (writers do not have to live in Rehoboth). The contest opens March 1 of each year and closes July 1. The cost is $10/entry. Cash prizes are awarded for the top stories and 20–25 stories are selected by the judges to be published in that year's book. Contest guidelines and entry information is available at: *catandmousepress.com/contest*.

Also from Cat & Mouse Press

Eastern Shore Shorts

Characters visit familiar local restaurants, inns, shops, parks, and museums as they cross paths through the charming towns and waterways of the Eastern Shore.

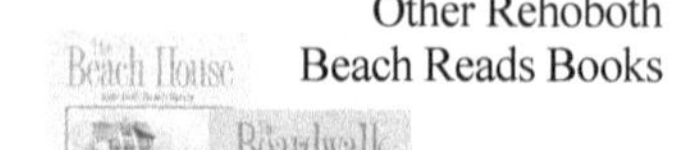

Other Rehoboth
Beach Reads Books

Beach Love

A diverse collection of beach romances, set in Lewes, Rehoboth, Bethany, Fenwick, Ocean City, and Cape May. Also available in large print.

The Sea Sprite Inn

Jillian leaps at a chance to reinvent herself when she inherits the responsibility for a dilapidated family beach house.

Fun with Dick and James

Follow the escapades of Dick and James (and their basset hound, Otis) as they navigate the shifting sands of Rehoboth Beach.

Children's Books

Sandy Shorts

Bad men + bad dogs + bad luck = great beach reads. Characters ride the ferry, barhop in Dewey, stroll through Bethany, and run wild in Rehoboth.

Online Newspaper for Writers

Jam-packed with articles on the craft of writing, editing, self-publishing, marketing, and submitting. ***Writingisashorething.com***

How To Write Winning Short Stories

A guide to writing short stories that includes preparation, theme and premise, title, characters, dialogue, setting, and more.

Come play with us!

www.catandmousepress.com
www.facebook.com/catandmousepress

When You Want a Book at the Beach

Come to Your Bookstore at the Beach

- Fiction
- Nonfiction
- Children's Books & Toys
- Local Authors
- Distinctive Gifts
- Signings/Readings

Browseabout Books
133 Rehoboth Avenue
Rehoboth Beach, DE 19971
www.browseaboutbooks.com